A Promise to Break

Kathy Springer

A Promise to Break

Love, Faith, and Politics in the 1930s
(Book 1 in Promise Series)

Kathryn Spurgeon

Edmond, Oklahoma

Published by Memory House Publishing
Edmond, Oklahoma 73034
www.memoryhousepublishing.net

Printed in the United States of America

ISBN 978-0-9973347-2-2 (Paperback) Christian historical fiction

Cover design by Krystal Harlow
Interior design and layout by
Front Cover Photo: Sibyl Pope, courtesy of Margaret Pope Akin
Back Cover Photo: Shawnee, OK, Pottawatomie County
Oklahoma Historical Society

To my mother,
Margaret Kathryn Pope Akin,
for the long hours she spent
recalling her childhood.

She is a spiritual rock and a loving,
godly mother due in part, to her
parents' commitment to the Lord.

Prologue

Shawnee, Oklahoma, April 1922

"Where're we going, Papa?" My father, Malcolm Calvis Trimble, Sr., placed his hand on my back and hurried me along.

"To a crucial meeting, Sibyl," he answered. "We've decided to support Jack Walton."

I was dressed in disguise, my hair stuffed into an old Cardinals baseball cap, Papa's bomber jacket swallowing my small frame. With the way I was decked out, I could have fooled any of the neighborhood boys into thinking I was one of them.

Papa stopped, pulled his fedora over his eyebrows and rubbed his fingers down his lapel. I straightened my hat. Papa often lectured about looking my best. "You must be absolutely mute, do you understand?" I nodded and he continued. "You must listen carefully because this man has good things to say."

"I will, Papa."

He smiled down at me like he was pleased, and I swelled with awe. Such a handsome and smart man.

Papa ushered me down an alleyway toward Shawnee's Convention Hall, a two-story, red brick giant with a basement and an elaborate cornice around the top. The building had a columned entry facing Union Street and another facing Ninth Street, where we approached.

"Some of our state Constitution was written in this building. Our own community leaders helped draft it in 1906." Papa's chest puffed with pride. "Nearly fifteen hundred people attended."

It seemed like that many people were shoving in now. Hundreds of men and a few boys around my age pushed around us as we neared the doors. There were no other girls, just me dressed like a boy. I held my secret close, intent on making Papa proud of my discretion.

I was only eleven years old but I understood political meetings. Papa had brought me to meetings before, but never one like this. There were so many people.

I clung to Papa's coattail as we pressed toward the entryway. Papa shook hands and traded words with several men, their conversations injected with words like *enlightened*, *reformist*, and *progressive*. These gentlemen were dressed like Papa in pressed suits with matching vests. Most of the others in the crowd were farmers—obvious by their overalls and the odors of sweat, hay, and cow manure that surrounded them.

No one acknowledged my presence as Papa dragged me inside and down a hallway. We went through a double door toward the front of the smoke-filled room. When we stopped about halfway down, I stood on tiptoe to peek between the men's shoulders so I could see the podium.

The buzz of voices hushed as a speaker approached the front. The Farmers Union president, John Simpson, spoke and then introduced Jack Walton. "Our Jack," as Papa called him, started slowly. As he got all worked up, he hollered for farmers all across Oklahoma to vote for him. He condemned the bureaucrats who gained from farmers' hard work and spent it all on their pride. My favorite part was his promise that if he was elected, there would be a feast for the hungry. Papa was a banker, so we never went hungry, but a feast sounded fun. I heard new words like *socialist*, *justice*, and *communism*. Although I didn't truly understand what "struggle for political rights" and "social justice for the downtrodden" meant, my heart beat fast and my spine tingled from the passion in the air.

Our Jack's voice grew louder until he screamed, "God wills it!"

The people immediately shouted back, "God wills it."

Animated men raised fists and their faces turned red in eagerness. They clapped and screamed, loud, deep voices reverberating through the building. Walton's promises were like bones thrown to starving dogs. I heard a man near me grumble, "He's touched a chord of discontent."

Walton yelled again, "God wills it."

The crowd, now in a frenzy, responded, "God wills it!"

"God wills it!" This time I yelled with them. I'd lost myself, carried away in the emotional tide. Yes. I pulled off my baseball cap and waved it in the air. My long hair fell loose around my shoulders.

Walton yelled out once more, "God wills it."

The crowd answered once again, "God wills it!"

Suddenly, everyone grew quiet and my childish voice screamed out alone, "God wills it!"

Men's laughter echoed and faces turned to find the culprit. Papa picked me up and set me on his shoulders, my long legs dangling over his chest. I swung my hat through the air. The crowd cheered. I felt like a heroine.

When Papa set me down, he gave me a look I had *never* seen before. Pride. In me. It shone on his face. He smiled and I grinned back, then I stuck out my chest and pulled my shoulders back. I had done well. I decided right then and there to join forces with Papa and this movement. I would make my life count. I would make a difference. I'd follow Papa's ideals to the letter. Why, I'd even follow Our Jack if that's what Papa wanted me to do. You could bet your bottom dollar on it.

On the way home, I scurried to keep up with Papa's long strides. He ranted nonstop. "Child, Our Jack made a lot of good points. We have a decentralized and self-contained society. Good towns. Main Street values. Children of the soil form the majority of our state's population. Most of the more than two hundred thousand people in Oklahoma live on farms. Jack means to help them. Sure, he's a Democrat, but what does that mean to us Socialists as long as our agenda is heard?"

He leaned over and whispered, "You'll see. Eventually we'll develop a utopian world run by the people. That is, if we band together for the benefit of all."

Papa glanced at me as if I might answer, but kept talking. "Your grandfather was an old-fashioned Christian socialist. He used to quote, 'If we all came from the same father and mother, Adam and Eve, how can anyone prove they're better'n we are?' After all these years, I agree with him. Socialism has changed during the past decade. It's our turn to make a difference. One way is with this coming election. We need Walton for the next governor."

I understood almost nothing he said, but it did not matter.

Papa suddenly stopped and knelt down to my level, taking my shoulders into his big hands. He looked me straight in the eye. "Remember this, Sibyl girl. You're part of the movement now, one of a select few who understands and can become a leader." He shook his finger in my face. "Promise me. Promise me, child, that you'll follow me and help change the world."

"I promise, Papa. I'll help you change the world."

He nodded and stood. "Nothing can stop you from stepping forward and doing your part. Nothing or nobody. Promise?"

Of course I promised. I would do anything to make Papa proud. Anything.

Chapter One
Shawnee, Oklahoma, May 1932

A steam engine chugged into the station from the north, pulling a massive wall of boxcars and several passenger cars. The brakes screeched as the train ground to a halt and the engine heaved, the roar echoing in my head like thunder.

Papa's train from Kansas City was late. He had attended another political meeting and seemed to be in good spirits as he descended the metal steps and tipped his fedora at me. He looked distinguished in his tailored suit and spit-shined shoes.

I tilted my cloche hat and hurried over to help carry his bags. We walked toward the front of the station, my high heels clicking on the brick portico. I wanted to hear all the details of the meeting. We would have only a little time to talk as we drove home in Mama's Chrysler through the center of the thriving town. The dark green vehicle sat in front of the rock train station on Main Street.

"Sibyl, wait here," he said.

Steam fogged the platform as Papa walked toward the train conductor. He shook hands with another gentleman, slapping him on the back, and I knew my wait might be hours long. Bored, I looked up at the forty-foot, castle-like tower and scanned the walkway and arches encircling the ladies' waiting room of the busy Atchison, Topeka, and Santa Fe Railway Depot.

The Santa Fe station, built in 1904, was made of two-feet-thick rock shipped in by rail from Bedford, Indiana. The ceiling was constructed from boxcar sidings. Meant to have a clock at the top, the city of Shawnee hadn't been able to raise the funds, so the Santa Fe

Railway Company had put up their emblem. Many people traveled by train to this busy hub to stay at the Norwood or Aldridge Hotels and shop on Main Street.

A cluster of flourishing men in wide-cut trousers, collared shirts, and two-tone brogues walked past me. As they laughed, they appeared to be jovial, agreeable and cocky in their wide-brimmed felt hats. Several nodded my way. Two ladies chose to ignore me. Dressed in stylish long scarves, gloves, and handbags, they twittered as they passed. A brakeman walked the line inspecting wheels while several boys scurried around to gather trunks and valises for the few pennies they could earn.

Then I saw him.

He was crouched on the opposite side of the train between two passenger cars. A hobo. Hiding. Most of the destitute rode the rails for free instead of purchasing a ticket. He wore a tattered homburg hat and had a bedraggled, youthful face. He was probably around my age. I watched as he stood and shifted his bundle, his arms bulging and his shoulders slung back in confidence. He tightened the rope holding up his too-short, worn-out britches.

Then, just like that, the tattered man took off running, crossing the rails in front of the steam engine.

"Hey, get away from that train!" A uniformed yard bull yelled as he chased after him.

I tensed. They were running right toward me.

The guard swung a club several times and it finally connected with the hobo's head. The thump of the club against his skull made my stomach turn as the hobo's knees buckled. He dropped his bundle and fell onto the red bricks a few feet in front of me.

"Go on!" the yard bull shouted. "Get out of here. We don't need the likes of you around." The yard bull was within his rights.

The vagrant scrambled to his feet and I backed away, scanning the area for Papa. Where was he?

"Don't worry, ma'am, I'll take care of him for you." The bull swung his wooden stick around again, encouraged by a growing audience.

The hobo was more muscular than most men. He cocked his fist and swung toward the other man's unprotected face, but his fist stopped in midair.

"Go ahead. Hit me!" mocked the yard bull. "Jail's the right place for you."

"He's just a bum. Push him out of the way!" yelled a voice from the crowd.

"I'm not a bum." the drifter shouted. "I'm a hobo!" He looked around at the noisy onlookers. "I'm able-bodied and I work for my meals when I can."

I stared at him. He wore filthy, dog-eared garments and his hair was long, curly and unkempt. Then his eyes met mine. Chills ran up my spine. His eyes were blue—sky blue—bluer eyes than I had ever seen. And they were serious. Intelligent. And so arresting. He straightened, standing even taller, and wiped the black soot from his face with his sleeve.

"Someday, I'll be somebody," he said.

I quaked as if shaken by an electric spark. I wasn't sure I understood his words, but I admired his small claim to dignity. A hobo might find a place to settle and prosper, but a bum had no future because he would not work for it. That small claim and his bundle might well have been all he had left in the world.

I looked aside, unable to maintain eye contact.

The moment, just as quickly as it happened, was over. The yard bull clubbed him again. Blood ran down the young man's hands as he tried to cover his head. He stumbled and rolled into a ball while the guard clubbed his back and shoulders.

"No!" I screamed before the guard finally stepped away.

Another drifter snuck toward the hobo's bindle.

I ran over, grabbed the sack and threw it toward where he lay.

Without rising, he reached for it. "Just wait," he whispered, snatching it to his chest, "Someday, I'll be as good as you."

"Sibyl!" Papa's biting voice came from behind me. "What are you doing? Come here this minute. You know better than to get near bums like that."

"But Papa, he's hurt." I said.

"I told you to stay put."

"Did you see his eyes—clear as crystal."

7

"Let's get out of here." Papa grabbed my arm and tried to steer me through the crowd.

I balked and glanced backward before Papa finally dragged me away. Everyone else went about their business, pretending not to see the poor hobo crumpled on the ground.

Chapter Two

Papa traveled for his job as a bank examiner, so he was gone a lot. Some days he arrived home snapping orders, throwing disapproving looks, and cursing as he stomped around the garden. Today, as Papa and I pulled into the driveway, I could see the whole family anxiously waiting for his arrival as if a tornado might come any time

Our state-of-the-art bungalow stood in a new addition on Beard Street. The veranda beneath the low, overhanging eave had a swing and rocking chairs where we congregated in the evenings when it was hot. A handrail along the front porch connected heavy columns holding up the low-pitched roof.

Papa arrived with gifts as he often did after a successful trip. His big voice boomed happily as my youngest sister Frances rode on his shoulders. I led him through the front door where the prosperity of the 1920s still graced our home. The troubled economy had not yet touched our extravagant lifestyle. Long tapestry drapes framed the windows, and a candelabrum dangled from the ceiling while artwork of promising vacation destinations decorated the walls.

He patted eleven-year-old Blanche on the head while Marjorie, just over a year younger than I at twenty-one, swung his briefcase in the air. Papa knew how to please his four girls, so his gifts raised the excitement to a crest. This week, he handed each daughter a box from Montgomery Wards. Inside, mine held a new wide-caped collar dress plus a matching hat and gantlet gloves.

"Thank you, Papa," I rubbed my fingers along the cool cotton fabric. A print rose-colored day dress. Ah. Lovely.

"Thank you." my sisters chimed as they held up new dresses.

"I'm going to show Grandma my new dress." Frances squealed.

Blanche was halfway out of the room when she called over her shoulder, "Did you bring a present for Grandma?"

Grandma and Grandpa Bennett, Mama's parents, had moved in with us the prior year. It was no secret they didn't get along with Papa. When he was home, they stayed in their room except for mealtimes. At dinner, we all crowded around the handmade table, sitting on the benches Grandpa had crafted. Neither grandparent made an appearance today. Naturally, Papa had not brought gifts for them.

Mama stood off to one side, watching, her arms crossed over her chest.

"When did you have time to buy all these things? You didn't use to." Her words were caustic as she picked up Marjorie's new dress. "I don't know another man who picks out fancy dresses for his daughters. I thought you worked too hard for such nonsense."

"I can buy what I want," he snapped. "And, I might say, you're giving them far too much freedom. Why can't you keep them in line when I'm gone?"

"It's you who needs to control them." Mama did not back down. She never did. "Gone for weeks at a time, then strutting in here like Fred Astaire, buttering 'em up with expensive gifts."

"You ought to have a little more appreciation," Papa said without looking at her. "I do pay the bills around here."

"Coming home once a month is not enough," Mama said icily. "Where are you when the girls need calling down? What am I supposed to do with Calvis, your son who sneaks off and plays in the band at the Masonic Lodge? I couldn't even find him today."

Marjorie and I grew silent, examining our gifts. In this home, no one made waves. Except Mama when she was upset. We lived by Papa's rules, at least when he was home. To keep the peace, we had to behave like Papa was king.

"You worry too much." A frown line creased the middle of Papa's forehead. "A man needs peace and quiet when he comes home. All I get is a tongue-lashing. You should be happy I'm here." With that, Papa stomped out the door towards the car. Could he be leaving? Had Mama driven him away?

In a few minutes, he returned with a package and shoved it toward Mama. Her eyes shone as she opened the white box and discovered a beautiful mink coat. She stroked the soft fur and looked at Papa. "Okay," she cooed. "But next time, give me my present first."

I loved being outdoors working with Papa even though he never allowed me to plant his newly-purchased flowers. He did allow me to tend the rest of the garden. "Can't be trusted with my irises," he explained, "Not with something this fragile." I often wondered with what I could be trusted.

His garden was truly something special. It showcased the largest assortment of irises west of the Arkansas River. I kept a list for him, noting when and where each rhizome was purchased. Papa had personally chosen these flowers which came from as far away as San Francisco and New York.

I lived to please Papa, even if he was bristly and pretentious, even when he didn't let me touch his flowers. He was the center of the family and I puffed with pride whenever I saw him march into a room, as he did most mornings, with his hair slicked down, looking sharp in a starched shirt and brocade tie.

I wanted to excel as he had. There must be some way to show him that of all his children, I would be the one to step out and make a difference in the world. I stabbed at the weeds which threatened the edge of the plot.

He plopped down a bucket of new bulbs and busied himself planting them. Now was my chance to ask my important question.

"Papa, can I talk to you?"

"Of course," he said, not looking up from the bulbs. "What's on your mind?"

"I don't know what to do. Men are so troublesome."

He acted as if he had not heard me.

I swallowed hard. "I need to talk to you about James, the guy I've been seeing."

"Mr. James Fleming is a man with the big ideas, always trying to impress. A well-to-do man. Understands our ideas."

Papa looked up from the red soil but seemed to peer past me toward the back of the house where stones surrounded a newly-dug fish pond. The right side of the pond bank was covered with tall Welch's Reward bearded irises. "Your coming engagement pleases me, you know."

"I'm not sure how I feel about him." I sat on a bench and leaned forward.

Down on his hands and knees, Papa held out an iris rhizome. "Look at this. They have to be handled very carefully. Rare. Cost me nearly forty cents apiece." He tenderly placed his new Susan Bliss Iris into a perfectly dug, shallow trench. "They will bloom early," he continued. "Irises either take to the soil and bloom or they don't. Each holds its own fate.

"You're a smart girl." He reached for another rhizome. "Remember, man himself holds the destiny of his existence on the earth." He paused and looked up at me. "Living together in peace means sharing the wealth, of course. The only way to save the human race is by entirely eliminating wickedness. It's up to the elite or chosen ones to do that. You, of all people, should understand this movement. Aren't we fighting for the underdog? The downtrodden? Haven't we always supported women's vote, even when it was unpopular? James knows this progression, so I'm sure your marriage will be convenient."

Convenient? The word filled my head as Papa rambled, droning on about how little the New Deal proposed for Oklahoma, the economic survival of banks, the recent Gold Reserve Act, which brought the price of gold down by nearly forty percent. Once he got going it was hard to get him to stop.

"Papa," I interrupted, wanting to ask a question but unsure of Papa's response. His answer would mean a lot to me.

"Well, go on," Papa said impatiently.

"I'm not sure I want to marry James."

He squinted his face in dismay as I continued, "Shouldn't I wait for an exciting fellow who makes my heart jump? Shouldn't I feel affection for a man?"

Papa's brow wrinkled further. "Girl, there's no reason to marry anyone who has no money. If James is anything like his father, he has *ambition*. What more could you need? He'll make a perfectly good mate for your life endeavors. And we'll need money to make the kind of changes this country needs." Papa spoke as if marriage were a business contract. "Also, he's not from the wrong side of town."

I didn't know what to say. Was money the only thing Papa thought I needed for a good mate?

He resumed patting his irises into place. "We need this marriage, Sibyl. Our cause needs it. The movement is going forward and as you remember from our last meeting, more funds are needed now than ever before. James' father has agreed to a certain amount of support." He looked at me sternly, "Don't cross him."

So our beliefs in equality did not carry over to my marriage? Would only a wealthy man do for me? Or rather, for Papa?

"But shouldn't I feel excitement or see lights or something? Marjorie says she can tell when she's in love."

He snorted. "Marjorie has never been with one boy long enough to know about true love." He shook his head. "As for you—you're different. I have high expectations for you. Try not to be too pushy or hardheaded like you usually are, young lady. Stubbornness is not a good quality in women."

Papa stood and dusted dirt from his hands. "That's enough. Go fetch a water pail so we can see these growing up. And tell your mother to find a gardener. I'll be gone most of the summer."

I watched Papa pick up another bucket. Papa knew everything about everything and everybody, even if he never seemed to understand me. He read *Esquire*, wore pinstripe suits, and frequently had his name in the paper. He was a man to be admired. Brilliant. I had seen him add down a column of four digit numbers in his head within seconds.

He had done well financially in the depressed economy, a task made even more challenging by the bankers who didn't like him. Who could blame them for resenting him? He audited their losses, which did not make him a bad man. Only disliked. I'd been trying my whole life to emulate him and win his approval. I wanted to make him proud—would it take marrying James to do that? I stood and walked toward the water bucket.

"Money and standing in society will make a difference in your life—maybe a difference in the future of Oklahoma."

I stood and walked toward the water bucket. Papa had been grooming me, taking me to strategic meetings, introducing me to liberal leaders, preaching his form of revolution. None of my siblings saw that side of Papa. I was lucky, privileged even. So why did I need more than James offered? James had also been indoctrinated into the idea that man alone holds the fate of our existence on Earth. We enjoyed discussions about how to alleviate poverty and the outrageous condition of Oklahoma farmers who lived on the brink of total ruin, thanks to enormous liens against their property. I wasn't sure if I should trust Papa in matters of the heart. However, marriage to a prosperous man would give me the freedom to pursue humanitarian efforts, something I longed to do. Not sure if living with him the rest of my life would be worth it.

I handed Papa the bucket of water.

"And Sibyl."

"Yes, Papa?"

"I'll talk to Mr. Fleming next week. I think the engagement should be soon."

Chapter Three
June 1932

A few weeks later at ten P.M. on the dot, Marjorie and I pushed back crisp sheets to swing bare feet onto the wood floor. Without a sound, we pulled silk stockings over our long legs, attached them to garters and dropped white petticoats over our heads. I slid on my favorite dress –an Alice Blue with the calf-length skirt flaring below my knees. Marjorie wore a décolleté, fitted dress. She had sewn sequins on the bodice without telling Mama. Much more sociable and curvaceous than I, she stood slightly shorter. Her faded blond curls shaped an attractive, pouty face, while my dark curls had one unruly strand whirling about like a windmill, wild and windblown no matter how hard I tried to control it.

We were going dancing but we had to be quiet. Mama and our grandparents were asleep down the hall.

Marjorie disappeared through the open window. "Come on, lovey," she beckoned. "The band's started."

"I'm coming. Just need a bit of perfume." When I opened the bottom drawer to reach for the Chanel, the drawer squeaked like an angry cat.

"Shh. What are you doing? You'll wake up Mama."

I grabbed my favorite black pocketbook and slung the strap over my shoulder.

I hiked my dress up to my thighs, turned and sat down on the windowsill before I drew my legs over the ledge. My feet dangled outside. The breeze blew my wavy hair around my face as I slid down to the soft dirt below.

Thankfully, Papa was traveling again. His endless talking about *the movement* would wear out an old mule. Don't get me wrong. I wanted to make my stamp on Oklahoma society, but with action, not talk. In the meantime, I found dancing an outlet for my energy.

The moonlight illuminated the lilac bushes on the side of the house where a massive blackjack oak tree stood like a shield. Silhouettes of neighboring houses appeared as we slipped around the bushes to the front. We passed Mama's Chrysler in the driveway.

"What took you so long, sis?" Marjorie said as we reached the street. "We should've been there already."

"Why are you in such a hurry?" I asked. "Papa would have our heads if he knew we wandered the streets late at night."

"Papa's not here." We had been sneaking out in the middle of the night for months and had never been caught.

Marjorie changed the subject. "Tonight we'll see the fellows, lovey. From what I've seen, thousands are waiting in line."

"There may be a line for you," I said, "but not for me." My sister's Carol Lombard style of flirting always attracted male interest. Boys didn't look at me the way they looked at her.

"Why don't you be a little friendlier? Guys like flattery, sis. It's their ego."

"Friendlier?" I raised an eyebrow.

"Hey, loosen up a bit. They just want to have a good time. Don't be so particular."

I shook my head. "You may be interested, but I'm not."

"Oh, I'm definitely interested," Marjorie said with a grin.

"I just want to dance all night long," I said and we both laughed.

We walked the six blocks south down Beard Street to Main and turned left. People scurried about going to a dance or a bar. Jalopies lined the streets while horses and buggies were tied up in the alley. At night, the east end of Main Street was busier than the business section of town on a Saturday morning.

As we crossed the street and drew closer to the Blue Bird Ballroom, I dragged my feet. Sure, I wanted to dance. I always wanted to dance, but my mind struggled with other things, too. I wanted to shake Marjorie and tell her there were more important things to consider than the nearby boom of the bass drum.

"James should be there, sis," she said. "You got lucky when you snatched him up."

James. Marjorie didn't understand that he was part of my struggles. "A suitable beau," Papa had said. Anyone would do, as long as he had enough dough and sufficient political clout.

However, no better marriage prospects hovered around and I was getting older. I was already twenty-two. James might be a good candidate for matrimony even if we shared no deeper feelings for each other. Something like love might have to be sacrificed if it meant furthering our cause. Not sure if I liked that thought very much.

We heard music before we got to the Blue Bird. Much of it was coming from other bars and dance joints along East Main. We had made our way to what Mama called *the seedier side of town*. Several nights a week, this speakeasy entertained the largest crowd in the area. Farmers, Yanks, and criminals showed up from surrounding towns, shacks, and hideaways. Railway men filled in the gaps. It was the place to be.

We climbed the stairs and Marjorie handed the man at the open door a dime. Through the blurred smoke, I could see a four-man band on stage thundering out a Benny Goodman song. The saxophone's wail overpowered the enclosed space. Several couples on the dance floor moved to the rhythm, but in the shadowy light it was hard to recognize anyone.

Edging around the side of the large room, we passed wallflowers and fellows with glowing cigarettes lighting up their faces as they leaned against the wall. Half a dozen booths framed the south side, each seating six to ten people, some with curtains drawn around them to provide privacy for the occupants. Everyone knew the booths were used for drinking bootleg liquor. Along the wall, wooden window shutters were propped open by a few boards, allowing much-needed breezes into this packed place.

While Marjorie arranged her dance schedule, I scanned the crowd. The self-absorbed, arrogant guys in my circle of friends annoyed me. Sons and daughters of doctors, bankers, and builders seemed superficial and unconcerned about the greater issues of life. Didn't they know society needed help? Did they not see changes that the world awaited? Was I the only one who felt trepidation about the

17

political scene and economic conditions? The visionless would take notice when I —

"Well, if it isn't the most gorgeous sisters in town." A squeaky voice teasingly interrupted my thoughts. "One blond and one brunette. What luck."

Kelley Walker looked up and down Marjorie's voluptuous curves and her low-cut dress, eyeballing the glimmering sequins. He boasted, "I'm all you need, doll face. You promised to dance with me first."

"You got one dance, big boy." Marjorie batted her dark-stained eyes. "Just make sure you're there when I'm ready, or I'll give your spot away." I thought Kelley was much too young and dangerous. I warned my sister but she never listened to me.

We wandered around the room until we found several of our friends occupying a booth. We squeezed in.

The band played an old 1920's song, "Bugle Boy Rag," and my feet tapped to the music. My mood lightened. Rhythm touched my soul in a way I could not explain. The drummer and guitarist competed for attention. The next song was a favorite by Yip Harburg and everyone at the table turned to listen.

Marjorie nuzzled some fellow's ear. Who was he? I turned away and searched the crowd for James. He was supposed to have the first dance, but he was nowhere in the room. I felt relief and then guilt for the relief.

A new dance tune began, Duke Ellington's "It Don't Mean a Thing (If It Ain't Got that Swing)." The whole gang caught the mood and hopped to the floor. Some fellow grabbed my hand and drew me into the crowd of swirling arms and legs and flashing smiles.

I danced as a dangling light bulb created circles on the floor around me in the hazy room, only resting when the band took a break. I would have danced even if I'd been alone in the room, not just because I loved music but because it helped me forget that my life followed Papa's plan, not my own. He insisted I follow my purpose in life to guide the masses of unfortunate people. I shivered thinking about it. I wanted to help others but not exactly his way. Dancing and music were a small relief from my thoughts.

Not to boast, but I never lacked for dance partners. I had a high energy level with an athlete's stamina as well as some pretty smooth moves. I executed a lot of intricate swirls and steps, which made me a sought-after dance partner even if I didn't flirt. Eager fellows shoved in for the next dance while I tried to ignore their interest. I knew it lay mostly in my long, shapely legs and dance moves, not my conversation. When I danced, I forgot my worries. So, ragtime to Charleston to swing, I danced.

An hour or more had passed when I heard a commotion. Men's voices rose near a booth along the southeast wall. A gangly man leaned against a corner post, his face shadowed, his long arms flopping awkwardly at his side. The dark wooden beams appeared like walls around him. Then he shoved at a table and stepped away from the booth, yelling. "Where do you keep your bootlegging stuff? Just give me a swig."

My heart sank. Not another dance hall ruckus. Why couldn't these guys find somewhere else to get drunk and fight?

"Not a fat chance!" A man's loud, slurred voice sounded through the room. "Go get your own bottle! What do you want, another raid?"

"Don't yell at me, you fool!"

"Go get your own booze!"

The music stopped and people turned to stare at the two drunken louts.

Sure enough, a brawl started. The last thing I needed was to be caught in the middle of a boozy scuffle.

I pushed loose curls back from my face and glanced around. An ominous mood hung over the room. My cheeks felt hot from dancing.

Tension sparked through the smoke-filled room. People screamed. Pushed. Booth curtains flew open. Chairs scraped against the bare plank floor as drinks toppled and spilled across tables. Glass crunched beneath people's feet as the crowd shoved one another to get out of the way. The smell of liquor filled the charged airspace. My feet felt glued to the wooden floor. My dance partner was gone. Suddenly, I stood alone in the midst of the increasingly agitated crowd.

Then someone pushed me and someone else tripped on my foot as we retreated.

I swung about looking for Marjorie, my heart beating along with the uproar. She was in a far corner with her arms wrapped around Kelley, oblivious to the fighting.

"Way to go," I muttered before she turned around, looking elated.

Across the room, another scrapper's arms flailed about. He viciously cursed and swung at anyone in his way. Across the chaos and haze, I saw Kelley pushing people aside until he reached the brawl. Marjorie, always in the middle of chaos, followed him.

Retreating to the wall, my heart pounded even as I sought to remain calm. The noise grew louder as people cheered for one brawler or the other. A man's body crushed against me, and I tried to lean away. The air became unbearably suffocating. My asthma kicked in, and I could hardly breathe. My head swam. Think, I told myself. *Think*.

Yells reverberated from the fight area, and onlookers panicked as the noise grew deafening. I inched my way along the wall toward Marjorie. The shouts grew more belligerent. Swear words flew around me as I pushed myself in next to my sister.

"Marj, come on, let's get out of here. Things are out of hand."

Marjorie's face flushed as she gazed transfixed on the scene. "It's just started. I've got to find out what's going on."

"The fight's getting out of control." I grabbed her arm. "The police will be here soon."

Marjorie balked and jerked away. "What about Kelley? We can't just leave him like this."

I shoved Marjorie toward the door. "He won't even miss you." I glanced back to see Kelley hit somebody over the head with a chair while others piled into the angry crowd.

We pushed our way through the front door and were scrambling down Main Street when we heard sirens behind us. We ran, not slowing down until we reached a dimly lit sidewalk and turned onto Union Street. Buildings on either side nearly obscured by the thin streetlight.

"Ah, sis, the fun was just beginning," Marjorie said.

I shook my head, relieved to be outside and quite thankful our picture would not be splashed across the front page of the *Shawnee News* tomorrow. Hopefully, Papa wouldn't find out about our escapade. From now on, I would keep our dancing to a minimum. I wasn't ready to give it up *entirely*, though. After all, fighting was common, especially when booze was involved.

Marjorie and I didn't speak again as we walked home. The night breeze had disappeared, leaving the air heavy and humid, our dresses clinging to our skin. We took a shortcut on Union Street, approaching a murky alleyway that smelled bad from the garbage behind the Walcott Hotel, its massive brick wall towering above us.

Suddenly I heard a racket that made me jump. Goose bumps raised on my arms.

"Did you hear that?" I peered down the alley and saw a blurry form leaning over the metal trashcans.

"Probably a dog," said Marjorie. "Come on."

A black man whizzed toward us from the alley.

Marjorie screamed and ran up the block toward the streetlight, leaving me behind. Just what I'd expect from her.

The man tripped and tumbled onto the concrete in a heap at my feet, the second man in two weeks to fall in front of me. In his tumble, several items scattered on the sidewalk.

The middle-aged man, kinky black hair hanging around his ears, looked up and stared up at me with wide eyes.

"Are you hurt?" I stuttered.

"Stay away, sis. He might have a gun!" Marjorie yelled from the lamppost where she hid.

I saw something in the man's hand. Was it a weapon? My heart sped up, thumping like a runaway horse. I took two steps backward.

"He's clipping in the wrong part of town," Marjorie yelled. "We need to go now!"

Looking closer, I saw the strewn contents of the spilled paper bag—half an apple, slices of moldy bread, and chicken bones. I breathed with relief.

"It's okay. I won't report you."

"Now's not the time to play caretaker, sis."

I ignored my sister as the man's big eyes stared at me. Scared silly, I thought. Any accusation on the part of a young white girl could get a Negro man thrown in jail—or worse. There were whispers of lynchings that still occurred. He would be in serious trouble if we made a fuss.

The man and I continued to stare at each other. His thin, gaunt face looked as if food had not passed his lips in days.

"Well, I'm going," Marjorie said, "even if you want to help every Tom, Dick, and Harry roaming the streets. He can't be up to any good." She took another few steps and stopped.

"If you aren't hurt, get on up." I bent to help gather the items, trying to be kind.

He grabbed the discarded food and stuffed it inside his coat, then scrambled to his feet. He stepped backward and bobbed his head up and down. "Thank you, miss. Thank you." He raced away, disappearing around the next corner.

I crossed the street and joined Marjorie.

"What's wrong with you to put us in danger like that?"

"No harm came to either of us."

As we walked home, I thought of the black people who had moved into the Oklahoma Territories. Some established black towns and built churches, schools and businesses with opportunities mostly in sharecropping or menial labor. When the economy worsened, the blacks most often lost their jobs first. Unemployed and barely scratching a living, many were so hungry they dug through trashcans.

"Maybe this man has a family so famished they'll be glad for the spoiled food. Have you ever seen such desperation?" Marjorie didn't respond but my heart ached for him. Why, black people could not even vote.

While I had been dancing through life as if nothing else mattered, others had been suffering. Could it be time for Papa's outspoken views about the equality of Negroes to be manifested? How could Papa's ideas that we should help one another and feed the poor be turned from *words* into *actions*?

Chapter Four

The Chrysler's body was long, smooth as silk and classy as a mink stole. A neighborhood mutt chased the wire wheel spokes, and a gardener turned to stare as the curved fenders and rear bumper guards passed by.

Through the speckled Saturday afternoon sun, I drove the sleek motorcar south under the tall oak trees past Wallace Street. Their limbs stretched high over the road like people standing on tiptoe, struggling to touch in the middle.

I was the only child in my family who knew how to drive, therefore, the only one allowed to use Mama's new trophy. The surge from the engine gave me an unusual sense of control.

As Marjorie and I eased up to Main Street, the car bounced over the trolley tracks. I over-reacted and hit the gas pedal instead of the brake. We shot toward the ditch. I slammed my foot down on the brake. Our shiny car skidded to a halt right where the red brick road ended and the dirt road began. Marjorie and I jerked toward the windshield and then back again, our hands gripping the slick dashboard for dear life.

"Pay attention, sis." Marjorie spit out. "If Mama sees you drive like that, she'll never let us take the car again."

I took a deep breath to calm myself. "Don't worry. We'll get there." Persistence overcame anything and I was *determined* to master this car.

The afternoon sun blazed and this trip no longer seemed the pleasant way to spend the afternoon I had envisioned. I wished I had not worn such a stiff conservative outfit. It didn't leave much freedom

23

of movement, but at least the light blue color showed off my clear olive skin and dark eyes. I managed to get the automobile under control and we continued down Beard Street.

"Marj, if that fellow from Maud corners me with his long-winded stories about the weather or politics or—heaven forbid—Herbert Hoover jokes," I said, "you'll rush to my aid. Agreed?"

"Right, lovey, and if your fiancé slobbers all over you, I'll grab him and tear him away." Marjorie smoothed her low, revealing red dress and adjusted her matching feathered cloche hat.

"Don't make a spectacle." I tugged on my gloves while trying to steer the car. The car swerved, causing my big brimmed hat to bounce. "And I will have you know, no engagement date is set. That'll be years away if I have anything to say about it."

Mr. Winters's filling station sat on the northeast corner of South Beard and Farrell. Mud-splattered windows flanked the screen door of the green-and-white-trimmed wood-frame building. Various sizes of worn-out tires lay stacked against a wall.

I steered toward one of the two round red gas pumps under the overhang. I turned too sharply and slammed on the brakes. We jerked forward again, the front fender missing the pump by a cat's hair.

"Can't you do anything right?" Marjorie pushed her red hat back into place. "We're in serious trouble if you dent Mama's car."

"I can figure this out." I shifted into reverse and rammed my high heel on the clutch. "Hold on." I yanked the steering wheel. "This blamed car won't go right." Just like my life. Frustration oozed because nothing purposeful was happening.

On the other side of the station, the open garage door revealed a disorganized collection of oilcans and assorted tools. Waves of afternoon heat bounced off nearby parked cars, and a Ford pickup with the hood propped open was parked in the garage, engine parts strewn nearby.

A young, broad-shouldered attendant stretched his arms as he stood, muscles expanding against his thin shirt. Perspiration wet his underarms and grease streaked the front of his clothes. His sturdy frame exuded strength. I tried to appear composed but I could feel my cheeks flushing as I glanced at him.

The attendant pretended not to notice the Chrysler's jerky movements. I watched him turn to lift the door of the large red Coca-Cola chest, the sign above promoting "Drinks 5¢." The freezer would hold soda so cold that slush formed in the glass bottles.

Distracted, I let the car veer right before I corrected it. The man reached into the ice, pulled out a pop and pried off the cap. He turned, took a long swig and wiped his mouth on his shirtsleeve as I pulled into position at the pump.

An older mechanic leaned his chair back on two legs against the building's front wall. He wore faded overalls and had his hat pulled down over his eyes to sneak a midday nap.

"Don't worry about getting up," the attendant yelled over his shoulder as the man roused long enough to nod his head. "I'll take care of this one."

As the handsome attendant sauntered to the Chrysler and leaned over, he seemed to check his comely reflection in the shiny hood. He stared at the chrome-plated headlights. I thought he was arrogant until I realized he was admiring the car, not himself.

He strolled around the front, his arm extended as if he wanted to touch the luxurious auto, but dared not.

"Good afternoon, ma'am. Mighty fine car you have here." His voice was smooth. "What'll it be today?"

I looked up at him, right into crystal blue eyes. My hobo! Still tanned, he had cut his long sun-bleached hair. His hair was darker and he was a bit more cleaned up, but I would have recognized him in a cornfield. I didn't want to embarrass him by letting on that I recognized him from the train station that day.

He still wore tattered clothes and looked poor as a boot-black. He stood straight, shoulders back, unruffled and his straight Roman nose and refined features made my heart turn somersaults. He was the handsomest man I had ever seen. His striking pale-blue eyes held mine. I hesitated for such a short moment that I didn't think anyone would notice, but his eyes took the challenge. I had never seen a man quite like this one.

"Ten gallons will do for now." I pushed back a curl from my face.

He smiled as he cranked the handle until gasoline filled the glass bubble of the pump, then he took a wet rag from a bucket of soapy water and began to wash the windshield. As he bent the wipers back, the rhythm of his arm remained steady, controlled. My heart beat faster than usual.

"Need your oil checked, ma'am?" he asked after he put the nozzle back in. His dark waves fell over his forehead.

"No, Papa takes care of that. Thanks, anyway." Handsome, self-composed men were hard to come by in this town.

"Oh, yes. Your papa," he said slowly, as if remembering something. He hesitated as though waiting for me to say something and then walked around the front of the vehicle to wash the other side of the windshield.

Did he remember me? Maybe his stealthy entrance into Shawnee was a secret we shared.

Marjorie's red hat tilted provocatively as she brazenly batted her eyelids at him. "Hey, good looking," she said.

I tried to hush her.

The attendant nodded, calm and respectful, but stood back a little as if he disdained silly, flippant girls. He glanced toward me. "Where you headed?"

"We're on our way to Benson Park to meet some friends." I leaned my head halfway out the rolled-down window as he walked back around to my side of the car. My hat bumped the top of the door. "Are you new around these parts?"

"Just got in town," he called. "Been traveling."

"Oh—I thought so. I've lived here several years myself." I ducked the hat back into the car and sighed.

The attendant held his broad shoulders straight back as he returned to the pump, replaced the gas cap and tightened it. He walked to my window. I was eager to gaze into those pale blue eyes again. Something about him intrigued me. Then I stopped myself. For Pete's sake, this man was a hobo.

"That'll be a dollar ten." He wiped his hands on the rag he pulled out of his back pocket.

I slid my gloves off and reached into my pocketbook. "Sorry, all I have is a five. Do you have change?"

"Yes, ma'am, sure do." He paused as though hesitant, and then took the five. "I'll be right back." He strode back behind the car to the station, pushed open the screen door and walked inside. The wooden door banged shut behind him.

"Well, what do you make of that fine specimen of a man?" Marjorie said. "Right here in our own backyard, too. I saw how you looked at him."

"I must admit, he doesn't seem like the usual attendant." I was meticulously scribbling the cost of gas in my notebook, keeping track of every penny I spent. "I wonder where he's been. Traveling around the country, you suppose?"

"Wouldn't you like to know?" Marjorie raised her eyebrows. Intellect held no attraction to her, but a handsome face did. "You've always liked adventurous men. I bet he's been around. From California, you think?" Marjorie giggled. "Aren't you glad you didn't run into the gas pump?"

I opened my car door.

"Wait, where are you going?"

I smiled. "I think I need one of those Coca-Colas." I hopped out of the car and went inside the filling station. Out of the bright sunlight, I blinked and looked around. Boxes of penny candy, a licorice stick jug, and a gumball machine with red and blue balls lined the dingy glass countertop. The rest of the filling station, though orderly, was blanketed with red dust.

The young man looked up, surprised. "Can I help you?"

"It's such a hot afternoon," I said. "I'd like to buy a drink."

"Of course. Anything you like." His eyes scanned my well-coiffed hair down to my sophisticated dress and two-toned shoes.

A silent space lingered between us while I waited for him to give me the change. He extended some crumpled bills in his dirty, greasy hand. He jerked the money back to his side and wiped his palm on his pants leg.

He counted the money back to me. Our hands contrasted as if they had evolved on two different planets. His was a large, powerful working man's hand, the kind you could depend upon to get a job done. Mine was pale with long, smooth, well-manicured, piano-playing fingers. He shifted slightly, accidentally touching my hand. Electricity charged through the touch. He raised his eyes to mine, and I felt like I had just met the most baffling man on the continent. Did he feel it, too?

He pulled a glass bottle from the ice chest.

"Thank you for the drink," I whispered as I took the offered Coca-Cola.

"It's my pleasure. I'm mighty glad we met."

My heart beat fast. I was glad too. Something drew me to this man, something more than just his handsome face and square jaw line. I felt an attraction I had never felt before.

"Have we met?" he asked. "I feel like I know you."

I turned and rushed back to the car. My heels clicked out of place on the scattered gravel. He followed me around to the side of the vehicle where I slid into the driver's seat.

I turned the engine on, shifted the car into gear and let it roll forward.

"Wait!" he yelled. "I forgot to ask your name!"

Looking straight ahead, I drove away without answering. My hands shook. Never had I imagined that looking into the eyes of another human could be so intense.

After all, who was this man?

Just a hobo, for heaven's sake.

Chapter Five

Marjorie and I arrived at Benson Park and pulled in beside rows of roadsters and coupes with tops pulled back. I drew a breath of fresh air and looked north, scanning the park where the swimming pool and opera house were open. A ballpark lay to the east.

Benson Park lay south along the trolley line, halfway to Tecumseh. People paid a nickel to hop aboard the interurban streetcar on Main, where it turned south on McKinley Street for a bumpy ride out of town. The pecan trees that shaded the park were so wide that a grown man could not stretch his arms around one of them.

At one of the dozens of picnic tables spread around the grounds, a large group of our friends were setting out the lunch: platters of fried chicken, bowls of potato salad, and relish plates of pickled beets and bread & butter pickles. Others laid out cold cuts, cabbage slaw, baked beans, and lemonade. We joined the crowd, exchanging hellos as we added two of Mama's homemade pies.

"This much food would feed all the people in Hooverville," one of the boys said as he stuffed a cold cut in his mouth

"That disgusting shanty town near Oklahoma City?" someone else asked.

"That's the one."

"You're right," said a red-haired girl sitting next to me. "I saw it. All those folks living in rusted-out cars or orange crates or whatever they could put together. The kids run around in rags. Unbelievable."

I listened to their banter, keeping my opinions to myself.

"Heard it's down by the Canadian River. Ten miles wide and ten miles long."

29

"Ah, they're just bums," a banker's son chimed in. "That trash just wants a handout."

"I disagree. It's bad everywhere. What do you think about this coming election?"

"Personally, I don't think Hoover stands a fat chance to win again."

"Roosevelt's my man."

"Think Thomas has a chance? He's running again."

"Nah, the Socialists will never make it in this country."

"I think they'll do better than the Communists. Foster's a joke."

We all laughed.

"What do you think's causing this depression?"

"I heard the big-wigs are causing it. Getting a mite too greedy."

"In my opinion, for what that's worth, Hoover's not doing enough to fight the depression."

"Times are tough, that's for sure."

As the discussion waned, the men lounged on blankets spread on the shady grass under the trees. They removed their wide-brimmed hats and fanned themselves in the heat. While the girls cleared the table, the men talked about the possibility of the Benson Park Opera closing and of the Olympics being held in Los Angeles.

I tapped James on the shoulder. He looked up. Although little romantic interest sparked between us, James had escorted me to various events and driven me on excursions to Sulphur and Turner Falls. He'd even once bought me a box of chocolates.

"Let's walk over to the stables," I said.

"Good idea." James stood. "I've been wanting to talk to you." As we walked to the stables, I glanced at him. His stylish clothes accentuated his nice-looking face and tall, slender build. He spoke in a smooth baritone voice and managed to look like he had just stepped out of a J.C. Penney's catalog.

We found a secluded bench and sat. In the distance, people waited for the trolley to take them back to Shawnee. James pulled a big Havana cigar from his pocket, lit it and took a puff.

I hated the smell of cigar smoke. More than once, tobacco smoke had brought on an asthma attack.

"I've been pretty busy lately, working part-time at the store when I'm home from college on weekends. Dad offered me a job managing his store in Oklahoma City when I graduate from A&M next year. So I'm considering the future. I think you're a good-looking gal, and of course, we get along just fine."

I looked away, uncomfortable. Our conversations typically centered around the declining economy in Oklahoma and what the undercover Socialist party could do to rectify it. We rarely spoke of a future together. The idea of being stuck in a marriage before I had a chance to make my mark did not appeal to me. I might lose my dreams. Although I wanted marriage, I had never been attracted to James.

"What are you getting at?"

James drew a long puff. "We've been seeing each other almost a year now. We do well together. I'll be making a more than adequate living. Your dad's a well-known man in these parts, which will bode well for our future." He placed his hand on top of mine. "I hope the wedding can be soon."

"We can take our time. There's no hurry." My heart pounded. "I'm...I'm not sure what I want out of life." I knew I ought to take this proposal seriously. After all, it might be my only chance at marriage.

James liked me, even if love had never been mentioned. Maybe I expected too much. He was not given to romance. Worse, he seemed interested in my thoughts only in how they related to his career. What would it be like to wake up in the mornings with this man, feed him fried eggs, and send him off to work? Was I overreacting? I shivered as if pieces of ice rolled down my arms.

I wanted no part of a marriage like my parents. Mama was dependent on Papa and stuck with all of us kids. She seemed to grow bitterer every day. Was I childish to believe in true love that contained some strong inner emotion or genuine attraction?

My mind raced. No natural affection existed between James and me. I'd never felt a spark with James. My thoughts wandered to the hobo turned filling station attendant. I'd felt a spark with him, a real something.

I stopped my runaway thoughts. The filling station attendant? What in blazes was I thinking?

31

At least James had money, which would be needed to change the world. But James had never even kissed me. I felt nothing when I looked into his eyes.

"Shouldn't we talk more about this later?" I avoided looking at him.

"We can talk anytime." James flipped cigar ashes to the ground. "Why don't you think on it and we'll talk again in a few days?"

We stood, and as if he could read my mind, James pulled me to him and pressed a hard kiss to my lips. I neither responded nor pulled away. I felt numb. What kind of marriage would this be? What kind of life?

As the sun set, Marjorie and I waved good-bye to our friends and pulled onto the dirt road toward town. I turned north onto Beard Street, the road that would lead all the way through Shawnee. Dust gathered on the shiny car while Marjorie napped next to me.

Shawnee was the largest town for miles around, but from a distance, the houses were specks of brown shingles. The palate scheme of the area seemed centered on one drab color, brown: a cowboy riding a Palomino near a wooden fence post, dust behind a tractor, and the faded paint of an old barn. All shades of brown. The dirt-packed road brought the dying landscape closer and led to the rich bottom soil of the North Canadian River.

I drove over the bridge toward the outskirts of Shawnee. I had just reached the stop sign at Beard and Farrell when a rusty farm truck to my left jerked, barely missing a couple of children in the street. It zigzagged off the road into the ditch.

I sighed. "I'm glad we live on the north side of town."

To my left was the poor part of town and to my right was the Negro section. An invisible line separated the houses on this side of the train tracks, south Shawnee.

A barefoot black boy scuttled across the field from the train tracks, barely concealed by the dusk.

He dared to enter the white people's side of town at night, maybe to gather coal dropped on the ground or to pilfer through trash cans.

Poverty. I shuddered.

Chapter Six

A few days later on another hot June Saturday afternoon, I left our house and walked south on Beard Street toward Riverside Park. I carried my bathing suit bag. None of my siblings had wanted to accompany me, but I needed some relief from the heat, relief that could be found only in a swimming pool.

I strolled on the sidewalk opposite the Ozark Service Station where I had encountered the handsome attendant. A rubbery musk filled the air, and a noisy fan whined from inside the building. I glanced that way but saw no attendant. I looked away, disappointed. How foolish of me, though. I didn't want to put myself in an awkward position again. Almost flirting with a filling station attendant. I adjusted my straw hat, straightened my print dress, and walked quickly down the hill past the cabins and camping area at the park.

On the west side of Beard, down by the slow-moving Canadian River, a swimming pool overlooked the broad river's banks where the water had receded in the summer's drought, revealing red sandy patches.

In the dressing room, I changed into a modest one-piece bathing suit and matching bathing cap that covered every strand of my flyaway hair. I stood on the diving board, pulled my shoulders back, and remembered my grandma's words: "A beautiful woman should never stand like a farm hand."

I dived off the board and cut through the water.

I surfaced a few feet from a sturdy young fellow. I shook my head, causing drops of water to sling into his face. He laughed, and our eyes met. I looked into his big sky-blue eyes that sparkled like diamonds and did a double-take. Was this the hobo?

33

He looked clean now and had darker hair. His California bleached blond must have grown out. Maybe I was mistaken but yes, this could be him.

I took a deep breath and asked, "Hey, have we met before?"

"You drive a new Chrysler, don't you?"

I cocked my head and smiled. He did remember, at least the encounter at the filling station. "And you're the guy who put gas in Mama's car."

"You're the brown-eyed girl with the high cheekbones and a big hat. Of course I remember. I'm mighty glad to see you again. Wondered what happened to you."

"Your eyes." I looked straight at him. "I remember your blue eyes." When I looked at him, my heart sputtered like a Model T.

"I thought you were mighty pretty," he said bashfully, running his fingers through his short dark hair, smoothing its unruly waves. He looked different with shorter hair, the sun-bleached hair cut off.

We both chuckled. I liked his laugh. It was open and cheerful. We swam to the side and held on to the edge.

"I'm Fremont," he said. "Fremont Pope."

"I'm Sibyl Trimble. Nice to meet you, Fremont." I forced myself to look away at a group of children splashing nearby.

We pulled ourselves out of the concrete pool and sat with our feet dangling over the side.

"Good day for a swim, isn't it?" Fremont asked. "Sure cools off a fellow in this heat."

"Great day," I felt as if a magical charm surrounded us, and then berated myself for being so foolish.

Fremont seemed playful, at ease with himself, which made me believe I could confide my dreams to him without shame. Not in any hurry to prove myself, I relaxed. I felt so much more alive now than I ever had with James.

Fremont's quietness disappeared quickly and we chatted, diving into the cool water when the heat overcame us.

When it came time to leave the pool area, I returned to the dressing room, changed back into my street clothes and shoved my wet bathing suit, cap, and towel into my bag. As I stepped out of the changing room, I shook my head, causing my hair to spin around my shoulders in waves.

Fremont met me at the gate. His eyebrows rose when he saw me. "Mighty days, you look elegant, even with damp hair."

"Mind if I walk you home?" he asked, drying his hair with a towel.

I hesitated, noticing his rugged clothes and work boots. Mama would disapprove, of course, as her sense of decorum forbade my socializing with people not within the appropriate circles. But, oh, his compelling eyes. His cheerful presence made me feel safe. I didn't want this magical day to end.

"Of course you may," I said.

We walked north on Beard toward Main, passing a cotton gin, King's Grocery, the Shawnee Ice House and the Shawnee Mill. Then we hopped over several of the south-side railroad tracks. Oklahoma's busy railroads junctioned in the middle of our town: the Atchison, Topeka and Santa Fe; the Chicago Rock Island; and the Katy, which went back and forth from Missouri and Kansas to Texas. Fremont's gait was slower than mine, steady and intentional, so I slowed my pace to his. Then I skipped ahead and waited for him to catch up.

"How did you—?"

"Did you—?" Fremont said at the same time.

We laughed, "Ladies first," he said.

"No. Your turn. I'll take any question. Only gentleman's questions, however."

"I just wondered why I never saw you during high school," he said. "You went to Shawnee High, didn't you?"

"I graduated in '27, months before the stock market crash. I was only sixteen. Got pushed up a grade."

"I knew I would have remembered you. I graduated in '31."

"That was the year someone played that genius Halloween trick, wasn't it? Pushed an old Coupe up the steps into the front hallway of the school?"

Fremont threw his head back and laughed. "You heard? Yeah, I was in on that. We never did get caught."

"*You* were in on it?" I stopped to look at him.

"Me and a few other fellows." Fremont was still grinning. "I'll never forget the look on the principal's face when he saw that jalopy inside the school."

When his laughter faded, he said, "You look mighty good for a woman older than I am."

I punched his arm.

Fremont's humor was endearing. My family didn't know the meaning of humor. What was his family like? They must be very different. We conversed like old friends.

Within minutes, we turned east onto the brick-layered Main Street at the corner dominated by the massive Roebucks Building. Strolling under storefront awnings, we passed the Ritz Theatre, a billiard's parlor and the Owl Drug Store, where the best fountain drinks in town were served.

"What did you do after high school?" Fremont asked.

"Papa offered to send me to any college in the state, but when it came time to enroll, I decided on Commercial College here in town. The one in the Whittaker Building. Business courses will help in the future, Papa said."

"Why's that?"

"Papa says I'm the only one of his kids who thinks before I act. He expects more from me than the rest of the family."

"So what about now? What do you do now?" he asked as we passed the Duncan Drug Store, Woolworth, and Rosenfield's Jewelry.

"I work full-time as a stenographer for a lawyer, Mr. Weston. Get paid four dollars a week—when he has it. I feel like I've been trapped here since high school. I want to leave Shawnee. Do something meaningful with my life. I promised Papa I'd help change the world, and look at me. Stuck."

"That's where religion helps me," Fremont said. "Gives me faith."

"What do you mean?"

"Gives me purpose—trying to help others and live a contented life."

Maybe there was more to this guy than his melting blue eyes. Maybe he deserved my attention. "So, what have you been doing since high school?" I bit my tongue. Maybe I shouldn't ask him about his past. No one could be proud of being a hobo.

He didn't seem upset about my question. "I'm from Shawnee High like you. I tried to get a job when I graduated, but jobs were mighty scarce, as you know. I worked on a wheat farm west of town, then did odd jobs here and there. Most fellows around town couldn't find work, much less earn decent pay to support a future family."

"Jeepers, what happened?"

"When the farming started failing, the owners couldn't afford help no matter how much they needed it. Many couldn't pay their mortgages, so the banks booted 'em off their land. They didn't need help after that. Hayfield work petered out. I heard talk of good-paying jobs in California and got caught up in the tales of adventures out west. So one day, I moseyed on over to the train station to see what was going on."

Fremont stopped and gazed at the Santa Fe Train Station. "I've always liked this tower. It's a welcoming sign to strangers. I'm not easily discouraged, mind you, but I was desperate—one more mouth for my family to feed. After the '29 debacle, rumors flew about the financial bust back east, and most folks thought times were bound to get worse here in Oklahoma."

Fremont chuckled as he watched a train slow as it approached the depot.

"I jumped on the next freight train. I didn't have clothes, cash, or food with me. Mighty unwise if you ask me now. Even forgot to ask God what He wanted."

I gasped.

"Yep, I jumped a train," Fremont almost whispered. "And I remember your kindness."

So, he admitted he *was* a hobo. I let a railroad bum walk me home. On the other hand, he seemed to be a go-getter, a determined man who was not afraid of the unknown. A person with gumption to hop on a train to adventure and employment on his own. Maybe he wasn't such a bum after all. He did exude a certain masculine politeness that was most appealing.

I glanced at him. His refined profile, that straight, aquiline nose and strong chin, was as manly as a shining knight. Maybe he was my knight. I felt giddy with the idea.

Fremont took my hand and led me toward the rails. He pointed. "Down that track, I caught a train and then another and another, until

I was so far away from Oklahoma I thought I'd never get back. The rail took me all over the country, all the way to the San Joaquin Valley in California. A beautiful green valley not too far from the ocean." He paused, balancing on an empty rail. "Nothing else like it."

"I've always wanted to travel." I teetered along the track behind him. "It's so confining here, stifling, not like other places in the world where things happen."

"You'd love California." He jumped down from the metal track.

"I might." I followed in his steps over the tracks. "Maybe I'll go someday."

"I'm planning to go back in a few weeks. Maybe sooner."

I nodded and regarded the man—the hobo—beside me. How would Papa react if he knew who was walking beside me? He would not understand. He'd glare at me with his burning eyes, and tell me I was ruining my reputation by talking to a bum. I could practically hear his voice in my ears. *You're reducing your chances of becoming a leader. I taught you better than that.*

Befriending a hobo—that's exactly what I'd done. Here stood a poor man needing a friend. Of course, he was remarkably good-looking too, which helped.

Fremont and I turned and wandered back through downtown. We had been walking and talking for a long time. Where had the time gone?

"I need to go home. I have four younger siblings I feel responsible for. It gets difficult."

"I have two little sisters, so I know the feeling. It's a mighty heavy load. I want to help them and all the tots riding the trains with their folks."

"Me too," I said, pleased that he also cared. He loved people like I did. "I'm just waiting for an opportunity to help society." I lowered my voice as if whispering the words would protect me. "I want more out of life. I'm restless, but I can't explain why."

"You and half the young people in the U.S.," he said. "Do you know your eyes sparkle when you talk?"

I laughed.

"Passion," he said, "I see a passion for life."

Fremont touched an emotion deep inside me.

"I remember the first time I saw the Pacific coastline." Fremont's face glowed as if he could see past the sky. "I watched the never-ending ocean waves. How small I felt. How awed I was that a great God would create something so grand."

"You seem mighty stable to have gone through so much," I said, extremely aware of his masculine presence. I wanted to touch his striking face but did not dare.

"And you—you seem so vibrant and full of life." Then his voice softened as he added, "but timid and sad, like a wounded bird wanting to fly away."

My heart melted right there. No one had recognized my true self like this before. I turned and faced him. "I'll always remember those words," I whispered.

Our pace slowed as we reached my house, secluded and partially hidden by shrubs. Lilac bushes sprayed an overpowering sweet perfume and an orange-tinged full moon skimmed the treetops, its shimmering rays enhancing the dreamlike atmosphere.

"This is it." I stopped on the sidewalk and stared at the porch. A lamp was on, revealing Mama clearing the evening meal. "I feel like I've bared my heart to you and we've only just met."

"Could I see you again?" Fremont ventured after a long pause. "If you want to, that is…" He wavered. "I don't mean to be too personal, too soon."

"Yes, well—yes." I stuttered, not wanting to admit that I liked the idea. My papa would be furious. "That would be okay."

"How about next Friday night?"

"Friday?" I hesitated and looked down the dark road.

"Maybe I don't have a right to see you again." Fremont clenched his rough hands.

"No. It's just…I have plans to go dancing at the Blue Bird Ballroom. Hey, why don't you meet me there? You know where it is, of course?"

"Dancing? You want me to go dancing?" His voice sounded hesitant. "I've never been dancing."

"Don't worry. I'll show you how. It isn't hard at all. I took lessons at the Blue Bird for years."

"I'll try." Fremont looked down at his rugged shoes. "I've enjoyed the talk, Miss Sibyl. And I'd be mighty proud to walk you home again anytime."

"I'd like that, too," I said softly. I thought of James, and the joy seeped from my heart. I told myself I was only trying to help a down-and-out hobo.

But I knew better.

Chapter Seven

Every Sunday morning, Mama, my two youngest sisters, Blanche and Frances, and my grandparents went to First Baptist Church, one of the most magnificent church buildings in town. It sported not one but two belfries and a dome on top. Massive stone walls flanked a steep staircase which stopped at a wide porch held up by six white pillars. Its members, like the people of Shawnee, hailed from almost every state across the country. Besides Mama's pleasure at being seen doing her religious duty, she enjoyed the fact that the new music director appreciated her operatic voice. The main reason she attended church was to wear an elegant royal blue robe and sing in the choir.

My mother, Mrs. Mabel Margaret Bennett Trimble, was proud of two things: being born back east in Michigan to a prosperous family, and having a powerful operatic singing voice. As a teenager, she had moved to Sayre, Oklahoma, to live with her older sister and brother-in-law, who owned the Opera House. In fact, she'd been singing onstage in Sayre when Papa first saw her. Papa worked across the street from the Opera House at his first banking job, working for the Thurmonds.

It was a long story, but I heard it often.

When Papa got typhoid fever, a handyman who worked for Mama's brother-in-law took the sick man flowers, saying they were from Mama. No one knows why. Maybe he was matchmaking. Even though they didn't know him, Mama and her sister decided to visit Papa to take him some soup. That's where their romance started.

Mama was impressed with Papa because he learned to dance for her and he never took any liberties.

Once they were married, Papa never attended church with Mama again. They argued about religion until Papa finally stopped trying to convince Mama of his views. "Social justice can and will be attained on this earth only when people of goodwill unite to live by the Golden Rule," Papa repeatedly said. It was not far from Mama's views. Their differences centered on "who are the people of goodwill?" and "what demonstrates goodwill?" Papa believed that being of goodwill meant seeking social justice. Mama believed in goodwill to all, especially to those who could do her a favor.

Mama was a Baptist and Papa, a Unitarian, and that was only the beginning of family differences. Grandma Bennett claimed to be Methodist and Grandpa Bennett was Seventh Day Adventist, which caused a little friction between the two. Fortunately, Grandpa was an easy-going humorous old man, and Grandma was dedicated and read the Bible more than the rest of us put together.

When Marjorie and I were younger, we had to go to church with Mama every Sunday morning. Now, like this morning, we were allowed to sleep in late. I believed religion was important, but church never seemed to benefit my parents, so I had set it aside.

When I heard Mama's car pull out of the driveway, I jumped out of bed. Marjorie was still asleep, of course. I enjoyed reading, especially when the house was empty and quiet, so I sat at my desk and pulled out a list of several books I'd recently finished. A Zane Grey novel and a discourse on the poet Edmund Spenser, *Spenser and Utopia*, by Merritt Hughes, one of Papa's recommendations. Papa's vision for the future was indeed Utopian. He believed if people would continue to improve the world, righteousness would one day rule. He could drone on for hours about the injustice of class hatred and the dawn of a new social justice, but he never once attempted to carry out any plan of action that might improve opportunities for the poor. Instead, he would accuse the powers-that-be of covetousness and pride, saying things like, "Rich men are estranged from compassion for the poor people."

Papa had never actually read Spenser, so he would not understand why I liked the way Spenser's Lucifera explained that the brightly lit

Court of Pride masked a dungeon full of prisoners. Like the smokescreen in our politics today.

I didn't know whether Papa's beliefs were merely fantastical rhetoric or something that would lead to real actions. People could never achieve perfection like Papa said. But he told me I was one of the elect, chosen to help alleviate suffering. Could suffering end without God's help, with mere men? I had a lot of questions. Instead of suggesting concrete answers, Papa bought me other books by Marx and Darwin.

"Society must evolve," Papa would lecture me in the evenings. "Find your place as a leader in that evolvement. Don't drag humanity backward like so many of the establishment bumble-heads."

Pondering my reading and Papa's lectures made me grow weary.

"I need to sort out my life," I mumbled as I rose from my desk chair. I tied back my hair and slipped into a pair of knee-knockers and an overlarge blouse before going out the back door to do my weekly chores. I walked under the flowering bridal wreath hedge that faced the garden toward Papa's pride and joy, his irises. Hundreds of different shades and varieties erupted from his meticulously arranged beds.

I wanted to have the yard sparkling before Papa returned next week. I pulled on work gloves, lugged over the stepladder and climbed it to trim the bushes. Someday, I would plant my own flower garden with all shades, shapes, and sizes of flowers.

"Excuse me, miss."

Startled at the man's voice, I lost my balance and tumbled from the stepladder into the hedge.

As I got to my feet, a thin black man, hat in hand, rushed over to help me up. "I didn't mean to scare you none. Is you hurt?"

"I'm okay. A little smudged is all." I stood and dusted the dirt from my blouse. "Can I help you? I can get my sister to bring some food." I didn't allow the man to answer but yelled toward the kitchen door, "Marj! Someone needs a handout!"

Mama occasionally fed hungry people. Tramps familiar with this side of town knew to go to the back door.

"No handouts, miss. That's mighty nice of you. But I was wondering if you be needing any work done here in the yard? Sorry 'bout letting myself in through the gate."

The bottom of his baggy coat was frayed and stains darkened the edges of the long, rolled-up sleeves of his suit coat. He pulled his jacket around himself and turned back toward the gate. Poor black people always offered to work. Their pride wouldn't let them beg. An image flashed through my mind of the man digging through the trash near the Walcott Hotel.

"We could use help pulling those weeds over there," I said. Papa had said we needed to hire a gardener but I hadn't found one yet. "And that pile of wood needs to be hauled to the curb if you want to work for some dinner."

He turned toward me and smiled, his smile huge in his gaunt face. "I'd be much obliged, miss." He put his hat back on. "Name's Lester Morris. Show me where they's work tools and point me in the direction of them weeds. I'll be the hardest worker you ever seen."

After I got Lester started, I returned to trimming the bushes. Before Oklahoma's statehood and for some time afterward, black towns thrived with their own schools, churches, and businesses. Unfortunately, the Jim Crow laws of the Deep South had moved west and Oklahoma's first law reduced blacks to second-class citizens. What could be done to change that situation?

When he finished weeding, Lester picked up a pile of wood and headed toward the front yard. I saw him readjusting the heavy load as he went around the corner of the house toward the gate.

Suddenly, a loud clatter startled me. I dashed around the corner of the house.

"What happened?" I asked. James and Lester were lying on the ground with a pile of wood scattered around them.

James' loud voice echoed down the street for blocks. "I reached for the gate latch and this bumbling fellow came charging through." He picked himself up and brushed at his double-breasted jacket. "He crashed head-on into me."

Lester took a few moments to recover his bearings. As he got up and bent to retrieve the wood, he flinched and brought one hand to his hip, then continued slowly.

"You let a dirty, stinking n—" he barely swallowed the word, "come around this house. Your papa would never approve. Sibyl, get the police while I keep an eye on him."

"Why, James, don't talk like that." I said, mortified in front of Lester. "I don't believe you've sustained any injuries at all."

James turned and surveyed my bare feet, dirty clothes and tousled hair. "You aren't in any condition to make a judgment call about this."

How dare James question my judgment in my own home. "I guess you haven't met Lester. He's helping with the yard work. Lester Morris, this is James Fleming." Nastiness coated my words.

I had never seen James this insensitive. Lester stood still, his eyes downcast as if prepared for a beating. Annoyance rose in my throat. I hated for anyone to be treated like trash. And I certainly wouldn't put up with it right in front of me.

"Come over to the back porch where it's a little cooler," I said. "I'll fix you some lemonade."

"Sounds good to me." James eyed the presumed intruder.

"I was talking to Lester," I said over my shoulder to James, "but you're welcome to join us if you like."

As Lester set down the wood and followed me to the back door, James stormed out the gate toward the front of the house. I heard his car tires screeching down Beard Street.

Chapter Eight
July 1932

The clop of horse hooves and the clank of bottles sounded through the early Monday morning quiet. Milk in glass containers with cardboard stoppers was delivered to the front door. The well-trained milk horse knew to stop at the Trimble's home.

Marjorie ran through the house to the kitchen and stuck her head out the door. The milkman stood beside the porch as she stepped out. "Hello, sweetheart."

I could see the young man from the living room window. Brown cropped hair, not quite comfortable in a white uniform, clearly impressed with Marjorie's red lipstick and revealing nightgown.

"I'll take these," she said.

I turned away from the window and tried to ignore their whispered conversation. Marjorie was probably planning yet another rendezvous. The milkman left. I heard the horse ambling on down the street as Marjorie put the milk in the icebox and disappeared into the bedroom.

I dressed for work in a freshly washed and ironed well-cut tailored linen frock. I fastened a starched, white detachable collar around my neck. Later this week, I might wear the same dress but change the look with a scarf, a sash, or a collar and belt. Sometimes I tucked in uncomfortable shoulder pads. I had only a few dresses appropriate for work, so changing accessories stretched my wardrobe.

I worked as a stenographer for Mr. Weston, glad for a permanent job. Last year I worked briefly at Kress's five-and-dime and before that I worked for Mr. Kerr, who sold oil well supplies from his house.

I enjoyed the job and his lovely French wife's company, but he decided he needed a man to take care of his stock. I lost respect for him when he let me go, but it made me more determined to prove myself.

The morning walk to the office would be the coolest part of the day. Mr. Weston's office was on the second floor of a bank building on the corner of Main and Bell. I earned good pay for a young woman, but my boss had not produced one complete wage payment. He promised all the back pay when his clients paid their overdue fees.

Jobs in Oklahoma City offered promises of higher pay, adventure and action, but we had no family members living there. A decent, well-to-do white girl with an overbearing, well-known Papa did not live alone, no matter how lucrative the job. I had to stay at home in Shawnee.

Shawnee was not such a small town. Its name meant "Southerner" in Algonquin, who were the Indians from the South Ohio Valley. Our town was settled in 1891 during a land run and in less than fifty years, had grown immensely.

I walked up the stairs and down the hall to my office. Mr. Weston, coffee in hand, greeted me as I came in the door. "Sibyl, you're late this morning." He always arrived before me and always greeted me the same way, as if he'd waited hours to say those words.

"I'm right on time, sir." Which was unusual, since I *was* normally late.

"Well, come sit down. We have work to do." Mr. Weston was a sleazy looking fellow with dark-rimmed glasses that slid down his nose.

I grabbed my stenography pad and a sharp pencil from my desk and followed Mr. Weston into his office where I carefully smoothed down my dress and sat in a straight-backed chair.

My job included receiving clients and offering coffee as they waited, but my main job was taking dictation. Mr. Weston talked while I quickly jotted shorthand: strokes, abbreviations and symbols. I'd learned Gregg shorthand at business school. When he finished talking, I would decipher my scribbling into typed letters and legal papers. I enjoyed the work even if Mr. Weston made so many changes on a document that I had to type each page at least five times.

Today, as we worked, he paced the room. I kept my eyes on my pad of paper. He walked over to me and placed his hand on my shoulder as I wrote. I hated the feeling of his hand there. He stopped speaking, but I refused to look up.

"You look attractive in that outfit, Sibyl."

I squirmed, pulled my collar closer around my neck. I'd heard rumors that his wife was jealous of me, but I didn't know why. Heavens, Mr. Weston was as old as my father. I had to be nice without seeming to flirt with him or his clients. It wasn't easy. Maybe I should marry James and settle down. Then lustful old men would leave me alone. Did James still want me after the big garden incident? The bigger question. Did I want him?

"Thank you, Mr. Weston. And you were saying?"

Politely rebuffed, Mr. Weston sat in his chair as if nothing had happened. He shuffled through his papers and then started to dictate again, a Power of Attorney form this time.

I'd gotten this job because of Papa. He and Mr. Weston were old buddies from the Masons and banking industry. Their friendship went back to when we lived in Clinton where they'd worked together at a bank. Often, Mr. Weston made me want to stomp my feet and walk out, but I had to be agreeable, for Papa's sake.

There were almost fifty lawyers in town. Surely there were better attorneys to work for. I just had to spend enough time working for Mr. Weston to qualify for a better job. *Soon*, I hoped.

I was paid every Friday, two or three dollars each week. I didn't complain because the pay was good, especially for a woman, especially in the depressed economy. I was lucky to have a job at all. So I stayed, expecting the back pay to arrive any day.

For a man who never seemed to have enough money to pay me in full, he sure spent a lot on new ties from the Johnson and Templeton Men's Store and on client lunches at Norwood's Café.

When we finished he said, "We have one more item that needs to be filed as soon as possible. I'm afraid it's another foreclosure."

Farm foreclosure papers were one of Mr. Weston's frequent filings. Almost weekly, he helped a bank file foreclosure papers when a poor farmer couldn't make the mortgage payments. Papa's name occasionally came up when talking about foreclosures. Both men evaluated financial situations in the same way—the strongest would survive. But how strong could these farmers be when crop prices and land values collapsed? They couldn't pay back loans they'd taken out when prices had been high in the 1920s, much less pay the taxes and interest accrued. These days, most mortgages were for more than the land was worth. I felt sorry for the farmers. I didn't know any of them personally, but I read about the atrocities in the newspapers.

My legs ached, so I stretched them out a bit, noticing a run in my stocking. There went another dime and a trip to Mammoth's Department Store.

"Why are there so many foreclosures this month?" I asked.

"The farmers' plight is a regular part of business in this economy," Mr. Weston said. "If a man can't make a go of it, then the bank has no choice."

"But the banks do have a choice." I exclaimed. "They could reduce the monthly payments while extending the time to repay, or they could forgive part of the interest." It seemed to me that no one was looking after the farmers. In fact, many were exploiting the situation to buy up land and mineral rights for themselves. "Shouldn't it be illegal to take advantage of a national financial collapse to take a man's livelihood, his land?"

He didn't answer and I went back to my desk to type the documents, clicking at the keys.

Later that morning, the bell on the front door rang. I rushed to greet a gentleman in a worn suit and a decade-old tie. He took off his hat and practically bowed to me. Arrogant as an English knight.

"May I help you?" I asked.

"I need to speak to Mr. Weston."

"Whom shall I say is here?"

"The sheriff." There it was, a rusty silver star on his worn lapel.

I stepped into Mr. Weston's office to let him know and turned around, practically bumping into the sheriff. The man strode right in, so I returned to my desk. I could hear the entire conversation through the cracked open door.

"This union stuff you're working on needs to stop."

"What do you mean, Sheriff?"

"You're a union leader. You know exactly what I mean. There are rumors that the mill workers and railway workers aren't happy with their pay and time off. They're talking about striking. Better not happen while I'm sheriff around here."

"And you think I can do something about it?"

"Don't go smart with me, Weston. Do something decent for once."

"You saying I'm not decent?"

"Listen here. You heard what happened in Detroit? Those union strikers getting shot at? Well, I'm telling you, they should've shut those threats down or none of that would've happened."

As I eavesdropped, I reorganized the lists on my desk and straightened the stacks of paper into neat little piles. I knew Mr. Weston supported the unions. Anyone who was part of the old guard of the Socialists like Papa could not help but be involved. "Is this a threat?" I heard Mr. Weston say.

"You better believe it. What's more, if that riffraff from the other side of town don't tighten their belts and get on board, we're aiming to have some trouble."

Did he refer to an incident when a well-organized bootlegging ring was busted? A ring rumored to be protected by law enforcement officers?

I had kept up with the liquor bust and the resulting trial detailed in the *Shawnee News.* Several city officials resigned after the cleanup. The Pottawatomie County Attorney was acquitted. Fox, the former sheriff, and two drug store operators were convicted. Maybe that was why this new sheriff was determined to make sure no trouble occurred in town. He didn't want Shawnee's name on the front page of the *New York Times* again.

Oklahoma was still a dry state. Liquor was prohibited, but the state functioned as wet. The flagrant liquor sales had been a tradition since before Prohibition. The county bordered tribal lands. And small towns like Box, Corner and Violet Springs were infamous for selling liquor across county lines. With the expansion of new rich oil fields, alcohol sales had flourished.

Which side did the unions support? Wet or dry? Was money laundered through them?

Their conversation seemed to settle down for a while. I worked absentmindedly on the typewriter, adding three carbon papers behind the document before beginning a clickety-clack rhythm of the keys. Suddenly the voices exploded.

"We don't need unions in this town," yelled the sheriff. "We handle things our way."

"Remember Chief Butler?" said Mr. Weston. "Police chief work can be very dangerous."

"Are you threatening me now?"

"No more than you were threatening me," responded Mr. Weston smoothly.

Back in April, Tecumseh Chief of Police Butler had been ambushed, shot, and killed while on foot patrol. Wounded twice, Chief Butler returned fire, but hit nothing. Butler was taken to a doctor's office, where he died a few hours later. Before he died, he identified the shooters and they were apprehended the next day, convicted of murder, and sentenced to life in the state penitentiary in McAllister.

Surely Mr. Weston wasn't threatening to *kill* the sheriff. They didn't seem to know I could hear them or that I was there at all. I peeked in the doorway and saw them standing eye to eye. The air crackled with tension.

I hurriedly poured two cups of coffee, knocked on the door, and entered the room. "Anyone want coffee? I made it fresh," I lied.

The sheriff spun around and eyed me coldly. "Tell your banker papa that I aim to see that anything he's mixed up in gets shut down immediately. He's in on this unionizin', I'm a-betting." He snickered. "Taking money from the poor people and promising those fellows better wages if they strike. What kind of bunk is that? Same as stealing, if you ask me."

He strode past me and slammed the front door on his way out.

Mr. Weston's face was beet red as he plopped into his chair. "I'll take that coffee. And I need you to run an errand for me."

He scribbled on a piece of paper. "Run over to the union offices and hand-deliver this message."

"Yes, sir."

Mr. Weston jammed the folded message into an envelope and handed it to me. Then he picked up the telephone and I overheard him say. "Better get on this as soon as you can,"

The union offices were two blocks down on West Main. After I watched the trolley go down Main Street, I stopped to look behind me before turning the corner out of sight of Mr. Weston's office building. I slipped the message out of the unsealed envelope, my nerves as tense as newly strung barbed wire. I continued walking and glanced about, then dropped my eyes to the messy handwritten note.

Tell the boys to lay low for a few days.
Sheriff's suspicious.
Meeting still on at Lodge.

Papa went quite often to meetings at the Masonic Lodge, but I was certain he wasn't involved in any activities that might cause problems. Not my papa.

When I finally looked up, I had wandered pretty far from my destination, all the way to the back of the Norwood Hotel. A small group of shabby women with thin dresses and straggling hair and dirty children huddled under the staircase. They all were too thin and probably hungry.

A young girl stared at me, her eyes revealing misery and fear, as cast down as a slave who'd succumbed to hopelessness. She held a lethargic baby against her breast, her emaciated body visible through her ragged blouse. I stared back at her, compassion filling my mind, tears flooding my eyes.

Then I saw the ragged men straying from every direction and forming a line that circled around the corner of the street toward First Baptist Church. Had my hobo stood in lines like this? Late morning, the church dished out bowls of soup or beans. With the morning's events and my haste, I had forgotten the time.

I still had my errand to run, so I rushed away. When I reached the address, I took the stairs two at a time and bounded into the crowded union office. The office had only come into existence in the past two years. Half a dozen Shawnee unions and people's organizations were directed from these two rooms. The Progressive Knights of Labor, United Brotherhood of Carpenters and Joiners, Brotherhood of Firemen, Enginemen, Railways, Clerks, and Trainmen, and even one organization for women, the Women's Benefit Association, were headquartered here.

The room hummed with people coming and going, talking and arguing. Many farmers and workers who had lost their farms and jobs dropped by, hoping to hear of places needing workers or to learn of government relief action. The farmers who faced evictions, the sharecroppers dealing with failing cotton crops, and the railway workers coping with declining wages all came together to commiserate.

"Unions should do more," a man said.

"Asking for more wages makes no sense in this economy," another replied.

"That'd just get you fired."

"We don't need more wages as much as we need more jobs."

"No sense thinking about striking. Too many men to take our place."

"Who said unions should be abolished? Ain't this a free country?"

"Where's that union money going to, anyway?"

Desperate men flocked to the unions because the unions offered hope. Many feared that the economy would get worse. Some said things might get as bad as they'd gotten on the east coast. I looked around at the people in this room. Many seemed to be teetering on the brink of despair.

Unions were run by wealthy men who liked power: bankers, attorneys, politicians. Men like Papa. Union leaders promised to find better jobs, to get these men off the street and out of the bread lines. Who knew if they would or could keep their word?

"Hello, Sibyl!" someone called from a desk at the back. "Glad to see another female around here." It was one of my mother's church friends, a perky middle-aged lady. She sat behind a mountain of fliers.

"Eula May!" I crossed the room toward her. "What are you doing here?"

"I volunteered for the Women's Association, and this is what they have me doing. Preparing union propaganda. I don't even know what it's all about. I'd much rather be out there handing out bread to the poor folks who need it."

"My sentiments exactly. I saw a woman on my way over who could use a loaf. I don't know how she and her children are surviving."

"That's just it. Let me get my hands dirty. Let me do something useful for a change. We don't need this busy work. All I hear is talk, talk, talk!"

Knowing Eula May, she was doing most of the talking, but I agreed with her. I wanted to help too, not just sit around and discuss the pros and cons of the new president's policies.

"Who are you looking for?" she asked.

"Sam McClaire. Is he here today?"

"You might look over by that wall." She waved her hand toward the back of the office. "Most of the big dogs sit over there."

I left Eula May grumbling to herself as she folded flyers.

Sam sat in the back, his desk pushed up against the wall. His was the puffy red face of a man who drank too much, and in his case, the red went up to the very top of his bald head. A friend of Papa's, he and his frail wife had visited our house several times during the past year. I didn't know him well, but my impression was that he had been around unions a long time and strongly believed in them. I never heard him talk of anything else.

I waited until I was near his desk before I asked, "Mr. McClaire?"

He glanced up. "Yes?" Then he recognized me. "Oh, Sibyl Trimble. What brings you here?"

"I have a message from Mr. Weston." I handed the note to him. "He told me to wait for a reply."

"Give me a minute."

Since I had to wait, I walked back to Eula May's desk. "I'd like to volunteer to help with the soup lines. Do you need any help with those?"

"Oh my, yes. We can use all the help we can get. Nobody seems to want to stand around for hours ladling soup for the down-and-outers."

"Just don't tell my papa. He's supposed to be home this weekend and you know how he is. He'd never let me get near anyone who is not on their way to becoming a millionaire. And remember that I work every day until five."

"Gotcha." Eula May pulled out a calendar and flipped it open. "How about Monday evening? We need help at the First Baptist kitchen. They serve a meal at six. You know where the church kitchen is, so just show up in the back."

"Oh, dear." Mama would disapprove if anyone found out. Her high society position would be compromised.

"What's wrong? Want a different day?"

"I'll have to find an excuse to give Mama. But I'll be there."

I picked up Mr. McClaire's sealed reply and left. I stopped into Owls Drug Store on my way and paid a quarter for a cold sandwich at the lunch counter. Then I went back to the stairs behind the Norwood Hotel where I had seen the young mother and her baby. They were gone. All the women and children were gone, seemingly carried away by the dusty wind.

Chapter Nine

Papa didn't show up early Saturday morning. For nearly a month, he'd been out of town for work, but we expected him home today. I paced the living room, played a song on the piano, and wondered when he would appear. At last, at almost two o'clock in the afternoon, a horn honked.

"It's Papa!" shouted my youngest sister Frances.

Books flew, pillows were tossed, and children jumped up, running toward the front door. I rushed behind them through the living room, flinging Mama's hat toward the sofa and my sisters' stockings under the embroidered throw pillows. Last minute straightening, I rearranged the vase of fresh cut flowers and hurried to the door, following my three sisters.

The spit-wax shine of Papa's 1932 De Soto shimmered in the sun, a glare bouncing off the windshield. We all greeted him at once, gabbling like a flock of geese as he carried his luggage into the house. No gifts this time.

I wanted to talk with him about the recent events, but I waited as he unpacked his suitcase and changed clothes then ate the chocolate cake Mama offered. Through each mouthful, he ranted about his awful week. That's why there were no gifts. When he finished, he shot me a look that said I should follow him to the garden.

Out in the yard, I plopped down on a stool while he dug in the soil. As he worked, he told me about the newly formed Oklahoma Iris Society. I nodded my head until he abruptly changed the subject.

"Marjorie told me when I telephoned, of course, about your rendezvous at the Blue Bird. You might as well be out with the whole business."

"Sorry, Papa," I gritted my teeth. That Marjorie. "We got bored and dancing seemed like fun. We left early. I made Marjorie leave before the cops got there." She probably blamed me.

Papa's brow crinkled into a frown. "I must remind you that Marjorie needs protecting. She's naïve, and I hold you responsible for her behavior."

Angry tears formed, but I blinked hem back. How could I explain that Mama did nothing when Marjorie stayed out all hours of the night with different men? That Marjorie was capable of getting into trouble, no matter what I did?

I changed the subject. "Papa, James is coming by tonight."

"Yes, I know. We have some business to discuss." His eyes sparkled as he glanced at me. What did that mean? I certainly did not see anything humorous about James.

"I'm concerned about the state banks," he said. "The State National Bank in particular, which closed during the Bank Holiday. I don't think it should have been, but at least it's being reopened. A conservatorship was set up under the name of American National Bank. Getting new owners, I heard."

He, like always, drew me in. "Are any other banks reopening?" All the Shawnee banks had closed during the mandated three-day bank closings. Some had not reopened yet.

Papa ignored my question. He clamored from subject to subject almost quicker than I could follow. "The unions have begun to take form now, and we must unite the people who have proved their loyalty."

I raised my eyebrows, thinking of Mr. Weston, but Papa kept talking. I wasn't sure what he meant by *unite the people*, but I knew I'd missed my chance to ask questions. I couldn't interrupt his soliloquy now, and I still had subjects to discuss. Why had the sheriff threatened Mr. Weston? Is anything unsavory going on with the banks or unions? How involved was Papa?

At precisely six o'clock that evening, James bounded up the steps and knocked on our front door. Blanche let him in and simpered a greeting. During his previous visit, he'd played chess with Blanche, tossed Frances into the air, complimented Marjorie on her new hairdo, praised Mama for her cooking, and then to Papa's political opinions for hours. Unusual behavior for James.

This evening, James was impeccably dressed in highly polished shoes and dandified clothes. I nodded a greeting from the kitchen door. He gave me a sisterly hug. "I'm talking to your father tonight," he whispered. No apology for his atrocious behavior with Lester in the yard. Like it never happened.

I turned back to the kitchen while Papa swooped in and pulled him away.

"James is here, a little overdressed as usual," I said to Mama. She had insisted I dress up for the occasion, so my favorite blue outfit had been washed and starched stiff enough to stand on its own.

"He's such a gentleman," Mama replied.

"I guess."

"Why Sibyl, I declare he's an excellent match for you. The other ladies in my clubs have put together outstanding, beautiful church weddings. At your age, it's time you walked down the aisle. James' father is one of the leading men of this town *and* county." Mama wanted her daughters married as soon as possible and into well-to-do families. She seemed more concerned about social position than affection or common interests, completely indifferent to my feelings.

"You've already told me several times," I said, "but he seems no different than so many others, boring and self-centered."

"Good Lord, girl, don't talk like that."

"Deep down, this marriage doesn't feel right."

"Your mouth is bound to cause you trouble one of these days." She shook a mashed potato covered finger at me. *Do as you are told* seemed to be on the tip of her tongue, but she managed not to say it.

"Why don't you worry about Marjorie getting married?"

"Oh, Marjorie will be the easiest to get settled down. Most likely she'll run off with one of the dozen boys she brings around. Her lovely face and sweet nature attract all sorts of fellows. She only needs to close her eyes and pick one. You're different. You want to discuss topics inappropriate for courting, like politics or the latest book you've read." She looked at me sharply. "You've run off most suitable young men."

"How can I help it if I have a mind of my own? Isn't that what Papa encourages?"

I was not in the mood to argue with her. All I could think about was the conversation going on in the other room between James and Papa. My nerves were frazzled.

"Papa wants you, Sibyl!" yelled Frances as she ran into the room.

I froze. The dreaded discussion had reached the point that I must be included at last.

Mama raised an eyebrow. "You'd better hurry now."

I hesitated at Papa's office door, glimpsing the back of James' head as he faced Papa, who sat in a low, comfortable easy chair.

"Come in, Sibyl. Don't be shy now," said Papa. "Sit down." He motioned me to the chair across from him, beside James. I sat down stiffly and avoided James' eyes.

"I'm sure you already know that James and I were discussing your marriage," he said. "He seems to have a good proposition—that you get married as soon as possible. I like his way of thinking. I think we'll have the wedding in...hmmm...let's say three weeks."

I gasped.

"Let's talk about where the wedding should take place? First Baptist, naturally, even though I don't agree with their doctrine. It is a large ornate building and the dignitaries who come would be duly impressed, especially those from the City who do not think we have enough refinement down this way. And that new preacher they have, um...Dr. Turner? I haven't met him, but he might be the best choice."

I scooted down in my chair, melting with dread, not listening to the details as my mind reeled.

Finally James interrupted. "I figure a man like you wants the best for his daughter, sir." He pulled a small box from his coat pocket, opened it, and held a shiny diamond ring toward Papa.

"Not to me. Give it to her," Papa said. "Give it to Sibyl. Don't be so nervous. Weddings happen every day."

James fumbled with the ring box and held it toward me.

I took deep breaths to keep from panicking. The diamond was gorgeous, the biggest one I had ever seen, even bigger than the one

Mama wore, which she proudly and habitually flashed in front of others. I felt too weak to say what I felt. I could not take the box because my clammy cold hands were trembling.

"Well, James, I do believe she's too overcome to react," said Papa. "It's a good thing I'm here. Go ahead and put it on her finger."

James did as my father said. He didn't seem to notice my reluctance.

"There now, that's done." Papa chortled. "Sibyl, all that's left is to tell your mama. She'll be downright glad to see the ring. Then you can show off that stone to your sisters and friends." Papa turned to James. "I spoke with your father at the last meeting downtown. Looks like he may have lined up a spot in the next election for you, all right." He turned back to me. "Sibyl, don't just sit there. Run on to your mama. You two have lots of planning to do."

"But, Papa...I...I don't know—"

"Nonsense. Your mama is dying to see it. Go on now. James and I have some business to discuss. I know how you girls like to show off these things."

Dazed, I fumbled for the door knob and stood there a moment to catch my breath. I heard James say, "What about that business we were discussing? My father wants to open a new store in town, and he needs a loan."

Papa said, "I think we can handle that."

I stood in the hall as tears streamed down my face, tears of frustration for not standing up for myself, for giving in yet again to please Papa and fulfill his expectations. Why did I fear losing Papa's regard for me?

I had made a promise on that long-ago night when Papa took me to hear Jack Walton's spiel for governor. I promised I would help Papa change the world. I could never break that promise—Papa was my hero.

Chapter Ten

The following Monday I walked to the First Baptist Church after work for my first day of volunteering at the soup line. I'd told Mama I was going shopping at the Mammoth and would probably be late coming home. She would be furious at me for wasting my time helping at the church. Earlier that day, during my lunch hour, I purchased some stockings to make my cover story seem real.

At five o'clock, an hour before serving time, bedraggled men already stood on the street in a line that meandered around the block. Many wore well-worn newsboy caps and jackets, but some were farmers in overalls. The dust was all-pervasive, surrounding the men like a shroud. Most of them were quiet and sullen, but a few chatted. When I heard some election talk, I slowed to eavesdrop. Three men discussed the coming election—two seemed to be for Roosevelt and the other for Socialist Norman Thomas.

I arrived at the church's back door, entered the kitchen, and asked a heavy-set woman who looked to be in charge what they needed me to do. She tossed me an apron like the one she wore. "You new here?"

"First time," I replied, looking around. Two decently-dressed women sliced loaves of bread and placed the pieces in a huge basket to distribute. Others diced potatoes and several huddled over a large boiling pan, steam rising above the stew. I didn't recognize any of the ladies, which was a relief. I didn't want my clandestine activity getting back to my parents for fear of their over-reaction.

"Well, for starters, you can set up a few tables outside to put the food on. About three tables will do. Get Pearl over there to help you."

She pointed to a petite girl whose hair was pulled back in a chignon. Pearl's lips turned up in a happy-go-lucky smile.

Pearl and I carried heavy tables out the back door and set them up to serve the food. Pearl knew the arrangements quite well. Her mother, I discovered, led this endeavor, so she often came to help.

For the next half hour, we worked together, carrying bowls and spoons to the outside tables and making a place for the stew and bread. Some men brought their own bowls, but most did not. My earlier fears about seeing anyone I knew faded. I felt silly. I had met so few destitute people in my life. These people had real fears of hunger and joblessness and things I could hardly imagine.

Just as the last preparations were being completed, there was a commotion near the back door.

"Sorry, I'm late. Can't seem to get myself together," squawked a woman as she burst in the room, several loaves of bread in her arms. My heart sank when I recognized her voice. It was Mama's friend, Mrs. Matthews. She strode through the room like she was the only saint in town. Her flashy glass beads glistened in the dark steamy room.

If I had not been in the middle of helping move a hot soup pan outdoors, I would've ducked away. Instead, I tried to avoid looking in her direction. She spotted me at once.

"Well, Sibyl Trimble. How nice to see you down here helping the paupers. Didn't think your folks would allow it."

"Nice to see you too, ma'am."

"Well, it takes all of us to help during these trying times." Mrs. Matthews dropped her loaves of bread on the cabinet then turned to leave as abruptly as she had entered. She offered no more help.

The serving started right at six. As I passed out one slice of bread to each person who came through the line, I fretted. Eula May might keep my secret, but I wasn't sure about Mrs. Matthews. If she mentioned my activities to Mama, Papa would find out, and if Papa discovered what I'd been doing, I'd have to find a reasonable explanation. He didn't think action meant associating with the poor and needy. To him, helping meant planning an overall strategy and hob-knobbing with the ones who changed laws. He wouldn't be satisfied when I explained that I was merely trying to put his social justice ideas into action.

Grandma Bennet beamed with pride when I confessed to sneaking out to help at the church. Her heart always understood mine. She would spend a few minutes with me in the evenings asking about my day. Tonight she sat on my bed while I curled up on a pillow.

"That's a gorgeous engagement ring. Have you chosen a date for the wedding?"

I gritted my teeth. "Papa says three weeks."

"You don't seem thrilled like a bride should be. Are you worried about the preparations?" Grandma had let her hair down and the gray, wavy mass fell over one shoulder. She wore a raggedy house dress but her eyes were the kindest I had ever seen.

Grandma always knew when I needed to talk. Maybe she could see the steam rolling around my head. "I'm not sure about marrying James," I said. "How do I know if he's the right one?"

"If you're doubting, child, postpone the wedding until you're sure."

"But Papa wants me to marry soon. He would be furious." I sat up, agitated.

Grandma turned and looked me straight in the eyes. "You know what I think about your Papa and his uppities. Just stand up to him. It's your life."

I wish I tell my papa exactly what I thought and have his support. I winced. Maybe tomorrow. I would have to think on it some more.

She kissed me on the forehead. "Don't forget to pray, child. Pray and ask for help."

Should I confess to Grandma about my strong feelings for Fremont, the hobo? No, I couldn't do that either. Later, I would dig down for the strength to go against the forces in my life. But not yet.

One comfort remained. Whatever happened, my Grandma Bennett would understand.

Chapter Eleven

On the following Friday night, I saw Fremont standing near the front door of the Blue Bird Ballroom. I was hoping he would be there. I'd even worn my dainty, wrap-over shoes to show off my long legs.

Marjorie and I had snuck out again. I warned Marjorie not to tell Papa this time or it would be our last dance. As I waltzed, Fremont gazed at me as if mesmerized.

I stopped in the middle of a dance and walked over to him. "Hi, Fremont."

"Well, I, ah…I'm amazed at how well you dance."

I motioned him to follow me to a table full of people. "Come sit with us." Hesitating, he peered down at his flannel shirt, pressed work pants, and heavy work boots. Compared to other men's double-breasted casual jackets, bold silk ties, and silver tie pins, he looked as if he had walked into the wrong establishment. Lining East Main were many speakeasies, bars, and clubs that catered to the poorer classes. The Blue Bird was not one of them.

Fremont sat uneasily at the table with my friends and me. The loud music made conversation impossible, so when a guy stole behind me and tapped me on the shoulder, I shrugged and followed him to the dance floor, leaving Fremont to fend for himself.

When the music ended, I pranced back to the table, flush with enthusiasm. Several men quickly surrounded me again before the next song began. I looked to where Fremont sat, hoping to dance with him.

Why did Fremont excite me when I was engaged? I ought to have felt guilty. After all, I wore another man's diamond. Wished I had stood up to my father. Oh my, here's James, and he looks handsome and all, but he's not Fremont…

Not knowing my predicament, Fremont stood to ask me to dance.

James snatched my hand, "Sorry pal. This one's mine."

I followed him to the dance floor. Despite how I felt about James, dancing with him was enjoyable. He moved like winged Mercury. Seconds after the song ended, he disappeared to the back of the room where the carousing was going on.

I danced three more times before I noticed Fremont stand and turned toward the doorway. He was about to leave. As the band began playing, "It Had to Be You," I sashayed over and grabbed his arm. "Ready to dance?" I asked.

"I suppose so," he said, reluctantly. His inexperience at dancing became apparent when he tripped me twice and scraped my shoes. At least we didn't fall all the way to the floor. Fremont looked mortified. When we arrived back at the table, he dropped into the chair with a look of relief.

I left him there for the next half hour and went back to the dance floor, where I danced like I couldn't stop moving. I watched him watching me. Our eyes met often, and I liked the attention. Then I felt guilty looking at one man while my fiancé was nearby drinking.

When I returned to the table for a break, Fremont said, "Want to step outside for a minute? Fresh air might be good."

"Sure. I'm ready for a breather." I followed him out the front door. Roadsters and sedans were parked along the street. Several couples stood around a Model A. Cigarettes flickered as guys puffed and then stomped the butts on the ground.

"Sorry about the dancing," he said, leaning against the wall. "Didn't mean to step on your toes. I never danced before, so I'm a mighty awkward partner."

"You just need a little practice." I leaned next to him. "I can teach you."

"I'm afraid it'll take a long time for me to be as good as you." A moment passed, and then he said, "I noticed every detail about you, from your hair clinging to your high cheekbones to your long legs, from your mighty flashing eyes and creamy skin to those slender arms. Oh, yes, I noticed."

His forwardness astounded me. Excited me. None of my dance partners had ever spoken to me so boldly, not even James. And I wore his ring. I looked over my shoulder. Where was James?

"Mostly I love your passion for life." Before I could reply, Fremont asked, "May I see you again sometime? Maybe away from the dancing?"

Should I even be talking to this attractive man? Then I responded just as boldly, "There's something different about you, Fremont. You're not like the others." I took a deep breath and turned to look into those baby blue eyes. "I thought I'd never see you again."

He smiled. "Maybe the miserable evening was worth it."

Neither of us said anything else, but the silence was electrifying. Our breathing slowed and we inhaled deeply at the same time. He leaned forward, his face close to mine. I could smell the Lifebuoy soap he used and the hint of Old Spice. His eyes sparkled. I held my breath, hoping he might kiss me, and then afraid he would.

The Blue Bird's door burst open and James' gruff voice sounded loud. "Hey, Sibyl." His eyes darted from me to Fremont and back. "Who's your new friend. Oh, the filling station bum."

"James, there you are," I stepped up and took his arm, turning him towards the smoky, booming room. "I was trying to entertain the lower part of society."

I hated myself for my haughty words. As I looked back over my shoulder to wave a slight goodbye, I could see the pain on Fremont's handsome face. For the first time, he seemed to notice the glaring diamond on my left hand.

James snapped his attention back to Fremont. "Been watching you. Don't think you belong around here."

Fremont stepped away from the wall. "Maybe you're right, maybe I don't. But that is one mighty fine girl you've got there, so you should treat her right."

"Now's a good time for you to leave," James growled.

Fremont stepped toward us. James put his arm behind my back and pushed me toward the ballroom door. Then he stepped in front of Fremont and shoved him roughly. Fremont stumbled, barely catching himself as the door slammed shut in his face.

Chapter Twelve

Two days later, I felt brave enough to visit the Ozark Filling Station where Fremont worked. I wanted to apologize for my behavior. I hoped he'd understand.

I drove up in Mama's Chrysler and old Mr. Winters lumbered across the lot. He filled my car with gasoline and washed the windshield. I looked around. No Fremont. Disappointment made my heart fall.

"Where's Fremont today?" I asked as I handed Mr. Winters my money.

"Couldn't afford to keep him," he said. "Said he was heading back to California."

My mouth fell open. Fremont left without telling me. Maybe he caught a train out of town after my unpleasant words. A sinking feeling settled in my heart. I needed to see Fremont, to apologize. Except it was more than that. Shouldn't I have felt relieved he was gone? Relieved I wouldn't have to face him? Relieved I could now focus on my impending marriage? But all I felt was a deep disappointment, despair even.

I needed to see him like I needed air or water. The connection between us hadn't been my imagination. It had been real, and I knew it was more than his good looks and kind manners. Those blue eyes called to me in a way that felt almost *divine*.

What could I do? After all, I was engaged. And a poor man, a man who would run off to California over a few ill-timed words, would never do for me. I had to pull myself together, forget about Fremont, and go back to the man Papa had chosen for me.

I drove around the block in a daze.

Papa said poor people were important, that all people were equal, no matter their financial status. Maybe Fremont needed financial help. Maybe that was why he was leaving town. I told myself that Papa would understand my desire to help him. I could at least check on him.

I drove back to the filling station and asked Mr. Winters for directions to Fremont's family's house.

His family lived on the other side of town, the south part. I cruised west down Farrell toward Pottenger Street. Skinny, ragamuffin children played in front of frame houses with patched roofs. Stools decorated long front porches like flower baskets might dot the porches of the houses in my neighborhood.

I stopped in front of Fremont's house, unsure what to do. I sat in the Chrysler for a few minutes. Just as I decided to drive away, he stepped onto the front porch with a suitcase in hand.

He saw me. Stared for a moment. Then he set his bag down on the steps. With a puzzled look, he came toward me. I couldn't tell what he was thinking. Was he angry? Or happy to see me?

"What are you doing here?"

I leaned out the window and smiled my best Marjorie smile. "Wanted to apologize and see if you'd like to go get a soda."

"Now?"

"Sure. Get in."

Shelves filled with boxes of cosmetics, new household gadgets, and the biggest assortment of pharmaceutical needs in town filled the walls of Owl's Drug Store. Beautiful, shiny glass countertops were lined with red cherry candies, lollipop sticks, and black licorice. As we entered, a drop-down ceiling fan waved away any gloomy mood, and the smell of coffee teased my nostrils.

We sat at a table and ordered cream sodas. I didn't want to delve into any serious talk, and he didn't seem to want to either, so I chattered away. "Hoagie Carmichael is one of my favorite songwriters. You remember, he wrote 'Star Dust' and 'Up the Lazy River'? He plays the piano and leads the orchestra down at the Blue

Bird sometimes. He's one of Papa's relatives, and his sister-in-law's father, Marshall Van Pool, owns the group, so Hoagie plays for us like we're family. Marjorie, of course, flirts with him. He sang 'Up the Lazy River' to her over and over before it was even published."

I talked on, hoping Fremont would smile, but his countenance remained somber. We finished the last of our drinks and decided to take a walk. As we were leaving, Fremont pushed open the heavy front door, and his arm brushed mine. The warmth of his touch thrilled me, but I quickly pulled away.

We meandered on a few moments without speaking. "What's wrong?" I finally asked.

"Why did you come looking for me?"

"I hated to leave things the way they were. Thought I might try to smooth things out a bit."

"Well, I'm not sure what the good Lord wants, but I've decided to let Him direct things. I keep falling all over myself with mistakes."

"Oh."

"I used to trust Him more, but I got away from church while I was traveling." He kicked a stone, and it sailed down the street and hit the tire of a jalopy parked in front of the Kresses. "My bags are packed to leave for California." He looked at me timidly. "I worked at a lettuce farm in the valley. It was owned by these old folks named the Rosens. They don't have any children and they favored me. I worked hard for them and tried to be honest, as I did in all my dealings."

"Mr. Rosen sounds like a good man."

"Well, the job lasted through the harvest season. I grew to liking it better than anywhere else I'd worked. After a few weeks, Mr. Rosen told me I could stay as long as I liked. He said they could use my kind of help." Fremont's countenance grew sad as he remembered. "He treated me like one of his own. And it's a job. It's mighty hard to find work around here. That's why I'm going back."

"Maybe you should put it off for a while."

"I'm worried about them. You heard about the strike out in the San Joaquin Valley, didn't you?"

"It was in Sunday's paper. Going on three weeks now. Three people got killed already."

"Imagine, people dying over a paycheck. Mighty dumb, if you ask me. The union fellows were only asking for enough money to support themselves." Fremont shook his head.

Neither of us said anything for a few minutes before I asked, "What does that have to do with you going back to California?"

"That's where the Rosens live. In the Valley. They probably can't get enough help now."

"You could try to get a job at another filling station here." Had I said too much? James' face flashed in my mind. James, my fiancé.

Fremont shrugged.

We stopped at a corner for a pickup truck to pass and Fremont looked at me. "Guess I could stay for a time. Mother tells me God has a purpose for everything. She's pretty wise, so maybe I ought to listen to her more and not be in such a hurry to do things my own way."

I hesitated. A purpose in life? Did God have a purpose for me? One not dictated by Papa? I wanted to rule my own life, but so far I'd done a lousy job. Should I break up with James? If I really wanted to marry him, what was I doing with Fremont? What about the wedding plans Mama was making?

The thought of following Papa's plan made me want to run for the hills. But what if God did have a plan for me? One different from Papa's, maybe even better? "Perhaps I should look into this 'purpose' you say God offers. It might be a worthy cause."

We rounded the corner at Union and spied the round red-and-white barbershop pole ahead. A wrinkle-faced black man sat on a stool outside shining boots. He'd been a constant presence in the Shawnee for years. Fremont nodded to him as we strolled past.

"What is this?" a thunderous voice said from behind us. "My sweet Sibyl two-timing me with a bum from the poorhouse?"

We spun around. James was standing in the open doorway of the barber shop. A hot towel wrapped around his face, a long sheet tied around his neck, and a white cloth hanging to his knees.

Faces peered around corners and the barber stuck his head out the door. Fremont and I stood still for a moment, too surprised to reply.

Then Fremont stepped toward James. "If you want to discuss this, tonight might be a better time."

"No siree." James yanked the towel away. "If I'm being jilted, I want this resolved right here and now."

The two men stood chest to chest, and then James pushed Fremont with both hands, causing him to stumble backwards. Fremont leaned forward as if to shove James back. A crowd began to gather.

My temper flamed. "Why, Mr. James Fleming." I stepped between them. "You're making a complete fool of yourself in front of this whole town. Mr. Pope and I just enjoyed a soda in the very public Owl Drug, and you accuse me of the worst possible things. You owe me an apology."

"Apologize, nothing," said James, glaring at me. "I don't aim to be the laughingstock of town with you prancing around with a hoodlum. Wait right here and I'll walk you home myself."

"James!" I stomped my foot. All the negative and stifling emotions about James and our impending loveless marriage instantly surfaced. "I'm going home right now, and Fremont is quite capable of escorting me!" James would never forgive me if I left with Fremont, but I knew I would probably never set eyes on Fremont again if I said goodbye now. I didn't care that a relationship with Fremont couldn't go anywhere. If I wanted to have a soda with him, I would do so. No matter what James thought.

"By the way," I said acidly, "I believe this belongs to you." I yanked the diamond ring off my finger and threw it at him. He scrambled for it while Fremont took my arm and we turned away.

"You'll be sorry for this someday!" James yelled behind us. "That poor bum can never make you happy."

I walked on without looking back, taking small steps to steady myself. James didn't understand me, never had. I trembled, shocked at what I just did. Maybe relieved. Maybe this wasn't about Fremont's blue eyes. Maybe I needed a reason to end things with James.

Fremont and I rushed through downtown Shawnee. When we got away from prying eyes, I turned to look at his face.

"I'm so embarrassed for that scene," I said.

"No. I shouldn't have been with you. You're engaged. Or were engaged. It's my fault. Will your family be upset? He does have a lot to offer."

"'He makes no friends who never made a foe,' said the lily maid of Astolat. Go on, Fremont, tell me more about your travels." Even if he was unsuitable marriage material, I enjoyed his company.

He almost grinned.

"You're a courageous man," I said. "You've explored the world. That takes courage. Would you tell me another one of your stories? Please." While he talked, I wouldn't have to think about life decisions and their possible consequences.

"I've never told anyone this before, not even my mother." He leaned toward me and whispered. "But it's downright lonely on the rail, out there by myself. Plain scary. Once in Kansas City, a gang of hoodlums knocked me over the head and took what few pennies I had. No, ma'am. I'm just plain folk. Courageous is not who I am."

As we walked, he told me about some of his jobs. He'd worked on a milk farm owned by a Chinese couple who couldn't speak English. He'd slept in the barn and woken before daybreak to milk cows. "I'd never seen a hundred cows needing milking all at one time. I wasn't too enthusiastic, so the first chance I got, I hitched a ride back into town and caught the next freighter."

I loved his contagious laugh and compelling voice. He took my hand, and I felt a chill up my spine. Suddenly, I almost jumped for joy. I'd had two fellows nearly fighting over me. Marjorie might have so many boyfriends she couldn't count them, but none of them seemed very committed to her, nor she to them. But here I was with two men who thought I was worth coming to blows over me.

My pleasure was short-lived and soon gave way to apprehension. What had I done? What if I'd made a mistake? Papa might have been right. Maybe I ought to marry a well-to-do fellow like James, settle down, use his money to lessen the world's poverty. My gait slowed and my feet dragged. Papa was going to be outraged when he found out I broke my engagement to James. How would he react to my notable public actions?

Chapter Thirteen
August 1932

The hem of my dress swished around my legs as I paced across the living room floor. Yesterday's fiasco with James had dampened my weekend. I dreaded having to tell Mama and Papa. "My life has absolutely no peace in it."

"Sorry, sis," Blanche said, "but talking to yourself won't solve your dilemma." My eleven-year-old sister stood in the middle of the room with her arms folded across her chest. Her caustic manner stemmed from believing she possessed the most active mind in Shawnee. That might have been true, but no one else wanted to hear about it.

"You're right. So I suggest you help me locate your little sister." I put on my no-nonsense, grown-up look. "Don't just stand there, help me."

"Poppycock. The truant doesn't want to be found, I suppose." She shrugged and stomped out of the room.

My two youngest siblings knew a different life than my brother Calvis, Marjorie, and me. Our parents seldom scolded or disciplined the younger ones, neglecting even to teach them proper manners.

Frances, a precocious five-year-old, was hiding to avoid my attempt at smoothing her unruly blond curls. Usually she loved dressing up and attending meetings with Mama, paraded as she was in front of others. This morning she thought it all a game.

As I headed down the long hallway, I heard little feet scampering through the house. Pink skirt tails flew around the corner of the room.

"You know better than to run from your oldest sister," I scolded as I caught her. "Papa wants all his girls to be good."

Frances giggled as she plopped on the couch. I brushed her wild hair into place, my long fingers working quickly and expertly, as I had done this many times before. With a little tug at a pink ribbon, I finished pulling her curls to the nape of her neck. I turned her around in a circle. "There, little miss, you're as good as you're going to get. A dear little bunny if I ever saw one."

"Can I dance for them today?" Frances grinned, twirled, and curtsied to her audience, almost knocking over a nearby lamp.

"No, silly girl. This is a grown-up meeting, and Mama's going to sing."

"Sibyl!" Mama yelled from the kitchen. "Come in here when you're finished. I need your help."

I sighed. I hated keeping secrets from Mama. Would she notice my absent engagement ring?

The aroma of cinnamon and apple pie grew stronger as I stepped into the kitchen. The delicious smell cascaded over me like sweet honey.

"Where's yesterday's paper?" Mama asked as I lifted the hot apple pie from the oven. She wore a stiff rose printed dress and a tea apron tied around her waist. "Lazy girl, you cooked the pie too long," she scolded. "Apples have gone up to a penny apiece. We can't afford to burn anything."

I cringed. "It appears okay to me."

Her anger over the pie was quickly replaced by excitement. "The notice of today's meeting should be in the paper. Hurry and read it to me."

"Right here, Mama." I snatched the newspaper from the table. "I've read it to you several times. 'Shawnee Chapter Forty-Three of the Order of the Eastern Star will hold services in the Red Room of the Masonic Temple. Newly Organized Eastern Star choir will sing'."

As I held the paper, Mama stared at my left hand. "Where's your ring?" Mama looked up at me like she could read my mind. "Is something wrong?"

"I'll explain later." I said.

Mama, involved with many organizations, attended every party, social gathering, and clothing sale in town. She loved being a socialite. "After this is over, we'll sit down and talk." She took a deep breath. "We have other things to do first."

Just like that my wedding was dismissed.

"We're going to sing today for the first time," she said. "After all our practice, we should be the best in the country. Do you know how many hours and days we've practiced?"

"Yes, Mama, I do know." I moved to the far side of the kitchen, my feeling unclear. For weeks now, and much to my chagrin, I had played the songs on the piano while Mama practiced them over and over.

"How did I sound?" Before I could answer she said, "That was a new version of 'Blue Steps' with a little more pep. I've never heard it before, but it was lovely, don't you think?"

"Yes Mama. Lovely." She had sounded really good, especially with her Marlene Dietrich-like voice. I loved to hear her sing "Let Me Call You Sweetheart."

"Hurry now, girls" Mama commanded. "This meeting can't start without me."

"I don't want to go," Blanche said, her lips turned down in a frown. "I'd rather go to one of Papa's meetings."

"Papa isn't here, so pack up your sour feelings and get in the car," Mama said.

They rushed through the door, and I followed them to the shiny Chrysler and laid the pie on the vehicle floor. I stood still and watched as Mama slowly backed out of the driveway. My mind was full, wondering about James, and Fremont, and Papa. Mama was too preoccupied with her own schedule to care much about mine.

It would be another week before Papa returned from his business trip, so I enticed Fremont to drive with me to Garrett's Lake to swim in the clear spring water. The lake was small and crowded, but it boasted a high diving board and an island in the middle, perfect for playing King of the Hill with my friends.

"I'm looking for a job at a filling station," Fremont said as we spread a blanket and sat down. "If I don't find one soon, I'll have to go back to California."

"Should be some kind of job around here." I ignored his comment about going back to California.

Hours after we finished swimming we ate at Van's Pig Stand, the best barbecue around. Tired from our frolicky day at the lake, we didn't talk much. Red sauce dripped from Fremont's chin, and I reached over and wiped it off with a napkin. He laughed.

I felt carefree when I was with Fremont, except when I thought of my family. His family. The future. This relationship, of course, could go nowhere. So why did I crave his companionship so much?

Late that afternoon, I dropped Fremont off and went home. When I pulled into the driveway, I saw Papa's De Soto. Frances rushed out the front door yelling, her pigtails flying behind her. I couldn't understand what she was shouting, so I jumped from the car and hurried towards her.

"What's wrong?"

"Papa's home!"

"Is he mad?"

"I've never seen him so angry. He asked Mama where you are." Frances's words came in a hurry, her face flushed red. "You better get in there fast!"

This was it. Had he heard the news about the broken engagement?

I found Papa in the backyard, stomping through the flower bed, grumbling under his breath. "This ground's as dry as a sow's bone. Can't I leave this family in charge of anything? I've been gone three weeks, and look at these irises. They're almost dead. Where's that gardener you hired? Doesn't he ever water these things?"

Sure enough, large cracks had broken through the parched soil. Lester watered twice a week, conserving water like the city suggested, but the flowers obviously needed more. With no rain in months, it was the hottest summer I could remember.

I knew more weighed on Papa's mind than his precious irises. I had seldom seen him so agitated.

"Papa, I'll water the flowers," I said. "I think they'll be fine."

"What do you mean, fine?" He barked. "Nothing's fine anymore. Your mother lets the house go to pieces. She can't keep you young'uns in line and begs for more money. All she ever does is complain. Never thinks about the rest of the country, about the thousands of indigents unfortunate enough to blindly follow the crowds to destruction. She never has any idea what I'm talking about. She's the stupidest woman I know."

After watering the flowers, I followed Papa as he marched around the yard. My body tensed wondering how I could tell Papa about James.

"And she tries to make me feel sorry for our 'poor little family.' Seems like the family's doing fine. Here I am out slaving, promoting the welfare of mankind. A bankers' job these days hinges on how many foreclosures he can instigate, legally or illegally. Do you think I like filling the coffers of the wealthy? Must I remind you of the bank holidays? The collapse of our national banking system almost destroyed the backbone of our country."

"Yes, Papa, I remember. But when you speak of mankind, does that include the hobos and the men traveling around by rail?"

"Mankind? No one deserves to be considered mankind if they are selfish and do not make the effort to overcome evil. Who do you think is out saving mankind from annihilation? Certainly not the double-minded Christians who lean toward the ways of Cain."

"But the churches help feed the poor," I ventured to argue, something I rarely did before. "Most Christians are good-hearted."

"Oh yes. Feeding the poor while filling their own pockets with stolen coins."

Arguing with Papa was useless, and I was afraid to push him too far.

When he finally quieted, I muttered so low I could barely hear myself, "I'm sorry, Papa," as if it was my fault I could do nothing to change the dry weather or to make Mama do as he expected.

"And you!" Papa turned on me. "I hear you fancied James was not good enough for you, so you gave him back his ring."

I stood speechless. I had known this was coming, but I had no idea what to say.

"What makes you think you're going to catch a better man than that?" His voice rose so loud, I was sure the neighbors could hear. "You know how important it is to marry the right man. The future of this state is at stake, maybe even the country. And what do you do? Throw away a perfectly good opportunity. Where's that under-used brain of yours, girl."

My hands were sweaty, and my heart flipped sideways. Papa's anger could turn me into jelly. But I could not, under any circumstances, marry James. I had tried to love him. I'd failed.

How could I make Papa understand?

"I can't marry James. I just can't."

"Well. What's done is done," he said, disgust in his voice. "Experience is the mother of wisdom, I suppose. I heard a few rumors about his flings."

Flings? How dare James lose his temper when he saw me walking down the street?

"Flings or not," Papa continued. "I'm sure you can't find a better man to put you on the road to success. Not sure you can ever find another wealthy man, or any acceptable man at all, the way you push fellows away."

"I'm sorry." I was unable to look at him. Disappointing Papa was the last thing I wanted to do but his words made me angry. I had tried so hard my whole life to please him, but in this one thing, the feelings of my own heart, I had let him down.

"You're on your own now." Papa spit out the words. "Don't look at me to find you a decent young man or a better way of life. I held high expectations for you, but it seems like you're determined to find your own way. I tried my best. If you amount to nothing, it'll be your own fault. You've made a big mistake!" He threw his shovel to the ground. "Let me know when you come to your senses. "Now go water those flowers."

Papa's unkindness festered in my heart all night long, so that by morning, I was so agitated, I awoke barely able to breathe. An asthma attack.

I ran into the living room. No one else was around. I finally found my grandmother. "Help me. I can't breathe." I was suffocating, nearly panicking. Why was this happening now?

Grandma Bennett took one look at me and directed me back to my bedroom. The moment Grandma sat beside me the severity of the attack and my sense of anxiety lessened. Her cool hand on my cheek eased the tension. Eventually she got me to calm down and I was able to breathe normally again.

Grandma Bennett, the self-taught natural-remedy practitioner, always knew what to do for the asthma attacks that had beset me for my entire life. When I was small, she sewed a flannel vest around my chest and wouldn't let me take it off except in extreme emergencies or for my Saturday night bath. After a bath, she would rub my chest and back with a mixture of turpentine, coal-oil, and lard. She showed Mama how to sew the vest back on again as tightly as possible. As I grew older, Grandma realized that the many layers of clothing kept me too warm, and when I left off some layers of undergarments, my breathing improved.

As I grew toward womanhood, the asthma attacks gradually became less severe and less frequent. Today's attack was the most severe I'd experienced in many years.

I spent the rest of the day recuperating, Grandma's orders. Even Papa didn't argue with Grandma when it came to health. She was my lifeline. And I thought about how much we had in common.

Grandma struggled with asthma for years herself. Maybe that was why she sympathized so much with me. She, my grandfather, and their family had traveled south by wagon train from Michigan in the late 1800s because of her illness. Her uncle, Dr. Clay who'd lived near Detroit, had believed the warmer climate would help with her breathing, so Grandpa Bennett sold their house, bought two horses, and rigged up a covered wagon. They loaded their furniture onto a box car to be recovered in Arkansas. They traveled about fifteen miles a day, and the farther south they got, the better Grandma could breathe. By the time they reached Missouri, Grandma felt well enough to walk with her three children, one of which was Mabel, my mother.

When they were older, around 1924, Mama's parents sold their farmhouse in Spiro, Oklahoma, and moved around from sons to daughters. I was pleased when they moved in with our family because Grandma Bennett was my ally. She believed in me and stood by my side.

I was feeling better after resting all day. That evening at dinner, we devoured Mama's delicious chicken fried steak and mashed potatoes.

"I'm about to finish Faulkner's book, *The Sound and the Fury*," I said to Papa. "It's tough to get through." I read the book to impress him. To get in his good graces, wanting to make up with him after our fight yesterday.

"I should have known you wouldn't understand it," he said. "That book reveals the fall of a distinguished Southern family, Sibyl. You should learn something from it."

Papa had obviously never read the book.

"It's a tragedy." I disagreed with him. "And the book *is* haunting, but the black maid, the last one featured, gives the viewpoint of a former slave. I think she's the strongest character in the book." Why was I arguing with him? I should be trying to relieve the tension in the room.

Papa pushed his chair back and said, "It's the principle of the matter, don't you see? Slavery had been the fabric of life for centuries and the Northerners interfered. Stupid people used the issue of slavery for their own benefit. Taxed the South, the poorer section of the country, to make a buck. The righteous-minded rose up against a bureaucracy that was taking away their rights."

I should have known not to get Papa started. I looked around the table. Everyone else had stone faces. They all stared at their food.

Politics was not off limits at dinner, although it should have been. The Bennetts had come from the North. Papa migrated from the South.

Grandma Bennett stood slowly and turned toward Papa with her hands on her hips. "Stupid people?" she said. "Are you calling my people stupid?" She was a small woman but looked severe in her dark dress with a round white collar and tight waist.

"One of the gravest errors committed by the North was arrogance." Papa, unconcerned, took a bite of Mama's angel food cake and swallowed. "Their potential was stunted and they failed to —"

"Insulting us again? You don't understand a hill of beans on an ant bed." She looked down at Grandpa Bennett, who pushed his chair back and rose to his feet to stand beside Grandma.

"You're like all the other do-gooders throughout history," Papa said. "You follow your own personal agendas instead of promoting the welfare of all mankind—"

"We're leaving!" Grandma's eyes blazed. "I'll never stay in a house with a man like this. I don't know how you put up with him, Mabel." She stomped out of the room. Grandpa followed. My body felt heavy, tied down with lead chains.

That night I begged Grandma to reconsider, even promising to read the Bible aloud to her. But once Grandma made up her mind, nothing could change it.

Three days later, Uncle Louie drove up from Sulphur and parked his pickup truck in front of our house. After loading their boxes and furniture, he tied Grandma Bennett's rocking chair securely on top. Grandma climbed on top of the pile and sat in her rocking chair, a grim look on her face. She wore a funny-looking bonnet with a round, flat top and a big ribbon tied under her chin. For an hour, with her homemade ruffled parasol sheltering her from the sun, she rocked back and forth until they were ready to leave.

I pleaded with her to no avail, aching at the thought of her leaving. They'd lived with us for several years and now I felt like they were abandoning me. When everything was loaded, my uncle pulled away to take my grandparents to a cabin in Sulphur. I would have chuckled at the sight of Grandma rocking away on top if I hadn't been heartbroken at losing my most loyal supporter.

Mama wept along with me. Everyone wept except Papa. Guilt ate through my pain. This was my fault.

Why did every disagreement with Papa end with discord and hurt feelings? Why was he so hard to get along with? I didn't know if I would ever be able to stand up to him. I felt torn between my promise to follow his desires and my need to be my *true* self. Not just torn. Flat out, double-minded, weak-kneed, wishy-washy torn.

The next evening, no one mentioned our grandparents. We knew not to discuss the disagreement while Papa was home. The house seemed as empty as a hay barn before harvest with no Grandpa whistling around the house or strumming his banjo, no Grandma fussing over the little ones.

We tried to have a semblance of normalcy at dinner that evening. Mama had been cooking beef stew all day and it smelled absolutely heavenly. A flower arrangement sat in the center of the table. My siblings and I took our seats but with my grandparents chairs removed, we didn't even touch elbows.

Mama brought in a steaming tureen of beef stew along with hot buttery cornbread and molasses. Glasses of sweet tea washed down the delicious bites. My mama knew how to cook better than Aunt Jemima. It helped ease the tension. No one spoke about our grandparents.

Spoons were scraping against the bowls when Mama said, "Sibyl, I had a talk with Mrs. Matthews today."

I stopped my spoon mid-air.

"Seems she saw you a few weeks ago down at First Baptist's soup line serving bread. But I told her that surely she was mistaken. I can't imagine why you would be over there around *those* people."

All eyes at the table stared at me. Papa was glaring.

"You don't say," he said. "I'd like to hear an explanation of this, too."

"Well, the women's union needed volunteers to help serve. I was at their office and..."

"Why were you at the union office?" Papa asked. "I told you to stay away from there."

Papa had not explicitly said that. What he'd said was, "Don't get involved with the working class." To him, apparently being in the union offices was too close to "those people." It crossed my mind that I should mention the sheriff had shown up at the law office to express his displeasure with Mr. Weston, and possibly Papa. I started to explain, but, as usual, Papa didn't give me a chance.

"I have warned you many times, Sibyl. This family should be above reproach—all its members." Papa's face got red in anger. "We have a reputation to uphold and an obligation if we are to be part of the future salvation of our country. The entire family's actions affect my career, and I want nothing to stand in the way. Our efforts must be to awaken the righteous-minded so they will begin to expand their good works, not to delve into the grittiness ourselves. We must seek a united strength to restrain those who do evil. Surely, some of the unfortunate souls have chosen the lower side."

On and on Papa ranted.

Mama and my siblings slid away, pretending to not hear his words. Probably irritated at me for starting another rampage. Blanche gave me a scornful look.

I remained silent, knowing anything I said would further inflame Papa. I thought he had forgotten my visits to the union offices and the soup kitchen until I got up to leave the table.

"Wait."

I paused, standing by my chair.

"If I hear of your gallivanting around at that union office again, I'll tell your boss. I'm sure Mr. Weston doesn't want his assistant anywhere near those grubby men. It's one thing to toss aside the only decent man interested in marrying you, it's quite another to hobnob with the tramps."

"Papa, my boss sent me there. And they're not all tramps. Some are just down on their luck and —"

"That's enough." he interrupted harshly. "You should seriously consider your actions. There will always be consequences, some which you will not like."

I gave up. Papa would never understand me. He did not see me as a separate person, much less a grown woman capable of making my own choices. I could not please him and be true to what I believed in my own heart. All he ever did was spout high-minded rhetoric and judge people without knowing them. He was incapable of recognizing my actions were in response to his insistence that we work to make the world a better place. He could not concede that my actions would make a difference.

Mama tended to avoid Papa when he was in one of his moods. She washed the dishes and would not look at me. I wanted to put my arm around her and tell her that everything would be all right, but I was not sure myself.

Papa didn't stay home that night. He re-packed his suitcase and told Mama he had to be in Oklahoma City by nightfall.

It may have just been an excuse but I was relieved to see him go.

Chapter Fourteen

L ater that week on Thursday evening, Fremont came to my window and whistled a special code we agreed upon. A bobwhite bird whistle. I climbed out the window and walked with Fremont down Main Street. I liked Fremont's strong yet gentle hand, which completely wrapped around my long, thin fingers.

I was tired of living under Papa's thumb, with putting up with his negative words. I decided to do as I pleased, no matter what Papa said. But I'd be smart, too. I wasn't going to get emotionally involved with an unsuitable man. Even though my family would never approve of Fremont, for some reason, I couldn't push him away. I liked being around him, and he seemed to like being around me.

A slightly chilly night, the wind blew leaves under the corner street lamps and along the darkened sidewalk. We walked past yards bordered with bedrock retaining walls, steps gracefully leading up to front porches with swings and rocking chairs deserted for the night. Slowly we reached the huge elm tree on Highland Street, its limbs leaning down, cloaking us.

"What makes you so different from other guys I've met?" I asked. "I mean, you're not out for a good time or always thinking about yourself."

"There's more to life than having fun. Not that I don't like a mighty good laugh here or there, but people should have a purpose. A higher purpose. More than everyday life."

"Yeah, I hope so," I said. "Papa expects great things from me. I don't know exactly what that means, but I have all these ideas. I want to work to change Oklahoma laws to help folks, or I might picket on the front lawn of the capitol building or hand out pamphlets on the street corners."

"Well, for me, if I follow God, that'll be my purpose."

Fremont and I would often meet for a soda and we'd discuss the distressful weather, our family quirks, and the national elections. We had not discussed religion again. He never invited me to visit the small, white-washed Calvary Baptist Church where his family attended. Instead, on Sunday mornings, Fremont went to First Baptist Church with me. He insisted we go, and I thought his dedication endearing.

I stopped and gazed at him. "Maybe that's the piece I'm missing. God."

He pushed back a wave of my hair and caressed my cheek. His blue eyes pierced deep into mine. Nothing could explain the turmoil in my heart that his look unleashed, and tears welled up before I could stop them.

I tried to rationalize my reaction. Maybe it was the excitement of someone new in my life. No, I had met other men and never felt this unsettled before. Maybe this feeling was an infatuation because Fremont could not share my dreams of changing the world. Or could he? No, even if he did have a heart for the poor, he had no money to help others.

"You're special," he said. "I've never met anyone like you before."

"It's you." I blinked away the tears, trying to resist the feeling. "You make me feel warm inside. I can't explain it."

"You're my sad little bird, and I'll always be here for you." Fremont lowered his head, and I felt his breath on my cheek. He put his hand to the back of my head, pulled me closer, and kissed me. My heart thumped wildly as his strong arms embraced me.

A few moments later we pulled apart and looked at each other. My heart raced so rapidly, I feared it would never slow down, and I would never think straight again. My lips tingled and my face felt warm.

No. No. This could not be happening.

We turned and strolled on, Fremont's arm around me. When we arrived at my house, he gently kissed me goodnight and left me standing in the front yard. I sank into the cool grass and looked up into the starry, moonlit sky, the full moon glistening.

"God?" I whispered. "Is this real? Are my feelings leading me astray? What am I going to do?"

I continued working for Mr. Weston, and dancing continued to be my favorite activity. I also fulfilled the social obligations expected by my family. In contrast, Fremont spent most days helping his father hoe potatoes and shuck corn. Finally, he found a new job at a filling station on the west edge of town. Fremont's family, the Popes, lived by stricter rules than mine. They took their religion seriously, so seriously that dancing, drinking, and playing cards were prohibited.

In spite of those prohibitions, every Friday night Fremont shined his boots, ironed his shirt, and came to the Blue Bird, where he would watch me dance with every slick fellow who walked in the door. He refused to step onto the dance floor after his embarrassment the first time he'd gone. Instead he simply sat and watched me dance a lively ragtime or boogie to a new tune. Other times, he watched me move to the slow rhythm of a waltz, close in the arms of another man. He often looked sullen and uncomfortable, but I kept on dancing.

Marjorie was seeing more of her friend Kelley now, although she still had other men lined up at the front door. As Fremont and I sat at a table, we overheard a discussion about Kelley and my sister from a nearby booth.

"Kelley moved here from Arkansas because of some trouble."

"Marjorie's too good for him.

"People say he'll never amount to anything."

Fremont and I listened quietly. I curled my arms toward my body in a retreat. I didn't want to hear more about Marjorie's problems. Her boyfriend Kelley caused a crevice inside me. I worried about the way she was headed in life and felt unable to change it.

When the conversation in the other booth changed to a different topic Fremont asked, "Are people saying the same things about me? That I'm not good enough for you? Not rich enough?"

"I don't care what people say."

Unfortunately, I cared very much what Papa said.

This particular late summer Friday night, the Blue Bird overflowed. Marjorie and I sneaked out again. Thanks to an out-of-town singer who'd come to perform, sweaty bodies packed close together. Fremont sat glumly at a round wooden table, watching the room. Usually, I felt at ease with people, but a hesitancy and melancholy surrounded me, as if the glamorous girl on the outside did not match the restlessness and desperation on the inside. Only Fremont saw that sadness. He'd said before that he wished he could make my life whole, to protect me from unhappiness. The only bright spot was knowing at least Fremont knew me.

I think Fremont felt like an interloper at the dances. When I wasn't dancing, I sat with him and listened. He loved to tell stories. As midnight approached, he told me a tale about why he disliked barrooms so much.

"About a year ago, I stepped into a joint much like this one. I'd jumped off the freight train near a cow town close to Flagstaff. Still a growing boy, my mighty empty belly had complained for several days. I was desperate for a slice of bread or a potato or *anything*. I would have eaten an old boot if someone had set it in front of me."

We laughed.

"But everyone in that town turned me down. I finally gave in and went to the local saloon."

Fremont stopped talking and watched the dancers for a moment. Then leaned in close. "You know, Sibyl, my family doesn't approve of these places."

I had gotten that impression. I nodded and he continued.

"The empty bar had trash all over the plank floor. Glasses cluttered every surface. It looked like a pack of raccoons had raided the place. This woman with a low-cut dress came out. I asked if she had any work for a strong-backed, hard-working man. She told me they took care of themselves, none too nicely, I might add. But I was hungry and didn't mind saying so. She looked me up and down and finally admitted she could use a little help. She'd bring me a bowl of hot soup if I worked 'til sundown. That sounded good to me. She also told me I had to bathe. She didn't want dirty scum hanging around running off the customers."

"What a rude thing to say," I said.

"It's all right. Folks don't worry about being nice to people like me. We struck a bargain and I started cleaning. One of the ladies told me I was the prettiest chap she'd ever seen and offered to keep me company later. Mighty embarrassing. Finally the matron shooed the girls off. I was right mortified. The matron offered me a cot behind the kitchen. That was the first clean bed I'd had in some time. I stayed on there and worked for room and board.

"I never saw much fun in carousing, but some nights I sat in the barroom and watched people. One night, a young girl was sitting on a sour-looking salesman's lap like a little girl sits on her daddy's knee. The next thing I know she paraded toward me and whispered in my ear. You know me, Sibyl. I wasn't interested in what she was offering. So she shouted back to that salesman, 'He says he ain't that kind' and everyone laughed."

Fremont paused and shook his head. "The salesman didn't like that at all. He came over and told me to get my hands off his girl. I stepped back but he'd had too much to drink. He popped me right on the chin. I didn't want to fight but the drunks were howling for a brawl. They started a ruckus and I snuck back to my room. Right then I decided to move on. The barroom and dancing kind of life holds no interest for me."

Fremont's story helped explain why he hated dancing so much. A tall, mustached man took my arm and practically pushed me to the dance floor. I left Fremont sitting at the table, staring off into space.

Right in the middle of a waltz, I saw James approach Fremont. He didn't look too happy. Behind James stood two of his buddies and the three loomed over Fremont, who hadn't bothered to stand.

"Hey, how's the poor boy doing?" James sneered. His low resonant voice always reverberated around the room. "You still trying to take my girl away?"

I made my way toward them. "James!" I yelled, trying to distract him.

Fremont shrugged. "She doesn't seem too concerned about it."

James grinned arrogantly. "She's leading you on." His words were slurred. "I know Sibyl. She's got more sense than to bother with a no-account like you."

Fremont stood and stepped toward me. "Let's get out of here," he said with a strained voice. His face flushed scarlet.

James stepped toward me. "Maybe it's time for my dance." He grabbed my arm. "Let's go for a spin."

I jerked free and faced James, looking at his starched white shirt and silk tie. I wasn't impressed. "I can make up my own mind who I want to dance with, and right now, it's certainly not you, James Fleming."

Fremont stepped between us. He pulled me behind him. "She's with me, so you better be off."

James motioned to his two toadies and they stepped toward Fremont.

"Now, who's about ready to leave town, smart man?" James glowered. "Take the hobo out to the alley, boys, and show him that he's not wanted around here."

They grabbed Fremont by the arms, but Fremont, his muscles bulging, yanked loose. I had forgotten his strength. One of James' cronies punched him in the gut. Fremont shoved him and the man stumbled backward. Then the band stopped playing and a crowd formed, everyone tense with anticipation. Girls backed away while guys stepped forward, as if waiting for a signal to jump into the brawl. Meanwhile, Fremont was scrapping with the other ruffian.

Then, it seemed like a flag dropped. Fights broke out all over the room.

I saw James trying to escape, but Fremont grabbed his shirt collar and pulled him near. I barely heard the words over the ruckus. "You stay away from Sibyl, you hear?"

James spit in Fremont's face as he swung his fist. Fremont ducked and the blow missed. He raised his hand to smash James' arrogant smile. Then he stopped, hesitating like he didn't want to hit anyone.

James stared at the fist and tried to get his feet.

"Time to get going, sis." Marjorie grabbed my hand. Boy was I glad to see her. "You said it before," she said. "We don't need to be here when the cops come."

I grabbed Fremont's hand and we rushed through the side door where Kelley stood waiting for us.

"Thanks," Fremont said to Kelley. "I'm surprised you're not in the middle of that."

"I know when it's time to skedaddle," Kelley said with a grin.

"See you at home." Margie's usual flamboyance was gone and I started to ask if she felt okay, but she and Kelley quickly disappeared into the darkness.

I couldn't stop thinking about how Fremont had protected me. About how strong he was. How brave he was. Once we'd run far away from the Blue Bird, we slowed our pace and walked down a dimly-lit sidewalk.

"You certainly were a killer-diller back there," I said. "Are you hurt?"

"Nothing a good night's sleep won't cure." His voice sounded low and angry. He froze on the sidewalk and turned to me. "It was self-defense, you hear? I never would have started a fight with him, but he started it. I just wanted to end it."

"But you didn't hit him."

"I couldn't."

"I know, Fremont. I saw what happened." I saw a lot more too. I saw a future with a man like Fremont by my side. A strong, protective man. "A man like you can do anything. Wouldn't it be great to do something different in life? Get away from all this turmoil. Look around the world. There's so much to do."

"Maybe." He sounded anything but excited.

"We could do something good for society. Assist the poor. Change the laws. Get away from these deadbeat fellows." I looked around our town, at the fancy buildings opposite the shanties on the other side of the tracks. "You see what it's like here. The poor need support."

With Fremont by my side, I could leave Shawnee. Leave home. Be free to follow my dreams. Help others.

We approached a four foot round concrete water trough in the middle of Seventh and Bell Streets. People still occasionally used it to water horses when they came to town. I pulled his arm to encourage him to go, left or right, his way or my way around the concrete trough. In the end, we went his way.

"What kind of a life do you want, Fremont?" I asked, feeling free to open my heart to him. "What about living in D.C. and becoming lobbyists? Or, who knows, we can find a way to feed the starving children in the New York slums."

"Noble causes, Sibyl, but the location doesn't matter as long as there's plenty of love and lots of children." He slowed his pace.

I hesitated. "I'm not sure I want children. I've never desired a big family. Too many things to do while we're still young, Come now, don't you want to do something great before you settle down?"

Fremont didn't reply. Instead, he walked even slower and stopped under the street lamp at the corner. The overhead light turned the dust into glitter suspended in midair. "There's something I need to talk about," he said. "It's mighty hard though."

I turned and examined him. He had been quiet since we'd left the Blue Bird. His large, pale eyes were grave, the usual sparkle gone. The brawl obviously upset him. In my excitement, I hadn't noticed his thoughtful attitude as I'd chattered about the future. I should have sensed something was amiss.

"What is it?" My heart beat unsteadily as I waited for his reply. I didn't want to let him know I'd dreamed about him during the past few weeks. I didn't even want to admit it to myself. I believed I was in control enough to get out of the relationship before it got serious.

The jingling of the change in Fremont's trouser pocket broke the silence. Then he spoke quietly. "It's about dancing, which I don't like. But it's more than that." He sat on the curb facing the street.

I stood in front of him and watched as he struggled to speak. "Have I done something wrong?"

"It's this kind of lifestyle. I was taught, and I believe, that dancing's wrong. Nah, it's more than the dancing. It's the booze and other stuff that goes on there. Like what just happened—you saw. Maybe I grew up with a different home life than you."

"What do you mean?" I sat beside him, relieved his concern was just about the dancing.

He said, as if to himself, "I can't stand all those guys hanging all over you. They beg to dance with you while I sit there and watch. Do you know how that makes me feel? And what do all those dancing buddies think about you? I don't mean you're not a mighty great gal, but I..."

"You need to learn to dance. I can teach you at home."

"It's more than dancing," he said. "It's us."

My fears surfaced. Did he not care as much as I did?

"What about us?" I asked.

"I don't want to watch you dance anymore. I want to try to live a godly life, and beer joints aren't part of that. You can go if you want to, but I'm not going."

Was he serious? He was. My fear turned to anger. "What do you mean, I can go if I want?" My voice rose. Was Fremont trying to control me like Papa did? "Of course, I want to go. I love dancing. How can you not understand that? You're jealous."

"I'm not," he said gently. "It ain't any blamed fun sitting alone watching you dance. I don't like it, not one little bit."

"So what does this mean for you and me? We have to do what you want to do?" I choked out the words as I stood and walked over to the lamppost and leaned against it, my arms crossed over my chest. Tears spilled down my face. Surprised at my reaction, I tried to wipe them away.

"I don't know." He rose to stand in front of me and took my face in his hands. "I care about you, but I can't see you like this anymore. Maybe I'm not your type. I'm not going to any more dances. I hope you understand."

"Can't a girl have fun once in a while without everyone looking down on her?"

"I've made up my mind." He took a deep breath. "If you want to keep on with this rowdy lifestyle, then I'm out. I thought you were trying to find a purpose in life. Dancing's not something that will make a difference. Maybe I've misunderstood, but I thought you wanted to follow God." His deep voice sounded determined. "You have to decide what you want."

I studied him, trying to see through to his soul. His bright blue eyes glistened with threatening tears. I knew Fremont didn't want to hurt me, and I hoped he would step forward, put his arms around me, and apologize. Or maybe he would walk away, back to his old-fashioned beliefs and safe way of living.

We started walking again, this time toward my home, more subdued than we had ever been with each other. Neither of us spoke.

He walked me to the front porch and started to leave without saying anything. Then he stopped and turned back, a somber look clouding his face. "If you still want to see me, I'll be sitting in our usual place in the church balcony on Sunday morning."

I stood, feet firmly planted, watching his straight back as he stepped into the evening's darkness. He didn't turn to look back.

I opened our front door and slid into the house, suppressing a scream. "How could he?" Tears started flowing again. Why did I always have to be the one to compromise?

I was supposed to be one of the elite, selected to make radical changes in the world. Fremont was acting like Papa, whom I could never please. And Papa didn't even know about him yet. I bit my lip. I couldn't understand why I was never good enough. I grabbed a pillow off the loveseat and threw it at the door. Life wasn't fair.

Fear lodged deep in my heart. How could Marjorie have all those boyfriends when I couldn't even keep one? What was wrong with me? Maybe Mama was right. I wasn't good enough and would never be good enough. I *did* want to choose my own path, to have my own way, to feel a sense of control over my own life. I also wanted to be loved. I wanted Fremont to love me. The panic came in waves. And so did the anger. And the self-doubt.

How could he not understand what dancing meant to me? I had relinquished so much for him already. I'd broken my engagement to the well-to-do man chosen for me by Papa. I'd gone against Mama's wishes by stooping to date a working man. Now that man wanted me to change my whole way of life. What arrogance!

I stomped into my bedroom, mumbling under my breath. I didn't want to wake the family down the hall.

The room was dark, and Marjorie was already in her bed, the covers pulled up over her. Great. The one time I needed her to stay out late and here she was. Home early. I yanked my dress over my head and tore off a button. I threw my high-heeled shoes, and each one bounced off the wall and crashed to the closet floor.

"What's wrong with you?" Marjorie sat up.

"I don't want to talk about it. Go back to sleep."

"Let me know when it's safe to come out," she teased. A green mask covered her face, and a towel circled her head.

"Why are you in bed so early?" I asked with a tinge of bitterness. "Early for you, that is."

"Not feeling too well, that's all. Can't a girl get some rest if she wants?" She pulled the quilt over her head.

I turned off the light and slipped into bed. Turmoil raged, and sleep eluded me for some time. I couldn't stop thinking about Fremont.

Chapter Fifteen
September 1932

When I woke the next morning, I noticed Marjorie's unmade bed and her clothes strewn all over the floor. She left late for work almost every morning. Not that I was ever on time either. On Saturdays she worked as a clerk at the Montgomery Ward store. Thankfully, I was off today. Paperwork would have been impossible in my state of turmoil.

Blue jays sang outside the window and brought hope as I pulled Grandma's quilt over my legs. I grabbed a piece of paper and made a list of Fremont's positives and negatives. The list helped organize my roiling thoughts.

On the negative side: his poverty, his stubbornness, and his puritanical attitude. None of those qualities fit my vision of a good partner. How could he fit into my dreams of doing something in the world to help the poor? For mercy's sake, Fremont *was* the poor! Would he support my endeavors, or would he hold me back? Perhaps while seeking something other than the shallowness of my friends and James, I had swung too far.

Despite those things, something powerful drew me to him.

On the positive side: his zest for adventure, his trustworthiness, and his clear thinking about right and wrong. He was straightforward, honest, hard-working, understanding, and probably could be relied upon in rough times. Not to mention good looking. Really good looking. And protective.

I sat back and mulled it over. The list didn't settle my restlessness so I decided to go for a walk. Looking in the closet for a sweater, I noticed my wide-brimmed hat perched on the top shelf. I stood on tiptoe, pulled it down, and walked over to the dresser mirror. I tilted the hat on my head, thinking about what I had looked like when I'd first met Fremont at the filling station. Was he thinking about me, as I was thinking of him? I remembered the first time we sat at Owl Drug Store. I recalled the films we watched from the Bison Theatre balcony. Somehow, he made even *King Kong* an enjoyable movie.

All day I remained in a foul mood. I stomped around the house, argued with my sisters, and snapped at Mama. I cried over the biscuits I burned. I grumbled about my useless job. Inside, I mulled over Fremont's words, Fremont's ultimatum. Nobody had ever challenged me like this. Nobody had ever suggested that I should choose a different way to live.

I thought of the self-absorbed rambunctious crowd I ran with. My friends were shallow, self-indulgent, and arrogant. They lacked concern for the well-being of others. Just like James. How had I ever thought they shared my vision of trying to better mankind?

Fremont strongly objected to how I entertained myself, but I couldn't picture a different life. Were my social trips to Turner Falls and Sulphur going to help me reach my goal? What about dancing every Friday night or driving about in cars with my friends. Would those endeavors help me find a purpose for my life?

If not, then what should I be doing with my time? And what would make a difference in the world? What did Fremont believe in, *precisely*?

Then, the memory of a long-forgotten event popped in my head.

When I was twelve years old, Marjorie and I attended a church revival. A preacher from Texas delivered the sermon, pounding the pulpit as he shouted about Jesus' amazing love. Listening to the speech, I felt a deep-seated pain, hopelessness, and yearning for acceptance. The evangelist spoke about a God who cared for me, who loved me beyond measure. Gradually, as I listened, I felt a quiet reassurance. *Trust me.* I heard the words inside myself and knew God did exist. Responding to the hope-filled message, I walked to the front of the church to talk to the preacher, deciding to follow Jesus. The next Sunday I was baptized.

A week later, Marjorie followed my example and talked to the preacher. Marjorie came home crying and carrying on.

"Marjorie's salvation seems more real than yours, Sibyl," Mama said.

"What do you mean?"

"You don't seem as emotional as Marjorie does."

My exuberance sank. My own mother doubted my new-found faith. She didn't think I was sincere because I didn't express myself in the way she expected. Since Mama couldn't see the change in my heart, I decided that spiritual matters should be something kept to myself, not shared with others.

I struggled with Marjorie winning over Mama, even in religion. Doubt crept in. Was my decision to let God in my heart even real?

Neither Marjorie nor I went to church much after that, except occasionally to attend the Baptist Girl's Auxiliary with our friends. Our spirituality faded. No one in our family except Grandma discussed spiritual growth or ever read the Bible. Life went on without much change or thought of learning about God's character or what Scripture taught. Papa, not God, decided what was right or wrong for our family. And right and wrong always depended on his mood that particular day.

Maybe, even after all these years, that seed of faith had not withered away.

That evening I took extra care with my appearance. Fremont might regret his words and arrive at the Blue Bird Ballroom after all.

"Sis, did you see that new fellow last week? The redheaded one with the broad shoulders?"

"I'm not sure I want to dance tonight." I used a hot pad to pick up the metal curler I'd hung on the kerosene lamp globe and rolled it into my hair. "I've got too much on my mind."

"Don't be a sourpuss, lovey," said Marjorie.

The band was booming at the Blue Bird when Marjorie and I arrived, and we heard a crowd of feet stomping to the rhythm. Marjorie sashayed in ahead of me, her new hat bobbing in time with her hips, and some young man swept her onto the dance floor.

I sauntered over to a table and plopped down to sip a soda. I studied the darkened room and tried to see the place from Fremont's point of view. Shadowy faces were hidden in dark corners while the smell of alcohol filled my nose. Cigarette smoke wafted toward me. Bodies twisted to a deafening noise.

From this spot, I saw what Fremont saw. And I realized this was not what I wanted from life. I needed to make a choice.

I had to do something about Fremont. He would probably leave for California if I didn't show up at church the next morning, since he always talked about hopping another train. I might never see him again. And maybe that would be for the best. Then I could follow Papa's dreams for me. But what were those dreams? What would they look like? I couldn't imagine my life would be spent in service to the poor, not like I wanted it to be. No, Papa would have me far from the folks who really needed help.

Where did I fit in? I hadn't been to a political meeting in weeks, but I knew I couldn't keep my promise to Papa and continue to see Fremont. My heart was with Fremont, but my promise to help Papa improve society jumbled my feelings all up. I wanted to make him proud of me.

Bing Crosby's song, "One More Time," bellowed from the band, and a tall, handsome dandy reached out to me. I hesitated. One more dance wouldn't hurt. I grabbed him and rushed to the dance floor. Tonight was not the time to think about serious matters.

Chapter Sixteen

Massive pillars supported vaulted ceilings throughout the auditorium of my church, First Baptist of Shawnee. The sanctuary boasted polished cathedral-style stained-glass windows donated by well-established families. People dressed in their Sunday best wandered in, and the church sprang to life. The pianist arranged her song sheets while a group of children sitting in the front pew giggled. Cooper's Funeral Home cardboard fans fluttered in front of overheated ladies. The new preacher, Dr. Chesterfield Turner, a stout Kentuckian, faced the audience, and I thought of the poor people who stood in the soup line behind the church. What a contrast to the folks inside the sanctuary.

Mama came in with the choir. They were all wearing navy blue robes, and she took her place in the second row. The pianist started a high-class church song, "He Hideth My Soul in the Cleft of the Rock." Sunlight streamed through the stained-glass windows, casting a surreal atmosphere on the whole congregation.

Today I had dressed carefully in a pale blue embroidered dress, which complemented my skin and golden brown hair. I tilted my straw wide-brim hat, its blue ribbon hanging down my back. I arrived late as usual, entering the side door in a hurry.

I gazed up, looking for him. Fremont sat alone in the balcony, right where he said he'd be. His eyes were on me as I walked slowly up the stairs to the balcony. I turned at the top of the stairs and slid in beside him. He reached down, took a rose from under the seat and held it out to me. Our eyes met.

The song leader prompted the congregation to stand and sing "O Worship the King." Even in this calm and beautiful place, my spirit was in turmoil. I dabbed my eyes with a lace-trimmed handkerchief, reached for Fremont's hand and gripped it tightly, my gloved fingers almost lost in his broad hand.

Perhaps my decision to follow Christ as a young girl could be as significant to my life as it was for Fremont. I had not followed through. I'd done nothing to learn or understand what might be required of me. All I really knew were the examples I had seen at home, and Papa didn't take organized religion too seriously. Salvation, to him, meant the salvation of humanity, stamping out evil until it was annihilated. He seemed to have no personal spiritual beliefs. Mama seemed to think church was a social club where she could show off her stylish clothes and her lovely voice. I had not been taught that God, in all His infinite wisdom, wanted me to lead a life serving Him. Not pleasing myself. Not pleasing Papa.

At that moment, as I stood next to Fremont and the congregation sang around me, I realized I had so much to learn about what God might want.

My feelings for Fremont were stronger than for anyone I had known. His magnetism, strength, and peace touched some vein of longing in me. Of course, he was the handsomest fellow a girl could lay eyes on, but more than that attracted me to him.

Lately, I'd had to search deep inside to see what I really wanted. Dancing meant a lot to me as an escape from my family's expectations and as a way to release my pent-up energy. Surrendering it felt like cutting off a part of me, like covering that energy with a wet blanket.

A relationship with Fremont felt worth pursuing. No one else had presented me with the challenge of a different way of living. He wanted to follow Christ fully and that seemed a meaningful ambition. I could learn from him how to pursue a Christian purpose even if our relationship did not end in marriage.

When the singing was complete, the deacons moved to the front altar where Mr. Jones prayed for the Lord to bless the offering. The organ played, offering plates were passed around, and I heard the clatter of coins dropping against the metal. When the offering plate came to us, even Fremont dropped in a dime. He may have been poor, but he was grateful. I had never known anyone like him before.

Even if this relationship didn't last, I could learn a lot from him. I couldn't bear to give up this man just yet.

Chapter Seventeen

I had never been poor. Papa had always provided our family with more than enough, while Fremont had been poor all his life. Though Fremont's attitude was a hundred percent better than Papa's.

Although Fremont didn't talk much about his travels as a hobo and I didn't push him for details, I was curious. He seemed to still be processing the hardships he encountered and the destitution he experienced side by side with thousands of other unfortunates riding on the rails or wandering the streets.

Our favorite place to walk was Woodland Park, with its flowerbeds surrounding large elm trees. Walkways wound throughout the park, and benches welcomed reflection. As we took a Sunday afternoon stroll, I thought about the day he arrived home, that day I had first seen him, beaten up at the train depot. I was still proud of my feat of rescuing and returning his bundle. I smiled as the train whistle blew. Fremont seemed to read my mind.

"I remember you, of course," he said. "I was at my lowest, and you looked like an angel standing there. A mighty pretty one at that."

I ducked my head, embarrassed. We sat on one of the wooden benches, and he began to tell me of his first day back home after being gone for almost a year. Listening to his stories was like watching a drama on the silver screen, a regular Clark Gable at his best.

"I pulled myself together, filthy and bone-weary, and hauled myself over the tracks to the south part of town. I went around the block several times but always came back to the tiny worn-out house on Pottenger Street. Finally I got enough courage to walk up the wooden porch steps and knock on the screen door. A barefoot twelve-year-old girl opened it and stared at me. It was my sister Irene. She screamed, 'Mama, Mama! He's back!' She ran back into the house, slamming the door in my face. I stood there, not sure what to do. Then I heard my mama telling her to stop that yelling. 'What's all this you're talking about? Who's back?' I wanted to call out to her right then, but I didn't. I couldn't. Maybe I was afraid. Or ashamed. My youngest sister Ruthie jumped up and down. Her cute little face alive with joy. I can't even say how good that made me feel. And then Mother came from the back room and stood in front of the door. She seemed mighty shocked and could barely whisper the words. 'Fremont? Is it really you?'

"I'd missed my mama so much. More than I'd even known. It's lonesome for a boy riding the rails alone. I was mighty happy to see her, to see all of them. I thought she was happy to see me too, but then she let out this wail. That cry echoed throughout the house, maybe the whole neighborhood. I was still standing on the porch, the screen door between us. I pictured myself as she saw me, a runaway poor boy come home in the guise of a hobo. My hair was long and bleached from the sun and I wore filthy, ill-fitting clothes. I had blood and bruises on my face. Someone had given me a pair of old high-top button boots with holes in the toes. Cardboard stuffing was poking out.

"Mama looked at me from my head to my feet. When she saw those boots, she burst into tears."

Fremont chuckled and tossed his head. "I don't know if I told you this, but my mother came from a proper English family, educated folk. She went to finishing school and took business courses and shorthand. Her father was a lawyer and her mother a schoolteacher. I imagine her worst fears were probably confirmed when she looked at me. I tried to hold back tears. I wanted to turn and run away. When I'd left, I'd had these big dreams. Foolish dreams. I'd thought I'd come back home with gifts for everyone, a new shirt on my back and money in my pocket. Watching Mama cry, I realized how far I'd fallen.

"Finally, Mama pulled me into the house and hugged me tight, and then she pushed me away, looked at me again and hugged me some more. So many times it hurt. I asked if she was mad at me, knowing I'd given her lots of worrying.

He shook his head. "She wasn't mad, just glad I came home. Before I knew it, she'd doctored my face and set me down with food. After dinner, she filled the tub. When I'd cleaned up in the backyard, she brought me back in the warm kitchen and scrutinized me again, dabbing her eyes, saying 'My son went away a boy and came back a man.'"

A wind picked up stray leaves and scattered them over our feet and under the park bench. Neither of us spoke.

Seeing poverty from his viewpoint made me want to understand what folks were going through. Were the newspaper and radio broadcasts accurate? What it was like for a woman not to have enough bread for the toddlers hanging onto her skirt? What was it like for the men trying to feed their families and unable to do so without begging for a handout? What was it like for children who never knew where their next meal would come from?

Fremont knew what it was like to be on the road searching for hope but finding none. The only way I could find out was to walk among the homeless as one of them. Papa would never approve, but I had to know. I didn't confide my plans to Fremont, afraid he would try to stop me. He would probably think it silly for a rich girl to want to know what it was like to be poor.

That week I went to the second-hand market and purchased a faded calico dress, a shawl, and a slightly battered bonnet. I shoved them into a bag to hide them from Mama. I rushed home and donned the outfit, slipped on my oldest loafers, and snuck out the back door. I stopped at the side of the house and rubbed dirt on my face, clothing, and shoes. The church offered meals on early on Wednesday evenings.

For as long as I could remember, certainly for as long as I had listened to Papa's discourses on saving the world, I wanted to make a difference in the greater world. I didn't want to live the mundane life of a housewife, cooking beans and potatoes, scrubbing the linoleum.

I knew there were poor people in town but I had never realized there were so many. Hundreds of people existed near my comfortable hum-drum life.

This day the food line stretched farther than the last time I'd seen it. No black people stood in the line. Where did they go for a bowl of chow? Lester still worked in the back yard twice a week, but no one could support a family on the quarters Mama paid him. How did he survive?

I couldn't go into the church itself, of course. I might be recognized. So, like I knew what I was doing, I walked to the back of the women's line, slumping like I saw the others do, folding my arms close around me like my belly ached from too little food. I recognized no one. Shawnee was a stopover for many people traveling the rails, so maybe she had continued her journey.

I looked ahead at the bonnets, scarves and tightly pulled shawls. None of these women wanted to be here. No one spoke. They slowly progressed toward the food, like a funeral procession waiting to view the dead.

In front of me was a woman holding the hand of a young boy. He gazed up at me from behind his mother's skirt and seemed to know I didn't belong.

"Hi," I said, bending down to his level. "I'm Agatha." It wasn't a lie. Agatha was my middle name. When his mother turned to look at me, I saw only a broken young girl with sad sunken eyes.

"Do you live nearby?" I asked the little boy. He stared back at me without answering. I looked at his mother. "Do you come here often for food?" I asked her. "Do you have other children?" I knew I should stop, but I couldn't. I had so many questions. I needed to understand how a woman could come to be in such a dire situation. The girl merely looked at me with those sad eyes, let go of a faraway sigh and turned away.

Discouraged by not finding answers, I decided to leave before I was either recognized or missed. The paved street felt grimy as I headed home. I could see the back of the Aldridge Hotel and the outline of the city, the tops of the buildings lining Main Street. A train whistled and screeched to a halt at the Santa Fe Station.

Had Fremont ever stood in a soup line? He told me that he'd gone for days at a time wondering where his next meal would come from. He told stories about working for food and shelter but never if he had resorted to begging. Had he bowed his head in shame as he asked for a scrap? My heart lurched. Hunger of the body could scar the soul.

In an alleyway near Union and Ninth, several grungy men huddled together, passing around flasks as I neared them. There were so many poor people. Many Oklahoma men like these were losing hope. I hesitated to pass near the men, frightened by tales of women being attacked. I considered crossing the street, when I overheard one of them say, "Big dogs up in Washington are trying to get us."

I continued slowly. I wanted to hear more, so I slipped behind a corner wall and stopped.

"It ain't only the ones back east letting us down. It's happening right here in Pott County."

"We keep paying them union dues and getting nothing for it."

"It's the only hope we have. No one's looking out for the little guy."

"Who's telling them to plow under the cotton fields anyway? What are we going to do now?"

"And they're killing cattle without giving the meat to anybody."

"Can't depend on our bankers anymore."

"Heard another man lost his farm today."

I was listening intently when a sedan drove down Union and stopped. It was Papa! Quickly I turned my back to him, certain he couldn't recognize me in these shabby clothes. I slipped behind a stack of empty crates and watched as one tramp walked up to Papa's rolled-down window. The contrast of the bedraggled man and Papa's clean shaven face and spotless overcoat reminded me of the difference between our new bungalow house and the hovel where Fremont's family lived. I couldn't hear what was said, but it seemed suspicious. Money changed hands. What was going on?

I could hold my curiosity back no longer. All the questions from the past weeks came bursting forth. I rushed across the street yelling, "Papa. Papa!"

I had never seen my father's face grow so dark so quickly. His countenance hardened, and it seemed that fire spit from his eyes and smoke poured from his nostrils.

"Sibyl Agatha Trimble!" he roared. "You get in the car this minute."

His anger stunned me. I had seen him upset but not this incensed. I had best do as I was told instead of peppering him with questions. When I got inside the highly polished vehicle, I immediately felt as grimy as the women with whom I had just stood in line. Only Papa could make me feel this low. The dirt on my dress and shoes soiled Papa's car.

Papa drove home in complete silence. When he pulled into the driveway and turned off the engine, he spoke, but without even glancing at me. "I need an explanation for your erratic behavior. And I need a good one." His voice was as harsh as his facial expression.

Try as I might, I could think of nothing.

"Now. Tell me now. Exactly what do you believe you are doing? Why are you pretending to be a pauper and gallivanting about the alleyways of this town? You know you will be recognized anywhere in Shawnee."

I decided honesty was my best recourse.

"I was curious," I said.

"Curious!" The word exploded like a cannon ball.

"I wanted to see what it was like for poor people. After all, you always said we should be helping them. Isn't that what you believe? That the well-off should change the world to make it a better place for everyone? I need to know what life is like for them so I can plan what must be modified."

He looked at me as if I was an incorrigible child. "Not this way, Sibyl. Not by pretending to live in the dirt with them. You've followed me to meetings all over this country. Do you see me stooping down and getting my hands dirty? No. I would never do that."

"But Papa—"

"Socialism is making a comeback with you young whipper-snappers. It's joined at the hip with labor parties. People seek a venue to put their ideals into practice. Well, this is it. But don't forget, unions push for peace and civil rights and jobs for all men."

"I wanted to see how it felt to be poor."

"You have to stay focused, girl, not go traipsing about town like an imbecile. I expect more from you, yet here you are, acting like a fool. I've almost a mind to have you committed. A few weeks in the asylum might wake you up."

By the time Papa finished his diatribe, tears ran down my dirty cheeks and made mud puddles on my lap. Part of me disagreed with him whole-heartedly, but my emotions felt otherwise. I had disappointed him. Disgraced our family and our fellow Reformers. Papa expected more from me.

Later, pulling a clean housedress over my head, I recoiled. Papa had been unconcerned about my feelings or thoughts. I had forgotten to ask Papa why *he* was driving around in that neighborhood. Why had he given money to a needy-looking chap? Papa had deliberately sidetracked our conversation. Maybe he was the guilty one, not me. It was time for a confrontation.

Chapter Eighteen
October 1932

I entered the living room having swept the back porch clear of fallen leaves. I had danced around Papa since the outing, skirting him and his likely displeasure.

I stopped in the doorway.

Papa's head popped up from his newspaper and he looked over his glasses. He didn't mince words. "Heard you're stepping out with a new fellow." he said, "Who is this man? I've never heard of him."

My sister Marjorie couldn't keep anything secret. Not that seeing Fremont was shameful, but I would rather have chosen my own time to disclose the news to Papa.

"Well, he's, uh, from the south side of town," I stammered, "and is the handsomest man I've ever met."

"Where does he work??

I hesitated. "He's a filling station attendant."

"You cannot be serious." barked Papa, a disgusted look crossing his face. Then he shook his head. "It's only a temporary fling. He's just a man to console you after that heart-breaking relationship with James. We all have flings."

"Flings? You think I have affairs?"

"Sibyl, don't be a dunce. Temporary relationships serve their purpose. They are *tem-po-ra-ry*." He sounded out the word like I didn't know the meaning. "You'll be sensible in the long run and put mankind's interest above your personal desires."

My hackles went up. I'd had it with my father and his pronouncements, his harsh judgments. He was my father, but it was not up to him to decide if my relationship with Fremont was temporary or not. I was having a more and more difficult time accepting that Papa expected me to set aside all my feelings for the sake of mankind.

His disappointment in my broken engagement seemed based on *money*, money that could support efforts Papa thought worthy. He didn't care whether James loved me, nor whether I had any feelings for James. While I was not sure how I felt about Fremont or even what I expected from my relationship with him, Papa's attitude made me even more determined to date him. Even if he was a man from the wrong side of town.

"I know you," Papa said. "Marriage to a man of low estate would be your undoing. Don't let this friendship last too long. I don't want you to get a tainted reputation. You're already on the edge, gadding about with the Union ladies and showing up in an alleyway around the trashy men in town. If I hadn't been there to pay the fellow who washed my car, you could have been molested. And girl, what would that look like for the daughter of a bank auditor?"

"What do you mean?" My feelings bubbled over like an unattended pot of water. What was more meaningful to him, that I might have been harmed or that he might have been publicly embarrassed by my actions?

"I met a gentleman in Seminole I want to introduce to you. He comes from the right kind of people and is quite well off." Papa turned the page of his newspaper. "I'll arrange a meeting soon. Maybe a marriage will keep you out of trouble."

Papa seemed quite eager to have me off his hands. So demanding. I would acquiesce on this, even if I disagreed with him. I disagreed with Papa? When did this opposition become about? Gradually? Maybe meeting this new man would keep him from interfering in my life. From interfering with the relationship I wanted with Fremont.

The man from Seminole proved to be old, in his thirties, and shorter than me. Papa didn't mind my marriage refusal when he found out about the man's Cherokee blood. Indian relatives were frowned upon in Papa's circle.

111

A few days after that, Papa went away again for work. For several years, he'd been traveling around Oklahoma, and he knew many small-town bankers personally. He also knew their list of delinquent loans. The last week he'd told me, "I've seen the bank statements of every busted farmer in twenty counties. Looks like we have to work harder and get this New Deal activated before there're no small farms left. Although trade unions may create a welfare state. May even rob Socialism of its working class base."

There didn't seem to be anything I could do about the state of our society except donate a few old clothes to the Lions Club clothes drive. My marriage, even if it were to the wealthiest man in the state, certainly wouldn't solve the workers' predicament.

And besides, dating Fremont could not be wrong. He was a welcome diversion from hoity-toity men and my father's quest to promote socialism. As long as Fremont looked at me with those beautiful crystal blue eyes, I would enjoy his company. I just hoped my heart would stay out of it.

One night while Papa was gone, Fremont and I decided to go see *Grand Hotel*, a new movie showing at the Victory Theatre on Main and Broadway. Our relationship contained elements of nervous tension, the kind you get when you steal candy from your mother's candy jar. Sweet. Tense. Sweetly tense. Mama didn't seem to notice I was dating Fremont. She kept Papa uninformed as much as possible.

"You don't need to go to see that movie. Just ask Blanche Harriet about it," Mama teased. "She can describe every scene in detail."

"I've seen it twice," Blanche said. "The movie takes place in an expensive hotel where Dr. Otternschlag states quite ostentatiously, 'People come, and people go. Nothing ever happens.' And oh, by the way, the Baron wins the dancer's heart."

I hoped we would enjoy the movie even if Blanche had relayed the entire plot. We cuddled in the back of the theater and ate popcorn along with the rest of the audience. The beginning newsreels played and then the movie started. However, the film broke often, causing eruptions of clapping, howling, and banging from the audience.

Marjorie and Kelley were supposed to meet us there. Where was that girl?

"Maybe they'll be at the soda fountain after the movie," I said, more to reassure myself. But they didn't show up at the Duncan Drug Store either. I couldn't imagine what had detained Marj.

Later, Fremont walked me back to our house, and we sat on the porch swing. Softly rocking back and forth, Fremont pushed for both of us. He was like that, carrying my heaviness with his own as if it weighed no more than a feather.

I kicked off my shoes, tucked my bare feet comfortably under my dress, and wiggled my toes. The neighborhood was quiet. Only a few dogs barked in the distance. Fremont stretched his arm around me, and I took a deep breath and moved closer. Warmth surrounded me like Grandma's quilt, only Grandma's quilt didn't smell quite as good.

"Folks expect good things to happen after this election. More jobs, more money for farming and such. I guess lots of people are counting on it."

Although normally passionate on such issues, I didn't reply.

"My dad, especially," he ventured. "He hopes to be able to keep his farm out in Waco. I'd like to take you out there sometime. It's about ten miles west of town and as pretty as a picture."

"Of course."

"You're mighty quiet." Fremont gazed into my face. "What's wrong?"

"I'm worried about Marjorie. She and Kelley are together and Mama was awful mad when she came in late last night. She threatened to tell Papa, so Marjorie promised to never come home late again. And she didn't meet us tonight. I'm not sure anything will do any good."

"You can't live her life," he said. "I'd say the problem is between her and your mama. Besides, Kelley seems to be an all-right guy."

"You don't understand." My voice quivered in exasperation. "Kelley doesn't treat her like you treat me. He expects her to do exactly what he wants." I stood and shuffled across the porch to sit on the steps. "She's in love, she says."

The clock in the living room chimed eleven times. Mama's head peeked through the front door, her hair in rollers and a kerchief wrapped around her head. "Marjorie should be home by now. She went to the movies with you, didn't she?"

Before I could say anything, Mama continued. "She shouldn't be too much longer."

"I'll wait up for her," I replied.

"I'm going to bed," Mama said. "Tell Marjorie we'll have a talk in the morning. And don't stay up late."

As the door closed, we heard Mama shooing Calvis to bed. A few minutes later, the lights dimmed in the front bedroom.

"I'd better be going," Fremont said. "It's getting mighty late. Will I see you tomorrow?"

We stood, and he turned toward me, touched my cheek softly and pulled me close, holding me in a tight embrace. Neither of us moved for several minutes, my head resting on his chest. He smelled so good. He must have purchased some of the new Barbasol shaving cream. I listened to his heart beating and felt safe, like this could be a lasting shelter in the midst of life's turmoil.

The contented feeling remained long after he left. But I also felt guilt stirring. How did I really feel about Fremont? Was Papa right that this was a temporary fling? Did I feel this excitement because Fremont came from such a different background? Was getting serious with a poor man a betrayal of Papa?

I was jolted awake by a screech of the window and heavy breathing. I bolted upright in bed and looked at the clock. Three-thirty?

"Marj, is that you?"

"Who do you think, lovey?" Marjorie climbed in the window. "A ghost?"

"And I suppose you're going to tell me not to say anything to Mama?" As Marjorie turned on the small lamp beside the bed, I noticed smeared mascara around her eyes and remaining traces of red lipstick. "Been with Kelley again?"

She sank on her bed and pulled off her shoes. "It's not what you think, sis. I'm not sure what I'm going to do, that's all."

"What do you mean?" I propped myself on a pillow. "Are you tired of Kelley already?"

"No, silly. He loves me." She rested on her pillow. "What more could I want than a guy who's head-over-heels mad about me?"

"A decent guy and maybe one not so flamboyant." I gazed intently at my sister. "So what's wrong? You look like your best friend died."

"Can you keep a secret?" She rolled over on one elbow and lowered her voice.

"Out with it, Marj. As long as you're not going to have a baby or something, we can deal with it."

"That's just it." She plopped her head back on the pillow, her disheveled hair lying in ringlets around her face. "I am."

"No!"

"It's true."

"How could you do such a thing?" My quick words sounded like staccato notes. "Mama and Papa will have your head."

"I love him. We were out at Woodland Park, and it got late. You know what can happen when jinxed by that totem pole. Besides, I always wanted a baby. Maybe Kelley and I should run off and get married and not tell anyone."

"That's disgraceful. I warned you to stay away from Kelley."

"It's not like I planned it or anything." Marjorie's voice rose, then she grew quiet for a few moments. "Oh, sissy, what am I going to tell Papa?" She turned over and sobbed, smearing mascara on her pillow.

"You need to tell Mama in the morning," I said. "She'll holler at you, but in the end, she'll forgive you. So will Papa. He'll lecture you, but your sweet talk always softens the blow."

I was confident in Marjorie's abilities to charm our parents even if I was disappointed in her lack of propriety. Nice girls did not find themselves pregnant before they got married. Marjorie was always forgiven for her wayward behavior, and she would be forgiven even for this. After a half hour of convincing, she agreed to talk to our parents.

Marjorie fell asleep while I stared at the ceiling where moonlit shadows moved across the room. Would our parents forgive her? What about marriage? What will they do with the baby? What does Kelley want? What will the townsfolks say? What about Papa's job?

I could not sleep. I could *never* do anything like what Marjorie had done. I couldn't risk becoming pregnant. I wanted too much from life. I certainly didn't want a baby for a very long time, if ever. My heart's desire was to prove to Papa that I was a person who could accomplish good works, move the masses. I wanted to change the world, not diapers.

Fremont was a religious, upstanding man with strict standards of moral conduct. He maintained control over his feelings and his behavior. I might dream of his arms around me, but a kiss and an embrace were as far is it would ever go. Until we married. If we married. No. I could never marry a poor man.

I was right. After crying, yelling, and haranguing for hours, Mama told Marjorie what to do. Get married. The family would be disgraced if she didn't do it soon.

When Papa came back to town, he agreed. "Since I don't have a shotgun, I'm telling you in no uncertain terms, a wedding will take place." It didn't take long for him to get distracted and off on a tangent. "It's these young people these days. If the government could just find them suitable jobs, these shenanigans would stop. Which reminds me, I hear boys like Kelley enjoy their booze. Better watch him, Marjorie. Kick him in the rear end if you have to, but keep him in line. We don't need more talk about you than we already have."

There were no admonishments about Marjorie's moral behavior, her lack of good judgment, or poor decisions.

Mama's biggest concern was about appearances, and Papa only cared about the inconvenience and his reputation.

Marjorie and Kelley married in Wewoka the following weekend. They moved into Kelley's small room above the dry goods store on the east end of Main Street.

Chapter Nineteen
November 1932

"Sibyl," Papa said, "our party may have been stamped out back in the twenties, but that doesn't mean the ideas have disappeared. That red scare debacle just about destroyed us. You remember that new newspaper I told you about? The one started last year by Oscar Ameringer? The *American Guardian*?"

"Yes, Papa." I had to walk fast to keep pace with him as we walked to the Convention Hall. He had invited me to go with him to a covert political rally. I hadn't been to a meeting in months.

"I read there's some disagreement with the party's acceptance of former Communists. Some young whippersnappers who think they know it all want to take over our agenda. Call us the *old guard*. Ha! What do they know? Of course, they've stolen our working-class base, and we don't have many good leaders left."

I felt Papa was insinuating that I, too, had failed to become the leader he expected.

The election did not go as Papa wanted. Roosevelt won by a landslide. Norman Thomas, the Socialist, had received only two percent of the total votes across America. The Communist Party fared even worse, receiving less than a half a percent. Papa was strongly in favor of Thomas, but I felt like Roosevelt was the best choice. I didn't dare share my opinion with Papa. I'd never hear the end of it.

"Listen," Papa said. "We need someone to type up and print out fliers for the next campaign. I told them you'd volunteer."

I had thought Papa wanted to spend time with me, include me in his life. But, being the master of manipulation that he was, he only

117

wanted my clerical help. Unless of course, he hoped I might meet some prominent, influential man to marry. More manipulation. Nevertheless, I volunteered. I loved being involved, no matter how mundane. What harm could it do?

Mama finally got her wish to travel out of town with Papa. He seemed cold to the idea at first, wondering why Mama wanted his company, until he finally gave in to her pleas. They drove the Chrysler to Hot Springs to attend an auction. Mama had lived in Little Rock as a young girl and was excited to show Papa the Ostrich Farm where she and her family would go dig for "diamonds."

I ran the household for the week. Unfortunately for the young ones, I took my job seriously. Blanche and Frances practiced their piano lessons early in the evenings while I washed the dishes. I loved listening to their attempts, even their screeching discordance or when they played the same measure so often I had memorized it myself.

I invited Fremont to come over to spend the evening.

"Come play us a song. Please." Frances begged in her sweet little voice.

Since my earliest lessons, my frustrations with life could be released by playing the piano. Marjorie had refused to practice and eventually Mama let her quit. Calvis preferred the drums or trombone. Several times a month, he played at the Masonic Lodge dance, fueling Papa's anger. Truthfully, I thought Papa was afraid Calvis would not follow in his footsteps and become a banker. But music was in our blood, and we all inherited some of Mama's vocal talent.

I sat at the piano and began to play "I'll Be with You in Apple Blossom Time." My sisters gathered around me and sang. Fremont sat in a corner of the room and listened, applauding and cheering when we finished.

"I didn't know you could play," he said. "That was wonderful."

"Come sing with us," pleaded Frances.

"You're mighty hard to turn down, but I have little musical ability," he said. "Once, while I was in high school, a band played outside in front of a drug store. They needed a drummer so they grabbed me. I'd never played before, so right in the middle of the song, I pounded too hard, and the drum stick went flying." Fremont acted out his story, pounding imaginary drums. "The fellows quickly asked me to quit, and that was the last time I ever played in a band."

Everyone laughed.

Soon, my sisters and Calvis stretched out on the rug before the Crosley radio to listen to the evening's programs. Fremont and I nestled on the couch. NBC news broadcasted regular news bulletins, stressing the recovering economy. Since the announcement of Roosevelt's election as president, people seemed more optimistic.

"Papa's taking me to see the governor next week," said Calvis.

"Why do you get to go?" Blanche jumped up from her seat. "He likes me better. He takes me more places, you know."

"If you haven't figured it out by now, he only takes you to the barber shop to show off your big vocabulary," said Calvis.

"That's not true!" she yelled. "He takes me to meetings sometimes."

"Stop, you two," I said more passionately than I intended. "Now what is this about seeing Governor Murray?"

Calvis explained that Papa had a meeting scheduled with the governor and wanted him to tag along. "Papa said we're going with his boss, Mr. Mothershead, the bank commissioner. Papa's hoping for a promotion, I think." Calvis' knee bounced up and down the way it did when he had to give a speech at school. He didn't want to let Papa down. I knew the feeling. "I'm nervous, but Papa said to sit there and say nothing. I can do that."

"You'll do fine," I said.

Amos and Andy came on the radio, and everyone stopped talking. We all laughed at the shenanigans. As soon as the show ended, I said, "Storytime's over. Lights out in ten minutes."

"We can stay up late since Mama's gone. She wouldn't mind." Blanche took her familiar rebellious stance.

"None of your back-talk."

My sisters didn't object when I tucked them into bed, and Calvis didn't complain when I told him to remain in his room. Satisfied, I walked to the kitchen and poured two glasses of iced tea. I returned to the sofa and handed a glass to Fremont.

"Tell me another one of your stories." I tossed a blanket over my stocking feet, pulled it up to my shoulders and nestled against him.

"You sound like one of the young 'uns," he joked. "Always begging for more." He started to put his arm around me but needed his hands to illustrate his descriptions when storytelling. I smiled and leaned back. Fremont's tales were more animated than anything on the radio.

Tonight Fremont's story centered around when he lived in Springfield, Missouri, as a boy. "We stayed with Mother's sister, Josie. Her son, Jimmy, was two years older than I was and taught me to ride a bicycle—among other things. That year, Babe Ruth played in the St. Louis Stadium. That's where Jimmy took me to my first big league baseball game. We couldn't afford tickets, so we watched through a hole in the fence. It was mighty exciting."

Fremont jumped from the sofa and pretended to be catching a ball. "Whoever could catch a baseball after a home run got a free ticket to the game."

"Sh..." I said, remembering my sisters sleeping in their bedroom.

Fremont hushed but continued to act out the scene. "So naturally, we all tried to catch one. That day, a ball flew my way. I ran for it, jumped, and caught it. I got a free ticket to watch the game. The other boys didn't like it that a 'country hick' like me had caught the ball."

I imagined the scene and laughed. Country hick indeed.

Then Papa's image came to mind. Papa wanted me to marry a rich man, a gentleman, a political leader. Fremont would not do. Papa would never approve.

But did I have to follow Papa? Couldn't I make up my own mind who I wanted to marry? Yes. That could change everything.

"What was it like?" I asked. "Being out on the rail? I mean, did you ever go hungry?"

He hung his head, the excitement from his baseball story gone. "I hope you never have to experience it, Sibyl. Never."

Eventually our whispers turned to traveling, which we both longed to do. I envisioned visiting every state in the country, being involved in promoting Papa's agenda. I felt cheated because Fremont had already seen so many.

It was after midnight when Fremont said, "Guess I should be going home. It's mighty late and I have to work tomorrow."

"Please, stay a little longer," I purred. "Tell me more about California and the Rosen family."

"I don't know."

"Just a little while, please," I begged.

Fremont shared a story about the San Joaquin Valley and how much he wanted to return. Instead of listening, I drifted away, content. For years, dozens of men had followed Marjorie around, some with lots of money and prestige. She could have chosen any one of them. Even Fremont's cousin Inez had gotten married this year, three months before she graduated from Bethel High School, and she was only seventeen years old. I had only this one man in my life, this destitute man, and I was still an unmarried virgin at twenty-two.

"The more I talk about it, the more I want to go back." Fremont's gaze fixed on a far-off vision. "California would be better than sticking around here with no prospects. I'm thinking of leaving."

"What?" I sat up. "Leave now? You would leave me?"

"It's not like that." He searched my eyes. "Don't you see? I could make good money. Make enough to come back, buy you gifts, and support you as you deserve."

I tried to slow my breathing, hoping to calm my pounding heart. I understood he might make more money—but leave me? Why? Panic pierced my heart like arrows.

"You would do that? Go off to California without me?" My voice broke and I swallowed back my tears.

"It'd be temporary. Only for a few months during harvest. I'll come back. You'll see." He patted my hand and stood. "Don't worry. But now I really better get on home."

I followed him to the door. My heart aching. My thoughts in turmoil. How could Fremont leave me so easily? Money, after all, couldn't be more important than me. Perhaps he didn't care as much as I thought. Fear fell over me like dense fog.

He turned to kiss me goodnight and our kiss lasted a long time, longer than usual. Much longer. I clung to him, desperate for reassurance of his feelings for me. Pressing my lips close to his ear, I whispered. "It's so quiet here. Please stay a few more minutes."

He hesitated but sat down again with me. "I like the way you smell of lilacs," he said, drawing me close.

The thought of Fremont leaving overwhelmed me. All I could think of was having him hold me tight. I pressed my lips to his, stopping his words as I moved closer. I felt his arm slide around my waist. He lifted a hand and tenderly touched my hair, moving to stroke my cheek and neck, setting my heart racing. I put my head on his muscular shoulder, and as I nestled on his chest, I felt the rapid beat of his heart. I had never felt as safe as I did at that moment. All the love I had ever yearned for seemed wrapped up right here in this man, everything I had ever wanted, and always missed.

He looked at me, the sweetest look I had ever seen. "I love you, Sibyl. I can't help myself. I just love you." All my resolve fell apart. His sweet blue eyes confirmed his words. I had never been loved like this before. Even though I wasn't ready to tell him I loved him, my heart echoed his words.

Our attraction grew beyond control. I yearned for him to need me the way I needed him. A warm mist crept into my mind, cloudy and muddled. The constant ominous presence of my father's unrelenting disapproval faded and then vanished from my consciousness in the warmth of Fremont's arms. He pulled me next to him, and we slid down on the sofa until we lay side by side. He drew me closer, closer than anyone ever had.

The lights went out in the rest of the houses on the street and the whole town became still. Fremont never left to go home.

Chapter Twenty
January 1933

The next six weeks hazed by in a cloud and before I knew it, it was a new year. I didn't see Fremont much over the Christmas holiday, and he stopped showing up for church on Sunday mornings. I thought sure he would come to our Christmas nativity program, but he didn't.

I was sorely disappointed in myself for my behavior that night. On top of that, I didn't know why Fremont was ignoring me. He didn't come by to visit me and he seemed distant, downright awkward, when I sought him out at the filling station. Did he feel guilty, too?

I woke up Friday morning and fear rushed through my body. I became acutely aware that my life was changing.

Not planned or even remotely anticipated, I should have known there was a possibility. Hadn't this just happened to Marjorie? Mama always said, "Don't play with fire, or you're bound to get burned." Well, I'd gotten burned. My heart felt as heavy as lead.

My family never spoke about sex. Even when my friend Mary Jane missed two cycles and everyone knew her boyfriend had fled town, the word *pregnant* was only spoken in hushed tones and never in front of children. Mary Jane's dilemma dissolved, washed down the toilet after a self-induced abortion. She ended up in the hospital for two weeks and would never be able to bear children, never face that problem again. I wondered what an abortion would feel like. I wondered if I would have regrets. Did Mary Jane?

I didn't want to think about an abortion much less actually do it. But a baby? Me? And Fremont? Shame and disappointment overwhelmed me.

If I took care of the problem now, I would not have to tell Papa or Mama. They would be disappointed. And furious. But no one would need to know, not even Fremont. Perhaps it would be better if it just went away.

Wait. Why would anyone want an unborn baby to just disappear? Because of the inconvenience? But wouldn't life be easier if it did?

I longed to talk to Mama, but she remained absorbed in her own struggle. Not interested in my struggles. She would blame me, not comfort me. And Papa? His rage and disappointment would leave a hole in me as huge as Texas.

After the evening meal, I sat down at the piano, banging out anger on the keys, releasing the frustration and confusion that overwhelmed me. The music dissolved in the cloud of gloom hanging over my head.

That night, my mind raced. I paced the length of my room, marching from the wooden dresser to the patterned window curtains and back, staring into the darkness each time. Marjorie's clothes no longer littered the floor. Nothing cluttered the spotless room except for the pile of books on the lamp stand. I wondered how Marjorie was coping. Unlike me, she had wanted a baby, wanted to marry and settle down. Marjorie never cherished dreams of grandeur or a higher purpose, never wanted to help anyone but herself.

My dreams of improving the world sank like fangs into my mind. Marriage to a hobo was certainly *not* in my dreams of the future. If I married Fremont because I was pregnant, I would never know if we were together because we loved each other or because we had no choice. My life would change in unimaginable ways if I married a poor man.

My anger surfaced. I threw pillows at the wall. How could he make love to me? A man I trusted. I had given up dancing because he thought it taboo. He wanted to follow God's way. He promised a better way to live. Some better way. If God had a purpose in all this, then I couldn't see it. Probably messed up His plan altogether. What was it Fremont said? God will work all things out for good for those who love Him? How? How would He work it out? This could never be from God.

I sat on the stool in front of the dresser and stared into the etched glass mirror. I looked pale. I slid the bobby pins from my hair and laid them neatly next to the bracelet Papa had given me last year when he returned from a Tulsa trip. I grabbed my hairbrush and, out of habit, counted one hundred brush strokes to make my locks shine.

I stopped brushing and leaned close to the mirror, peering into the red puffy eyes of my reflection. Nausea struck hard. I hadn't been able to eat much, and I looked terrible.

"What am I to do?" I asked my reflection.

As far as I could see, in my society, I only had two choices: get rid of the baby or get married. Prepared for neither, heaviness hit the pit of my stomach and weighed my whole body down. I shivered, and tears welled in my eyes again.

How could this have happened?

Once—we were together only once!

What about my dreams?

My life?

I needed time to decide about marriage. Oh, if only I could change what had happened between us!

My heart felt like it would burst. I lowered my throbbing head into my hands, pressing hard to hold back tears. I had wept off and on all day. Having a baby consumed my thoughts.

A whistle called from outside the window, and I jumped. It was Fremont's bobwhite sound meant only for me. I hadn't heard our secret code for a night-time rendezvous in what felt like forever. What was he thinking? Was he disappointed? Did he still care? Would he be better off without me? Right now, the world might be better off without me. I could never help the poor in this condition. I was useless.

The wooden window screeched much too loudly as I pushed it up and peered out. Bedtime meant everyone was asleep.

Fremont's silhouette, the outline of his hat under the street lamp, and his deep voice beckoned. "Sibyl," he called. "Come outside. It's safe. All the other lights are out."

"I can't come tonight," I whispered through the open window. "I'm not ready." This was true. I was not prepared for what lay ahead

125

of me, and he might not be either. I wanted to see him more than anything. I'd missed him—his sane, sensible self and his warm, sweet kisses. But I was nervous. What would I say?

"I have to talk to you." His voice sounded urgent. "I have to tell you my plans."

I didn't know what to do, what to say. I watched him, wondered.

"Sibyl—"

"Wait a minute."

I sank on the quilt that Grandma Bennett hand-stitched for me, relieved that she didn't know what I'd done. She would be disappointed in her favorite grandchild. If she'd still been living in our home, this never would have happened.

What would Fremont do if he found out about the baby? At least I knew he was an honorable man and would want to do what was right. Marry me.

But could I disrupt his life like this?

How could I tie him down with a wife and child he could not support?

Glory be, he couldn't even support a field mouse.

Papa would be furious if I married a filling station attendant who was a former hobo. I couldn't do it. It would break his heart and the promise I made to him all those years ago.

I should just let Fremont leave, push him away, tell him I never wanted to see him again. I would handle the crisis myself, solve my problems alone like I always did. It would be best.

"I can't come," I whispered through the window. My voice carried, and I wondered if anyone else heard. "Not tonight. I don't feel well." My heart pounded violently. Could he tell the difference in my voice?

Fremont came and touched the windowsill with his fingertips. He whispered—his voice a gentle caress. "What's wrong? Can I help?"

No. I couldn't tell him. I couldn't tell anyone. Fremont, a good, solid-minded man, had not an ounce of pretense about him, not like other men I knew. His voice pulled me, drew me out of my space, my shell. He would respond honorably, of course.

Was it fair to force such a good man into marriage?

Would he think I'd tricked him?

The tone of his voice had drawn me to him in the first place. His kindness was irresistible. Perhaps, just perhaps, I would take a chance and tell him tonight.

Yes. I would face this problem instead of ignoring it.

"All right," I leaned over the ledge. "I'm coming."

I dropped to the ground, and Fremont stood with his hands in his pockets. He looked so handsome that my heart felt like it might burst. Tears came to my eyes. I had missed him so much. The last weeks had brought heartache, guilt, and turmoil. Overwhelmed by feelings of loneliness for him, I took a step toward him. He reached out and, without speaking, we held each other close for a long time.

We walked our usual pathway, down Beard toward Main Street. Fremont stopped at a bench in the park but didn't sit down. I could hear the beat of the band playing in the distance, and I pulled my jacket around me as I stopped next to him. The crisp air seemed to betray my numb feelings.

"I won't keep you long," he said. "I need to tell you something. I'm sorry for what happened. It won't happen again."

I didn't listen to his words, my emotions tossed about in a stormy sea. Once my mind was made up, I was determined to blurt the news out as soon as possible, so before he could speak again, I took a deep breath and said, "I didn't want to tell you but—

"I'm going to California—"

"I'm pregnant—"

We stared at each other, mouths open.

His jaw dropped. "You're what?"

"I didn't want to tell you."

"No...no," he paused, ran his hands through his hair. "No. I'm glad you told me. Of course you told me." He settled on the seat beside me, seemed to absorb the news.

Of course he'd been distant. He'd wanted to distance himself from me, to break it off before... "You're leaving."

"I *was* leaving. But now..."

"What?"

"I can't just up and leave you like this, now can I?"

"I don't want to saddle you with a wife and family. I mean..." I fought the prickling in my eyes, but tears slid down my face anyway.

127

He stepped close to me, and I fell against him and sobbed like an injured child. All my wailing expended, I buried my head in his chest. My strength faded away.

He stroked my hair. "We're in this together, and I'll do whatever I have to do."

"But you wanted to leave me." I shook my head slowly. "This is not how it's supposed to be."

"I was planning on coming back."

I never wanted to marry Fremont or anyone out of desperation. How foolish I had been. Even my visions of helping hungry people vanished. What would I do with my life now, have a dozen kids and grow useless like Mama?

My life was a failure. And the whole world would soon know. I sobbed out loud.

"Quiet down. The Lord'll take care of us," said Fremont.

I didn't know what God he was talking about, but the God I knew did not like to find young unmarried ladies in this predicament. Guilt surrounded me. Guilt for getting pregnant. Guilt for hoping Fremont would rescue me in marriage. Guilt for failing Papa. *Especially* guilt for failing Papa.

As far as I was concerned, life was over.

Over.

I dropped to the ground.

"It's getting a bit too cold for you." Fremont took off the scarf around his neck and gently put it around me. "I'll take you home. We'll get married soon—tomorrow if you want."

Chapter Twenty-One
February 1933

Fremont parked Mama's green Chrysler in the driveway of his family's small frame house late in the afternoon. He opened the side door, and I slid out. I wore a calf-length pale yellow crepe dress and a jacket to match. Somewhat bewildered, I removed my gloves and squashed them together in one hand. He wore a jacket and freshly shined shoes. His thick, curly dark hair was oiled down and combed back, revealing his handsome aristocratic profile. I had never seen him so attractive.

We walked across the yard and onto the wooden porch. Fremont opened the screen door and motioned me to enter. I had never been inside a house on the south side of town before, and theirs was larger than I'd expected with simple furniture and a big potbellied stove in the kitchen. Cozy and warm, the only noise was the crackling of the fire and whistling from another room.

"Mother!" Fremont called out. "I'm home."

Mrs. Pope strolled in from the back bedroom and stopped when she saw me.

"You didn't tell me we had company. Lands 'o living, I need to cook more corn for supper. It won't take too long." She rushed to the sink and began washing up.

"Wait, we've got something to tell you. Is Dad out back? Can you ask him to come in?"

Two young faces, Fremont's sisters, peeked out from a bedroom. Mrs. Pope shooed them out to get their dad. Meanwhile, I looked around the room. The floor of the living room was covered with gray carpet and handmade rag rugs. Unusually warm for February, long sheer drapes fluttered in the breeze and bounced over two yellowish straight-backed chairs. A round end table fit between the chairs, and a pink-and-green swirled vase sat on top. The home was nicer than I'd expected.

The smell of a meal cooking permeated the room. Dishes clanged. Water boiled, and steam made the room warm and humid.

Mrs. Pope stirred back and forth around the kitchen. She was a tall, striking woman. A worn apron was tied around her neck and behind her waist and covered a blue flowered dress. Long braids wrapped around her head, framing a kind, warm face. Matronly, yet refined.

Mr. Pope stomped his feet and brushed the dirt from his coveralls before walking inside. He was about five-foot-ten, with broad shoulders. I could see where Fremont got his muscular build. "What is it, son? You've been gone since before daylight." Mr. Pope hung his hat on a nail on the back wall and sat on a small wooden chair. He looked his son up and down. "You're all spanked up now. Going somewhere? And who have we here?"

"Well, I...I mean we, Sibyl and I, want to tell you something," Fremont said.

I perched on the edge of the living room sofa, my fingers folding and unfolding the gloves in my hand.

"We just got married." Fremont's voice was low.

Mrs. Pope burst out crying. Her large frame fell back into the chair, and she gripped her apron tightly. I froze, not wanting to make the situation worse.

"I don't understand. What is this? You got married?" Mr. Pope's forehead creased.

"We're married. Today, Sibyl and I drove over to Chandler, and the Justice of the Peace married us. We just got back."

Mrs. Pope snatched a handkerchief from her pocket and dabbed at her eyes and blew her nose. She did not look up.

"Mother, it isn't that bad," Fremont said. "I love Sibyl and she loves me. Please don't carry on so."

I had never proclaimed my love for him, but when I looked at his sincere face, I thought it could be true. Maybe this was the man God wanted me to marry. I just wished it hadn't happened this way.

Mr. Pope seemed delighted. "Well, I'll be. Congratulations son." He stood and shook Fremont's hand. "Maybe we can build you two a little house out there on the land in Waco."

"You want to move to Waco?" I asked.

"It's the prettiest land in the whole cross timbers. Golden wheat and huge pecan trees. We can plant a large garden and support a dozen young 'uns. Of course, you might have to wait 'til this here dry spell's over, but come a year or two down the road, it would make a fine homestead for you two. The missus and I aim to be moving back out there soon. It's not much, but it's home."

Mrs. Pope sniffed and looked up and the room seemed to tense in anticipation.

She studied Fremont and ignored me. "I don't understand. Why did you do this? We could have discussed it, announced it, and had a big church wedding, if that's what you wanted." Her voice quivered. "Is there some reason you couldn't wait?"

"We couldn't wait," he said, almost in a whisper. The moment both Fremont and I had dreaded. "We're going to have a baby."

His mother wailed again and threw her apron over her head. Fremont rose and knelt down on his knees in front of her. He wrapped his arms around her.

I sat still. Tears fell down my face. I felt like an outsider in their close-knit family.

Earlier that day we had told my parents. They had not been so kind. Marjorie's pregnancy and wedding had been extremely unfortunate but predictable because of her behavior. Marjorie and Kelley Gargas ran off and got married on January tenth, 1933, at the same place Fremont and I married, Lincoln County Clerk's office in Chandler. She wanted to keep her wedding date a secret since she already showed a baby belly.

We were standing in the sitting room when we told Mama and Papa we were married.

131

Mama responded quickly. "Why? Why did you get married? You've always been the serious, thoughtful one. Now, when will I be able to throw a shower, host a fancy church wedding and invite recognized guests? That was terribly inconsiderate." Her sharp words cut like a blade.

Papa exploded. "You have ruined your life. Thrown away your potential. After all the effort I put into training you to be a leader of this next generation. You, of all people, should understand that you cannot act carelessly and be of use to anyone."

"Papa, I'm sorry." I tried to smooth the atmosphere. Papa, always rude, still managed to surprise me with his hatefulness. Was he getting worse or was I becoming more aware of it?

"At a time when the banks are failing at alarming rates, you do something this stupid," he snarled. "Do you know how close to financial collapse this country is? Why, we're discussing not reopening many of the banks in the state, or at least putting restrictions on them until we can determine their status."

I gasped. For the last few weeks I'd been preoccupied with my own catastrophe. Emotions ruled my thoughts. All I wanted was to get through the day.

"After all the promotions for women we've discussed, how women are smart enough to be equal to men, now you go and prove how *stupid* women can be. Going off and marrying a penniless, good-for-nothing bum. Not using that head of yours."

I stood and stepped away from him. "Papa, don't talk like that in front of Fremont."

"He knows what I'm talking about." Papa pointed at Fremont, who stood with his shoulders back near the door. "How in blazes does he plan to support you? Answer me that. Do you realize how many people are unemployed?" He seemed downright disgusted by his eldest daughter's mistake. "Why would you do this?"

I had hoped to keep my pregnancy a secret from them, but I knew it would not happen. I wanted Fremont to defend us, but he didn't speak. I wanted him to punch Papa in the gut for saying such awful things, but he didn't move.

"Papa, I'm pregnant. What do you think I should have done?" I asked.

Mama gasped. "No."

"Have done?" Papa yelled. "You should get rid of the problem, annul this marriage and get on with your life. You still can, Sibyl."

"But, Papa—"

My father's disapproval and harsh words weighed like lead in my heart. After trying so hard to please him, he was capable of dismissing me as being as useless as Marjorie. Just because I got pregnant and married. Why did he judge me so harshly? Wasn't this my own decision?

Someday I would show him that I could be valuable. But at that moment, the future looked helpless. A rock of self-pity sat in my stomach, and any self-esteem I had left burned away like vapor.

At the Pope house, we waited for Fremont's mother to calm down after hearing our news. When Fremont's sisters slipped into the room, Mrs. Pope hushed everyone about the pregnancy. Every adult unconsciously understood that it would not be spoken of again in front of the children. Earlier in the day, as we were driving, Fremont laughingly told me about his parents wedding night. When Mr. Pope had reached to take off her garter, she slapped his hand and said, "Now, listen here…" Culture could bind women to an almost prudish mold.

"Where will you two stay?" asked Mr. Pope.

"Why, they'll stay here with us, of course," Mrs. Pope said. "That is until they can get on their feet."

They determined that we would spend the night there and move my belongings into the back bedroom the following day. Fremont's sisters, Irene and Ruth, would sleep on a makeshift pallet in the enclosed back porch until we could find a place to live and move out on our own. The Pope's small house contained little furniture and boasted none of the conveniences of my family's home, but it was clean, and they were welcoming.

As the conversation died, Mr. Pope turned and spoke gently to me. "I guess you'll be one of us now. If Fremont here married you, the least I can do is make you feel welcome."

I felt the warmth and sincerity of the older man and, as I looked at Mrs. Pope, I hoped my new mother-in-law would welcome me too.

I had never faced such a difficult and embarrassing situation. Had I done right by telling Fremont? I had disrupted the Pope family along with Fremont's life. My bottom lip trembled as I held back the tears.

Sleeping arrangements were made, my bag brought in, and after dinner Fremont and I were shooed into the back bedroom. I looked around at the simple surroundings, an oil lamp, a wooden flat, and a feather bed. Primitive compared to my family's house. Fremont quickly skinnied down to his shorts and jumped into the bed. I pulled a nightgown out of my suitcase and slowly began to undress.

Uncomfortable in front of him, I turned my back to the small bed. Flustered, I bit my lip as I slid off my dress and hung it up. After I pulled my gown over my head and slipped under the covers, I sunk down into the soft feathers and turned toward Fremont's warm and inviting body.

"It's all right, Sibyl," he reassured me. "We'll be all right,"

Fremont made me feel safe, more secure than in my own home. Yes. Part of this arrangement might work out perfectly. Who wouldn't want to sleep beside a gentleman like Fremont?

A loud gasp woke me in the middle the night.

"Fremont. Fremont! What's wrong?"

"A nightmare," he whispered, shaking all over.

I pulled him close and felt the moisture on his skin.

"I get them sometimes."

"What was it about?"

Still shaking, he took a deep breath and explained, "From my hobo days. I see the fellows, weary fellows in tattered clothes. And women, oh, I hate to see the women. Hollow-eyed women with starving children holding onto their ragged skirts. You can't imagine, Sibyl. There were so many. I saw mamas carrying their dead babies in their arms." He rested his head on his pillow and sobbed.

It had been months since I'd first seen Fremont, months since he'd jumped off a train and staggered home. He had told me some, but I didn't understand. Maybe I'd never understand what he'd been through.

"It haunts me." Fremont's breathing finally deepened. He shook his head as if shaking the cobwebs free. "The fear of being poor. This is not the time to thrive in Oklahoma, what with the dust blowing like a banshee and sweeping people out west."

I didn't speak. I held him tight, wishing the nightmares would disappear, wondering if they would come every night.

"How will we survive?" he asked.

I knew he didn't expect an answer, but his fears fell on me, filled me. How *would* we survive? How could a poor man like Fremont support a wife? And how, dear God, could he support a child?

Chapter Twenty-Two
March 1933

The next few weeks flew by in a blur. I threw myself into work. Mr. Weston kept piling forms on my desk and I ran all over town delivering messages, filing legal documents at the courthouse, and purchasing office supplies. Married women were discouraged from working outside the home, so keeping my marriage secret from my boss was important. We needed the money my job supplied.

While I had been worried about being unmarried and pregnant, the banking industry was having a challenging time. I didn't know how bad it had become.

The federal government passed the Emergency Banking Relief Act to try to stabilize the banking system. Oklahoma followed the example of fourteen other states and restricted its banks, creating chaos through Shawnee. It seemed the whole world collapsed. Then disaster became personal.

Papa's boss, Bank Commissioner Barnett, had been in the news, accused of lying about the financial position of insolvent banks. I hoped that Papa, a bank examiner, had not been part of Barnett's mess. Surely, there was nothing to worry about there.

The federal government passed the Emergency Banking Relief Act to try to stabilize the banking system. Oklahoma followed fourteen other states and restricted its banks, creating chaos throughout our town. It seemed like the whole world had collapsed.

Then, disaster became personal.

On the morning of March twenty-ninth, a loud, insistent knocking sounded on the front door of the Pope's house. I opened it. Mother Pope stood right behind me, alarmed that a red-faced disheveled child was pounding on her screen. My sister Blanche leaned on the side of the house, her chest heaving as she gasped for breath.

"What's wrong, Blanche? What happened?" Something about her expression made me steel myself for bad news. Only something urgent would cause Blanche to run across town and arrive in such a state. "What happened?"

"Come in, child," chimed Mrs. Pope. "Can I get you something? Water?"

Blanche nodded yes.

"It's Grandma Bennett." Blanche wheezed between breaths as she slumped into a chair. "I ran all the way to tell you. Grandma died this morning."

I couldn't move. It couldn't be true. Grandma couldn't be gone. The truth of the words engulfed me in a shroud of pain. Just two weeks ago, one of Papa's sisters, a woman I'd never met, had died back in Alabama. Now, my precious grandma was gone. Not my grandma. Not her.

It was too sudden.

It was all too sudden.

I was still adjusting to married life, looking for a new home, and living away from my family. I suffered horribly from morning sickness. Working long hours. Trying to fit into this new home with this new family. Trying to figure out how Fremont and I were going to survive once the baby came.

Now this. My heart crumbled in a thousand pieces. I turned away from Blanche and sobbed. Mrs. Pope put her arm around me, and I leaned on her, helpless.

Blanche and I walked back to Mama's house. We were still nearly a block away when we heard Mama screaming. Except for the whine in her voice, you would have thought she was angry by the way she carried on. She ranted on about how Grandma Bennett should have been at our house, about how Papa had antagonized her. "You never cared about her," Mama screamed. "You never cared about any of us."

Blanche and I reached the house, where I pulled Mama into a hug. She sobbed onto my shoulder.

Papa merely shook his head and turned away. Not concerned about Mama's pain. His arrogance irritating.

I drove Mama's Chrysler down Highway 59 to Sulphur to attend the funeral. Mama was too upset to drive, and Fremont couldn't leave his job. Marjorie had stayed behind, too far along in her pregnancy to venture so far from home, but Frances and Blanche rode with Mama and me. Papa, of course, acted like he had more important business to attend to and Calvis disliked being near the emotional goings-on of the family. So it was just the four of us that morning as I focused on steering through the mist and dense fog. Rain pelted the windshield.

Mama and I wore black dresses and hats that had black netting pulled down over our faces. The younger girls wore Sunday clothes. We spent the two-hour trip reminiscing about Grandma.

"My mother was a beauty, wasn't she?" said Mama as she dried her tears, a total wreck since she'd received the news. "No one else in the family was so cute and petite or had her dark complexion. I should have been with her." Before the trip, Mama had been relaying the details of her great loss to every neighbor and church friend who stopped by the house to offer condolences. Even Mrs. Pope brought by a platter of fried chicken, sharing in our grief.

I didn't comment that I was a bit like Grandma, inheriting her dark hair and complexion. "Can you believe, at almost seventy-six-years-old," I said, trying to control the tremor in my voice. "Her hair was still as black as a raven's wing, hanging down to her waist with just a few sprinkles of gray. She looked good."

"Oh, what will I do without her?" wailed Mama.

"What about you, Blanche?" I asked. Helping the family cope took precedence over my feelings. "What do you remember about Grandma?"

"Her lively blue eyes that bounced with fire when she spoke. I liked that."

Our chatter fell silent and a memory flashed through the haze of my grief.

"I remember when I was fourteen," I said. "I went by myself to visit Grandma and Grandpa Bennett on their farm near the creek in Spiro. We gathered firewood, hoed string beans and okra and milked the cows, new experiences for a city girl like me. But I loved it. I enjoyed the outdoors and working beside them." I almost smiled. "When the chores were finished and Grandma grew tired, she would pick up her worn-out Bible and stroll to the creek, where she sat and read for hours. One day she stayed an extra-long time and when Grandpa came back in the late afternoon, he asked about her. 'She took off that away,' I told him as I pointed north. 'Well, go on up the creek and find her.' So I did. I found Grandma asleep, leaning against a tree with her open Bible on her lap and a fishing pole in her hand."

Truth be told, she never read any other book but the King James Bible. Grandma's prayers would probably impact the family for generations. She was with Jesus now, where she wanted to be. But I wished she hadn't left us until years down the road.

At the funeral, I sat stiffly on a wooden pew at the Sulphur First Baptist Church, brooding like a baby chick that lost its mama. Pain gripped me inside, and I thought my heart would explode. I grieved, feeling abandoned and left alone in a world empty of Grandma's prayers.

Tears ran down my face as they sang her favorite hymn, "The Old Rugged Cross." The tears continued as Uncle Louie told how strong Grandma had been in the face of hardships and how much she had loved her Lord and her family. Grandpa Bennet, sitting on the front pew, looked lost without her.

The graveside service was held at Oak Lawn Cemetery, which lay northwest of Sulphur. Most of the Bennett family attended, shaking hands, hugging, and weeping on each other's shoulders.

The event seemed to devastate everyone, especially me. My one supporter in the family had left me. What would I do now? The only comfort I had was that at least my dear Grandma never heard about the baby conceived out of wedlock or my quick marriage. She would have been terribly saddened. Then my heart fell, thinking that she would never see my baby, and Fremont would never know her.

My wobbly knees provided little strength as I leaned against one of the oak trees on the cemetery hilltop and let the tears flow freely.

Death.

All my grief and pain and loss jumbled together like the yarn scraps in Grandma's knitting basket.

The end of my dreams.

The loss of my grandma.

These events would be tied together forever in my mind.

I felt unsettled. What about everything else? Would we drop further into the weak economy as my banker father prophesied, obliterating hope for a meaningful future? What about the childhood promise I'd made to Papa? Would I ever be able to fulfill it? Would I ever do any good in this world?

According to Mama, Grandma Bennett died of a broken heart. Too many catastrophes in her life, one after the other, just like mine. Maybe, I thought, Grandma bequeathed the sadness to me, the sadness of trying to cope with my dreams while all around me life seemed out-of-control. How could I cook bacon for Fremont and sneak out to distribute fliers for Papa with this sadness in my heart?

No. I would not give up.

Chapter Twenty-Three
April 1933

A few weeks after my grandmother's funeral, Fremont and I moved into our first house, a rental on the south side of Shawnee. Sad because we couldn't afford anything nicer, I sucked in my breath and didn't complain. At least we had a place to live, a place to ourselves. Although the Pope's had been kind, I wanted privacy. And a kitchen of my own.

"The house *must* have an inside toilet, plus running water," I had insisted, and Fremont had agreed. Most homes in the poor part of town still had outhouses and outside wells. Even the Pope's house had not added indoor plumbing.

The house we rented had a toilet and running water, but no electricity. We had it put in within a week. The rent was five dollars a month, which was reasonable since Fremont and I both worked. I took care of all the bills. After all, Papa had taught me how to handle money, and I did have my business degree.

Our tiny two-room house on West Forrest Street stood on a hilltop, several blocks east and north of the Pope's home, up and over a rolling dirt street lined with oak trees. It may have been the smallest house on the street, but it was ours. Several steep steps led up to a concrete front porch where we liked to sit and talk after a long day. The bathroom tacked onto the back of the house included a shower, albeit one with only cold water. My new life was a lot different from my old one. Within two months, I had moved from a promising, comfortable life of anticipation to an almost pauper's life with a former hobo.

How quickly life could change.

After a while, Papa's anger almost subsided. His disappointment had not diminished. Fremont would never live up to Papa's standards. However, Fremont's natural confidence showed through as bright as a lamplighter's wick, flickering with promises. Papa recognized his potential.

Fremont's level-headedness presaged a much better future than that of Marjorie's husband, Kelley. Papa felt that Kelley needed a steady job, not a hand-out. He said that money given to Marjorie and Kelley would likely fuel the fire of carousing and drinking moonshine. He saw Fremont differently. He gave us fifty dollars to help with buying furniture instead of renting it. It was an extravagant and surprising gift.

We found a sofa, a dining-room table, and two high-backed chairs for sixty-five dollars. We paid forty down and agreed to pay the balance a little at a time. With the remaining ten dollars, we purchased other needed household items like linens and a cast iron skillet. Mama loaned us a bed, and I added a touch of home by laying Grandma's quilt over the end of it. Fremont's mother brought over some violet-designed dishes, pastel with shaped edges. Though old, they had no chips or cracks and felt like new. I loved them immediately but wondered why she would give me such a gift, since they had so little. She must have raided her jar of savings to buy them because even used dishes wouldn't be cheap

We spent all day cleaning and arranging our home, and by that evening, I was dog-tired from the hard work. "My blue heaven." I exclaimed. "There's still work to do, like sewing a few curtains and scrubbing the stove in the kitchen, but I love it already."

"Do you really like it?" Fremont asked as he fell into one of the chairs. "I mean, it's nothing like you're used to."

"It's a little doll house." I said, pleased with our work. I wiped my brow and brushed the hair back from my face. I was surprised at the level of happiness I found in something so mundane. Establishing a household of my own brought unexpected contentment. Perhaps marriage could assuage my restlessness, offer some form of peace.

Maybe marrying Fremont *was* the right decision for me. His love was evident and his laughter cheered me up.

His face lit up in a big grin. "So, you think this will do?"

"Any place with you is a good place to be. Do you like it?"

"Feels like I finally came home," he said contentedly. "Hope this feeling lasts forever."

An unruly noise emanating from the front of the house startled me. Pots and pans banging. Loud yells.

Fremont and I glanced at each other, puzzled. Horns blew and people shouted. Several voices sang raucously, "He's in the Jailhouse Now."

"Oh, no, it couldn't be." I said, looking out the window.

Thunderous, discordant music sounded. A shivaree!

News of our marriage must have spread. My family was often mentioned in the social section of the *Shawnee News*, so I should have known that my marriage could not be kept quiet forever.

How humiliating.

I hoped my pregnancy was not also the talk of the town.

"Where're the newlyweds? Come on outside!" one of my friends yelled from the porch. Others pounded on the front door. I grimaced and motioned for Fremont not to answer, but the noise grew louder.

A loud thump sounded on the side window, and we heard footsteps scurrying toward the back. Fremont laughed and said, "Guess we can't hide all night."

As he flung open the front door, Marjorie stood there surrounded by some of my old gang, youthful men and women dressed in bowler hats and fur collars. Some of Fremont's buddies mingled with them. "Surprise!" Marjorie yelled, her belly huge and her lipstick bright red. "We're looking for some newlyweds."

Fremont and I looked at each and laughed. "I didn't think this would happen to us."

Amidst whooping and hollering, Kelley picked me up and carried me outside. Embarrassed, I hid my face in his wool overcoat while two other fellows took Fremont by his arms and legs. They dumped us into the rumble seat of a roadster. Neighbors watched as the line of automobiles followed us through town toward Main Street.

143

The fellows honked their horns, waving to people along the way who gathered to watch. I ducked, trying to hide, but despite myself, I was having fun.

Eventually we arrived at a friend's house north of Highland, where the party continued. Several of my society friends were conspicuously missing. James, of course, was not in attendance, but I thought a few of my other dancing buddies would show up. Of course, some would reject me because of my choice to marry a lower-class man. I'd expected it, but I hadn't realized it would upset me so much. I tried to put the negative thoughts aside and enjoy the moment.

Typically, our gang's get-togethers brought serious conversations that carried no practical resolutions. This evening was no different. I overheard bits and pieces of the fellows talking, like a one-sided news flash from business owners' sons and lawyers' daughters.

"The Communist Party is mobilizing so fast they'll soon be bigger than the Democrats."

"I heard there were seven thousand in Oklahoma City."

"What's the government doing about it?"

"Didn't you know? They arrested some of the leaders."

"What about that food riot in Henryetta?"

"Those guys were protesting unemployment. Now, if that isn't the most useless thing to do."

"At least that demonstration was peaceful. They're not always."

The greatest catastrophe we faced, the worsening economy, was mentioned by no one. Of course, the topic was probably avoided on purpose, as my father was a bank examiner and banks were under suspicion.

Along with the typical talk of politics came the opinions about marriage. "Friends and acquaintances, it's sheer madness to marry. No offense, Sibyl."

Everyone laughed, even me.

"We're living in a period of uncertainty and insecurity, which might last a long time. However, I must admit, marriage provides a good excuse for a celebration."

"Here, here!" the group agreed.

Marjorie got us back on track, and the "pounding," unexpectedly, was amusing. Each friend provided a pound's worth of practical items we could use. They carried in baskets of flour, sugar, vegetables, and other staples to set up housekeeping. They even added a pound of nails for Fremont.

One additional wedding gift proved to be my favorite. Pooling their funds together, our friends bought us a desktop model Crosley radio. Later, I read the pamphlet to Fremont. It had a round wooden case and five tubes. I had to keep Fremont from taking it apart to see how it worked.

Several hours later, we all climbed back into the sedans, coupes, and speedsters. It was a regular derby lineup, as Fremont said, when they returned us to our little home on Forrest Street.

"Good luck!" friends called as they dashed back to their waiting jalopies, shouting well-wishes as they drove off.

Marjorie, her pregnancy obviously showing, should have been tired after all the ballyhoo, but not her. She could keep going all night. She energetically hugged me before she ran out to the car, jumped in, and waved goodbye. Fremont and I stood at the front door, waving back.

"Can you believe it?" I said. "The food! And how did they know we'd love a radio?"

"Friends are mighty amazing sometimes." Fremont put his arms around me, and I could feel his warmth through his cotton shirt.

"Do you think they know?" My pregnancy could not be kept secret forever. I just hoped Marjorie would keep it undercover for a while longer.

Fremont shrugged, glancing down at me as he smiled. "The good Lord'll take care of us, Sibyl. Don't you worry none."

Chapter Twenty-Four
May 1933

I rushed to Mr. Weston's office building. Late again. I was always running late these days, detained because I was sick or something in the house absolutely needed to be done. Every dish had to be washed and put away before I left the house. My rules, not Fremont's, of course. He never complained about anything. He was always easygoing, even jovial at times. I had never seen him so content. When I was with him, I forgot all my worries.

I hoped Mr. Weston didn't send me on another errand to the union offices today. He made me promise not to tell anyone that I carried messages for him and Mr. McClaire. Nor was I to breathe a word about the discussion he and my father had about the enlarging union bank account amidst the disruption of bank closings. Over the months, I had lost faith that their actions were honorable. They said they wanted to help the unemployed get their jobs back, but requesting union fees seemed like stealing food from the mouths of members' children.

"Sibyl Trimble!" said Mr. Weston when I arrived. He did not know about either of my conditions – being married or being pregnant. Many days I could hardly accept them myself.

"Yes sir?" I rushed to my desk and began straightening up the papers I had straightened before I'd left yesterday. It was a habit of mine. Creating these lists and then stacking them in order.

"Come in here. I need to talk."

I picked up my pad and a sharp pencil and walked in. I smoothed down my dark tailored skirt and rearranged the scarf around my collar and sat. Only then did I dare take a deep breath. Poised to take shorthand, I expected the typical hour or more of dictation.

"Sibyl, I have a serious matter to discuss with you," he began hesitantly. "It may be a bit unpleasant, but there are some um... delicate things that need to be addressed."

My eyebrows shot up. My pencil dropped. What delicate things would I discuss with my boss?

"My wife, er, Mrs. Weston, came by the office yesterday. You remember?"

I nodded.

"Well, she noticed a little something. I don't want to embarrass you, but, well, I'll just say it. She thinks you may be in the family way. Are you?"

I cleared my throat and looked out the window behind him. I could not lie, but I'd also hoped I could work a few more months before the baby came. We needed the money. Badly. Even if Mr. Weston didn't pay me everything he owed each week, my salary helped pay the rent.

He waited for my response.

"Sibyl?"

I couldn't look at him.

"That brings up another matter. If you do happen to be in the family way, you are either not the girl I believed you to be, or you have married without telling me. Either way is inappropriate behavior for an attorney's secretary to behave."

"I'm very sorry, sir. I should have told you I got married."

His wife, a jealous, unfriendly woman, had wanted me gone as soon as I had started.

"I'm very surprised your father didn't tell me. As you know, we don't hire married women. No one does in this town. Too many family men lined up in dire need of jobs. You should understand that."

My papa didn't know about my pregnancy. He would find out soon enough. Somehow I knew what Mr. Weston was going to say next, but I held my breath anyway.

"I really like your work. But I'm afraid I'll have to let you go."

I took a deep breath and turned my head away. "I understand," I almost meant it. Too many disgruntled family men in the soup lines, their wives and children begging.

Since I had married Fremont, I'd put myself in the same position. I could end up as one of these poor people. Except Fremont had a job, essential for survival, even with its meager pay.

I walked back to my desk and started to gather my personal belongings. "Wait!" I rushed back into his office. "I almost forgot. What about the $27 you owe me? The back pay you were going to give me when your clients paid up."

"There won't be funds anytime soon. I'll let you know when it changes."

"But we really need the money, sir."

Without looking up, Mr. Weston shook his head.

I knew our conversation was over and I walked out feeling two feet tall. I couldn't contribute to my new family any more. Pride reared its head. I was a Trimble. How could this happen to me? I felt poorer than ever. I *was* poorer than ever.

I stomped down the sidewalk like a mad bull, muttering under my breath. The more I thought about being fired because I was married and pregnant, the angrier I got. I would show him. I would find another job, a better one. One where they actually paid me. I was glad—no, *relieved*—to be through with the repetitive shorthand, the exhausting errands, the demanding boss.

On my way home, I stopped by Attorney Lawson's office and asked for a job. He knew my work, knew Mr. Weston. "I heard you were married. You know we don't hire married women. Not our way. Too many others needing a job."

No other attorney in town would hire me because I was married and pregnant.

Now I had to tell Fremont.

I stomped back home. We *would* make it. We *would* succeed. I was not sure how, but strength and determination bubbled up inside me.

Chapter Twenty-Five
June 1933

Seven months to term and pregnancy still proved unkind to me. I queasily stirred when my sister's husband Kelley delivered the ice, one of the recent odd jobs he had taken. Wearing a little billed hat, he hauled in an ice chunk with enormous magical ice tongs. He cut off a piece to fit into the square wooden icebox and put it in the top compartment above the drip pan.

I was too sick to see him to the door.

Mornings were downright disgusting. Some days I had to remain absolutely still and hope the nausea would disappear. Any movement, even walking around my house, made me feel ill.

While Fremont spent his day at work, I passed my time making lists on every scrap piece of paper in the house: baby needs, baby names and Christmas gifts even though it was months away. The list-making helped me feel more in control, more organized. By evening, I usually felt well enough to prepare dinner for the two of us. When Fremont came home, we would eat, and I would ask questions about his day down at the filling station. I asked who came in for gasoline, who needed their old jalopies fixed, and what family had loaded up to move out west.

On the days when the nausea wasn't too bad, I walked to the Popes' where Mother Pope fed me, her down-home cooking better than what I could make. She always took time to pray for me and her coming grandchild. Other days, I visited Mama and listened to her talk about society life and who was going to sing the next church solo. Some days, I sewed baby clothes. Most days I day-dreamed alone, listening to tunes on the radio and thinking of how life could have been. The loneliness sometimes overwhelmed me.

The radio became my constant companion. Daily news provided a glimpse of events in the larger world. Pretty Boy Floyd shot four FBI agents. Churchill believed the real threat to England was Japan, with their new machine gun firing an unbelievable 1,000 shots per minute. The economy was worsening. The climate was almost desert-like. The terrible winds continued to blow, whipping up dust storms unlike anything I'd ever seen. I felt distressed for the farmers, those men in overalls planting crops and watching the grain disappear in the squall, gambling on FDR's new policies. The whole world seemed to be disintegrating around me.

Governor "Alfalfa Bill" Murray got elected the ninth governor of Oklahoma by making big promises, talking warm and friendly on the radio, assuring us that life would improve. Controversial and colorful, with a boisterous flair, Murray dwelt at the center of public affairs. I might have laughed at him with my old society friends, but now that I belonged to the host scraping by for daily food, his promises seemed empty. When the dust started blowing and the corn started drying on the stalk, Murray reminded people of the early days of fresh dreams for people making a living in Oklahoma. Murray was a legend, a man who feared nothing and no one. I could have admired him if his policies made more sense and he quit calling out the National Guard for every squabble.

The Trimble family argued about the governor, either liking or hating him. Mama loved his outgoing style but Papa despised him. "Murray's fighting all of Roosevelt's public work programs and federal assistance," Papa complained adamantly one Sunday when we joined the family for lunch. "Doesn't he understand the state needs the money for economic survival? That's the government's responsibility. Social justice can be attained on this earth, but we must remember we're all brothers and help each other. Can't he see that?"

Mr. Pope also disliked Murray, but for a different reason. "It might help the poor if Murray'd let a few of those federal projects into the state. Folks could at least earn their own food. Course, that New Deal might likely change things 'tween us and the government.

Land o' Goshen, the needy'll want someone up in Washington to take care of 'em."

Our families passionately discussed the times growing harder in Oklahoma. Roosevelt labeled Murray as "crazy as a bed bug" and on this one issue, we all agreed. So far, the governor had accomplished nothing to help the people and the situation had grown worse. Even our beloved Will Rogers made jokes about the predicament. "Heroing is one of the shortest-lived professions there is."

I agreed. It was time for a different governor. Murray was a short-term man, and his time was over.

My days became routine. Some days, during lunch hours, I helped out in the First Baptist Church kitchen. I didn't tell Fremont, or anyone else, for that matter. I feared they would think I was trying to be goody-two-shoes or impress people. Or that I shouldn't be fraternizing that part of town because of supposed danger.

I tried to smile and encourage the poor women who stood in line for a bowl of hot soup, their sad eyes haunting me. Sometimes I added an extra potato to an emaciated fellow's cup. Although I tried to make their life a little bit easier, I knew my efforts did not help this growing mass of needy people. There were downright too many needs. What could one disgraced girl do? Fremont and I barely had enough food for ourselves. I felt helpless. At the same time, I felt drawn to the people who came to the soup line, and I looked forward to volunteering. It helped me feel useful for the time being.

Marjorie gave birth to a baby boy. I didn't hear about my new nephew, Larry, until the next day. Nausea still struck me, especially in enclosed spaces, so I didn't go to the hospital, but a few days later I visited her at home. Marjorie and Kelley lived in a small apartment above Kib Warren's Hardware on East Main Street, and it seemed like a long walk from our part of town.

"Sis, I was at a movie at the Hornbeck that night, can't even recall the name of the flick now," said Marjorie. "Remember how it rained a watershed? My water broke and I knew it was starting, so I ran all the way to Mama's house and got completely soaked. Since I didn't have a doctor, Mama rushed me to the emergency room at the ACH Hospital downtown."

"I tried to tell you, Marj," I said. "You needed to see a doctor, and then you could have given birth at home instead of at the hospital." If a woman had a doctor caring for her, she could give birth in the privacy of her house, but if she did not have a family doctor, the hospital would take her in.

Marjorie was already out of bed and washing dishes by the time I left. I wasn't sure I could be as nonchalant about a new little life as she seemed to be.

"Oh, I forgot to tell you about this," she said before I walked out the door. "I ate three big dishes of homemade ice cream the day before he was born. He was born purple—about frozen to death!" Marjorie's chortles rattled the cups on the dining-room table. "Mama worried until we finally got him warmed up."

I shook my head, and we laughed together.

I held my new nephew and it stirred my heart. What would it be like to care for a baby? Was I ready to be a mother?

Full of joy, I went home and waltzed around the living room alone, listening to Benny Goodman and Louis Armstrong on our radio. I fondly remembered dancing to Duke Ellington's "It Don't Mean a Thing If It Ain't Got Swing" at the Blue Bird Ballroom. I missed those days. They felt like a lifetime ago. Closing my eyes, I glided around the small house, captured by the music, exhilarated by the rhythm. Dance steps came as second nature. I didn't have to think. Forward, backward, circles, and twirls, I danced, reveling in the freedom.

When life improved, I decided, I'd teach Fremont to dance, even if we only practiced in our bedroom. We could waltz together, just the two of us. I would do it for me, for us. Maybe we would dance to "It Had to Be You," a song that rang true to my feelings, and hopefully, to his.

Soon I became too big to dance and my belly too heavy to twirl.

Chapter Twenty-Six
August 1933

Mid-August, and my baby was due any day. One Thursday, Marjorie lifted my boredom by coming to visit. Unhealthy as I thought it was for her to push a buggy across town with a newborn, I was glad to see her.

"How do you do it? Stay all chipper and happy about a baby? And it's only been a few months." I sipped my coffee. These days I had to forgo the cream and sugar, the cost of such things prohibitive.

My sister snickered. "Lovey, having a baby isn't too bad. It's taking care of one that's so hard. Without Larry, I'd go nuts. Nothing else to do." Marjorie picked up her tiny boy and held him close, rocking back and forth in the chair. She offered to let me hold him, but I shook my head. 'Baby' still seemed like a foreign word to me, but his presence made me question myself. Could I mother a child? Did I even want a child?

I hadn't seen Marjorie's husband in months. "How are you and Kelley doing?"

"If you ask me, lovey, marriage is not as grand as I thought it would be. Kelley's a bit on the jealous side. Doesn't like me to have friends around." She shook her head full of blond curls. "He got mad yesterday when I talked to Doyle at Kresses. You remember him, don't you? Oh, and guess who I saw the other day? Remember, the good-looking guy you almost married, James?"

I would rather not have discussed James. Why did she bring him up? She didn't even think about how his name could bring back uncomfortable feelings. "How is he?"

"I was up at the Silver Station in the City, you know, that new dancing spot. He was there with some fancy-dancy girlfriend. He pulled me aside and told me all about his new store. Seems he's doing quite well, even in this economy."

I stared at the linoleum floor and did not look up. It needed mopping. Again.

"He asked about you."

"Oh."

"Yeah, he insinuated that if you ever wanted to pick up where you left off, he might be interested."

"Marjorie, stop," I said sternly. "I'm married and having a baby any day. I hope you set him straight."

"Why? Always keep your options open. You never know what might happen in the future."

I had no idea what James had in mind. I hoped my reputation had not sunk too low.

Marjorie laid the sleeping Larry down on a blanket while I changed the subject. "So you're still dancing? Shouldn't a grown-up, married woman stay home? Take care of her family?"

"You know me, I'm always ready for a good time," said Marjorie. "Life is too short not to enjoy."

It was hard for me to be mad at Marjorie, even if her good-timing, still-dancing lifestyle irritated me. We switched to stories of our childhood, reminiscing late into the afternoon. We laughed about Papa's stubbornness, like when he tried to preserve a bushel of cantaloupe. It didn't matter to him that everyone told him it could not be done. He peeled and cut the fruit into pieces, heated the cantaloupe in the pressure cooker, and packed it into glass jars. His pride only deflated three days later when all that canned fruit turned black and moldy.

In the earliest hours of August 19, 1933, my labor began. Both sets of grandparents, all soon-to-be aunts, uncles, and relatives, and lastly, Dr. Fortson, waited impatiently in our home for my baby to be born.

The labor and delivery lasted more than fifteen hours. Good gracious, was it difficult! I writhed in that borrowed poster bed. I was told they could hear my screams resounding down the street. Our small bedroom was cramped, barely enough space for the doctor and my mother and mother-in-law to squeeze around the big bed.

Fremont, a jittery, nervous, about-to-be-father, paced the house. I could hear the pennies jingling in his pocket when I relaxed during contractions.

Finally, the baby arrived. A girl, a healthy eight-and-a-half-pounder. Her tiny head was squished to a point on top, and her tiny wail filled the room.

"What's wrong with her?" I mumbled as Dr. Fortson held up my new squirming infant. I had never seen a newborn without a perfectly round head. "Is she supposed to look like that?"

"It's nothing, dear." Mama patted my hand. "Sometimes this happens when it's a long delivery." I sank exhausted onto the pillow, worn out, and ashamed of my weakness that brought about the baby's life.

Mother Pope washed my plump, tiny girl. Her unusually long, black baby hair softly clung to her pointed head. She quieted when wrapped tightly in the hand-crocheted blanket my mother's sister, Aunt Adah, made.

"Here," Mother Pope said as she handed me the baby, "just hold her. I believe she looks a lot like Fremont."

I shook my head no. I didn't want to hold my baby. I turned over to my side and stared at the wall as tears streamed down my face and soaked the pillows. Thoughts swirled senselessly in my head. My emotions had been on one big roller coaster, my exhaustion bringing out the worst. I was not ready to be a mother. How could I be happy about this? All the plans for my life disappeared in one night of pleasure. I felt worthless, useless to the world, a letdown to Papa. One mistake had cost me my dreams. Why had God let this happen?

"Just leave me alone," I muttered.

Mother Pope summoned Fremont. His brow furrowed when he turned to me, his blue eyes gentle and worried, I am sure, about his wife and baby and how to pay the doctor. He sat on the edge of our bed and said in a low, sweet voice, "Don't worry, Honey, you're going to be a good mother. You'll love this baby."

He reached out, took our infant in his arms and rocked her back and forth. His face lit up as he gazed at her. "We'll name her Margaret Kathryn, after our mothers' middle names. They'll like that."

My admiration for Fremont grew as I watched him hold our baby, but I did not have the strength to respond. I rolled over.

Later. I would deal with my feelings later, when I felt better.

Right now, I just needed to sleep.

I could not nurse my baby. My body refused to make milk. Marjorie produced plenty of milk for two babies, so she handled the task. Seeing my need, she wrapped up her own three-month-old baby, brought an overnight bag and prepared to stay.

"Don't you fret, Sibyl," said Mama. "I did the same for your Aunt Adah when she had Gladys. You're lucky to have Marjorie here to help you."

Why did Marjorie always do everything better?

After two days, Marjorie scolded me for my despair and lack of energy. "Lovey, you just have to crawl out of that bed and take care of this baby. She's yours even if you don't want her."

But my sister's pleading could not reach my heart. The pain went deeper than I could admit. I felt guilty for getting pregnant. I finally agreed to try to nurse baby Margaret again, but I still did not have enough milk. I handed her back to Marjorie.

"I'm so tired," I said, too exhausted to even cry. Every muscle ached, and my head felt full of clouds.

"You're probably depressed, lovey," Marjorie said kindly. "Many gals feel that way after giving birth."

I roused slightly, unsure if I wanted my sister's company. I felt guilty. I felt angry. I felt useless. I couldn't even care for my own child.

Then I heard the front door open. Fremont had come home from work, and I could hear him mumbling to Mama in the other room.

Marjorie, her ivory-white breasts showing, sat in the rocking chair beside my bed and rocked Margaret. She swayed back and forth nursing the tiny newborn. My anger surfaced like a hot flash. I didn't want Fremont to see my sister unclothed. Had he already seen her half-dressed and nursing his infant?

The chair creaked as it rocked. Marjorie held my baby close, almost as if Margaret were her own baby. Larry lay asleep nearby. I pulled myself up, threw my feet over the side of the bed, and sat still, staring at my child. She looked like a Pope, round and sturdy. She wasn't dainty like a Trimble.

"Seems like your man has taken a shine to this baby," said Marjorie, "even if you haven't." She set my baby on her lap and began to wrap her up.

Fear and panic rose within me. Irrationally, I was afraid of losing Fremont. After all, Marjorie had just nursed *his* baby. I stared at my sister until Fremont's muscular silhouette covered the bedroom door.

"Honey," he whispered softly. He paused as Marjorie wiggled her almost bare breasts back into her clothing. His faced turned red.

I was horrified.

"Wait a minute." I whispered back, a little harsher than I wanted.

He turned and quickly left the room.

"I'll take her now," I told Marjorie.

"That's okay," she whispered. "I think she likes me."

"But she's mine. I can do this."

Marjorie hesitated.

My pink bedclothes clung to my skin as I stood. Usually I would be embarrassed for anyone to see me in this state of undress, but I demanded, "Give me my baby."

She raised her eyebrows, a look of surprise on her face, but she didn't say anything as she handed me Margaret. I sat on the bed, leaned back against the pillows, and held my baby in my arms, looking down at this tiny life. So fragile, I thought, and such perfect miniature hands and feet. The baby's serious eyes looked back at me in bewilderment and something tender touched my heart. Here was a sweet angel, my own child, pink cheeks and soft hair. Then the little one let out a loud scream, and I jumped, not sure what to do. I looked up at Marjorie.

"You can do this. I'll go help Mama cook dinner." She hurried from the room.

By the following week, I accepted little Margaret as a reality in my life and got to the task of motherhood. I learned I could love a tiny person more than fancy petticoats and social balls.

Marjorie still came for feedings and saved her milk in glass bottles while Mother Pope supplemented with warm goat's milk. I saw no way to change the situation. Someday I would be a good mother.

I may not have known yet how to care for my new baby, but there had to be something I could do. Then I had it. I decided, right then and there, to start saving money, every penny I could, in case I might need it someday for my child. I brought out my small black pocketbook, dropped a penny into it, and hid it in the back of my dresser drawer. The action carried me through. I was comforted by knowing I had a plan. I would save money in case our family needed food or, unlikely, needed to move west. We would be fine. We would not turn out like some of the women I saw in the soup line.

Faded dreams of helping the world tossed about in my head, seemingly unreachable. Smiling through clenched teeth, I shook off the depression to walk like a queen, with my chin in the air, making the best of the situation. I hoped no one noticed that underneath the well-coiffed exterior beat an unsure, aching heart.

I was determined. My heartache was *not* going to destroy me. I would survive. *We* would survive.

A few days later, I woke to the smell of chicken pot pie baking. A biscuit-topped chicken pot pie at that. Fremont's mother was the only one who could whip up a pie out of nothing and create that old-fashioned, homemade aroma. While the pie baked, Mother Pope sat at our kitchen table with her Bible in front of her and prayed.

She must have thought I was sleeping, but I watched through the cracked-open door. Strands of damp hair slid loose from the bun at the back of her neck, and she reached back to tuck them in. My admiration for Mrs. Pope had only increased since I found out she helped raise funds for the Oklahoma Baptist University's ministry for women, supporting young girls who wanted to attend college. As I turned to go back to sleep, I heard her voice. Right there at the table, Mother Pope bowed her head.

"First things first, Lord. Help me love this girl like my own daughter. Fremont and his family's future rests in Your hands, but I'll try to do my part. Lord, the whole kit-and-caboodle needs a heaping lot of love. Please, give me an opportunity to show how great You are and put the right feelings in my heart so Your love can shine through. In Jesus' name. Amen."

Yes, I thought, we need Mother Pope's prayers. Our marriage did not start off well, even if Fremont loved me more than honeyed sweet potatoes. I knew little of homemaking, but I knew even less about how to teach a child the important things in life. A desire to succeed at motherhood rose within me. My life's tasks and goals may have been altered, but I would see it through. I may not have wanted Margaret Kathryn at first, but she had touched my heart. Her head had rounded as Mama said it would, and I warmed at her preciousness. Her sweet, tiny face opened a tender spot deep down.

Later, with potholders, Mother Pope brought a plate of warm pot pie to my room.

I ate while Mother Pope settled into a chair holding Margaret and explained how to strain food for babies, how to clean a burned cast-iron skillet, and how to follow the Lord even when you didn't feel like it. Then she bustled around straightening the room, washing bedsheets, and feeding Margaret her bottle while I boiled water and took a long, hot bath in a big metal tub.

Chapter Twenty-Seven
October 1933

Two weeks later, Papa dropped by our house. I thought he was there to see the baby, but all he did was complain about Roosevelt, how he had written Roosevelt a letter recommending Socialism, how Roosevelt had rejected his ideas, rebuffing all the social models Papa had promoted. Then, after his tirade, he blasted me for getting pregnant.

"You are foolish to find yourself in this situation."

"What do you mean? What else could I have done?"

"Done?" he yelled. "You could have taken my advice, married James, or gotten rid of the problem and gone on with your life. Maybe you and Fremont could have made a success without a child, but there is no way you can support yourselves now beyond the necessities. What with our failing economy, this is not the time to start a family. You should have taken precautions."

I did not respond. Did Papa think I didn't want my child? How could he be so insensitive? Maybe he was not the Papa I had always admired. Thankfully, Fremont had gone back to work and was not there to listen to the hateful words.

Papa ranted on and on, mostly about Roosevelt. The more I listened, the more I began to hate his rhetoric. I was sick of hearing about our president's incompetence, but his next rant was no better. He talked about Wiley Post's untimely death in an airplane crash in Alaska, almost as if it were Post's fault for daring to leave Oklahoma while people hungered. I was glad when Papa left. He had hardly looked at his new grandchild the entire hour he was visiting.

The Popes' ordered home-life differed significantly from the Trimble's haphazard way of existing. Two homes could not have been so extremely opposite. Love and acceptance exuded from the Popes' home, even in the face of our indiscretion, and nothing more was said about the beginning of our married life.

Papa had not been so forgiving. Every time I saw him, hateful, condemning words spewed from his mouth.

The Popes talked about God as if He sat with them at the dining table eating potato soup. I had never heard anyone speak as if Jesus was a real person, caring enough to spend time with a poor family.

I needed reassurance and looked to Fremont's mother, who listened and acknowledged me more warmly and completely than my own mama. Since a strong bond of respect existed between Fremont and his mother, I wanted to draw close to her too. I also wanted closeness because here I found acceptance. The only acceptance I've found since my grandma died. Here, I felt loved.

Monday morning. Wash day. I rose early and pushed the baby stroller to the Popes' house, walking past the faded crimson cannas Mother Pope planted along the street in front of her house on Pottenger Street. She had already donned a wrap-around frock with ample room for her full-size body and had lit a roaring fire in the wood stove.

"My, she's going to be a beauty," Mother Pope said as she cradled baby Margaret. "She looks so much like her daddy."

Sturdy, blue-eyed Margaret looked so much like a Pope that there was no doubt the child was Fremont's. Dark, soft baby curls surrounded her sparkling blue eyes. She was not dainty and fragile like the Trimbles nor had she inherited my olive complexion or big, brown eyes. I wondered how a child I bore could have no resemblance to me at all. Even Margaret's temperament seemed like Fremont's—calm, not energetic and emotional like mine. I stared at my baby girl. Chickens waddled over too close to her, and she looked frightened.

"Shoo. Get gone all of you!" Mother Pope waved her hands and flapped her big apron at the chickens.

At the water well, thirty feet behind their house, I lowered a metal bucket tied to the end of a rope and filled it with water, then pulled the bucket up again. Mother Pope did not have a wringer washer like Mama, but she'd already put the big black pot on the fire to boil water for the washing, whistling as she worked.

I enjoyed my mother-in-law's companionship. Mrs. Pope had been Eva Katherine Castleman before she married. She was educated up to the eighth grade, and since she passed the state teacher exam, she could teach school if she wanted to. Her family was strictly English, that is, as she said, natives of England.

She was born in 1888, the youngest of seventeen children. Both of her parents died by the time she was fourteen and left her an orphan. As a child, she was passed around to her older adult brothers and sisters. For a while, she lived with her brother George in Phelps County, Missouri, and she became the fastest with Morse Code at the St. Louis's Telephone Company. Then she moved to Chickasha, Oklahoma, to live with her brother, Bob, who was the sheriff. That's where she met Ollie Pope, Fremont's dad. They married in 1910, and she never made it back to Missouri.

Mother Pope and I chatted freely as we washed the laundry. As it turned out, I knew quite a bit more about homemaking than I'd thought. As eldest of five, I had helped Mama from a young age. Still, there were a lot of things I didn't know, so I soaked in Mother Pope's advice. After spending the day with her, I jotted down notes in the evenings.

"For wounds," she told me, "crush fresh peach leaves and wrap them in a clean cloth, dip them in a pan of cold water, and bind the wound overnight. For colds, boil milk, butter, and garlic and drink it, and be sure to use vinegar on bruises or pinched fingers."

"I can't remember all this," I said hopelessly.

"You'll remember when the times come," she encouraged. "Oh, and remember this. The good Lord will always be there to help you. He's your rock and your shield." She stopped and took a deep breath. "Ah—there's nothing like the wondrous smell rising from freshly laundered clothes."

I washed the colored clothes the same way Mrs. Pope laundered the whites except in addition to scrubbing on the rub board, the white clothes were boiled. Hard work. By noon, my arms ached. My back felt like an oak tree after a tornado, bent and out of form. And the diapers. Oh, my. How could one baby go through so many diapers in one week?

After we had hung the clothes on the line, we sat with a cup of tea and homemade shortbread cookies.

"Child," Mother Pope said.

Why did everyone call me child? I was twenty-three-years-old and had not been a child in years. Heavens, I was a mother now.

"Child, remember God has a plan for you. Never forget that."

I didn't even smile. Tired from the heavy work, I leaned back and closed my eyes. I knew she meant well, and her kind words always encouraged me, but I couldn't see how God was going to do anything good in my situation.

By mid-afternoon, the laundry was dry. We pulled sheets and diapers off the clothesline and folded them. I packed up everything and pushed it home in the baby stroller, exhausted but satisfied.

Chapter Twenty-Eight

January 1934

Unusually warm for January, I dressed six-month-old Margaret in a print dress with a pinafore over it and carried her jacket. "Hurry, now, we're going to take lunch to Daddy down at his work." She squealed in delight at the word 'daddy' and squirmed as I put on her scruffy black oxfords. She'd been a Daddy's girl since she was born.

Fremont saw me pushing the baby carriage up to the Champlain Filling Station. He pulled his head out from under an Oldsmobile, stood, and dusted off his pant legs. Oil smeared his clothes, and his messy dark hair fell over his forehead. Nothing could disguise his good looks. My heart still leaped when I saw him.

Being so dirty, he didn't pick up Margaret but smiled and tussled her dark hair.

Fremont followed me to a bench in front of the station, and we sat. There were black soot marks on his face and he smelled of gasoline and grease. Around the garage was an assortment of tires, tools, and gas cans. Fremont spent most of his time here, patching flat tires and making old jalopies run again. Often he spent long hours at the station, just in case work showed up.

"What kind of a motorcar is that?" I pointed toward a station wagon stopped on the corner of Beard Street. Clueless about vehicles, I wanted to learn as much as I could. This was a big part of his life, after all.

"That's a '28 Ford. Has a wooden body—maple and birch. And the seats can be removed to change it into a truck. That's what ol' Mr. Clark did to his."

"I saw an advertisement on the Buick 60," I said, wanting to impress him. "They're supposed to go pretty fast. It has a straight eight engine. What do you think?"

"I don't rightly know. Never saw one of those." He pointed to a car puttering north. "Look over there. That's old Mr. Denmar's Overland touring car."

"I recognize it. Papa used to have one." Although cars did not interest me much, they were my husband's livelihood.

"I can't believe Mr. Denmar bought that old thing," said Fremont. "It has one windshield wiper, you know, on the driver's side, and that's operated by hand. You snap the side curtains on in bad weather."

"Mama put hot bricks under blankets to keep us warm," I said.

He laughed. "That's one way to stay warm. Things have changed a mighty lot in the past few years."

I handed him a bologna and onion sandwich slathered with mustard. I took out Margaret's sandwich and mine, the same only minus the onion. I had also packed a glass jar of sweet iced tea and pulled out a few apples. Fremont gobbled it all down like he hadn't eaten for days.

When we finished, he leaned back on the bench. "I get mighty frustrated with these vehicle owners. They don't understand that you can't drive a jalopy 'til it quits, then expect me to work miracles."

"What do you mean?" I asked.

"Drivers don't stop to check their oil. By the time they come to me with a broken down engine, the oil's as thick as molasses and as dirty as a henhouse. Oil gets old. And with the dust blowing the way it does, carburetors get clogged up easier'n drain pipes."

Fremont could talk about automobiles all day, and I would not understand half of what he said. He knew more about cars than anyone I knew. A skilled mechanic, he had a natural ability. Men noticed his skills, too, and discussed engines with him like women talked about babies. My husband could fix anything, given enough time, and I began to appreciate him and his talents more.

We watched Margaret play with a stick for a few minutes, the quiet interrupted only by a pickup truck passing by. She started crying, and I lifted her out of the carriage and patted her on the back. Fremont looked at us gently, as if he wanted to put his arms around us for protection. He had such a tender way about him. Nothing like my papa.

I remembered an article I'd read in the paper that morning. "The CCC may be able to employ thousands of fellows. Roosevelt's making good on his promises, don't you think?"

"CCC?"

"The Civilian Conservation Corps."

Fremont seldom had time to read but would listen when I read articles to him or summarized a book.

"Roosevelt's also proposing a Federal Emergency Relief Administration. I think that's going to help the needy, too. Lord knows, it's about time the government helped out people who can't find jobs. I just hope Oklahoma gets some of the money."

"I don't know much about those things, Sibyl. I don't keep up as much as you do."

"Considering your past, I'd think you'd be more interested." The harsh words popped out of my mouth before I could hold them back.

"That's not fair. I care about people. I just don't get involved in all these politics, is all. And it's mighty difficult to figure out what's good for people and what isn't."

"Why don't you go down to the union offices to hear what people have to say?"

"And when would I do that?"

He was right, of course. "I'm sorry. I know you're working hard."

Truly, we both worked hard. I glanced at my hands. They were not dirty like Fremont's, but I had calluses now from all the heavy housework.

"I got a mighty lot of work to do, Sibyl." Fremont shook his dark waves. "I got a family to feed, and I don't have time to sit around and discuss the weather, much less figure out what the government's going to do next."

"A woman with three toddlers came begging yesterday, and I only had a few biscuits to give her. And that family living two doors down are having a hard time. I spoke with the wife, Alice, the other day. She said they don't have money to pay the rent." I paused. "Wish we could help more, but we barely have enough to keep ourselves alive."

I looked down at my worn loafers and immediately regretted my words. I didn't have to tell Fremont about our situation. I bit my tongue, trying to stop more nasty words before they went from my head to my mouth. Fremont understood hunger and hopelessness better than I. Did he struggle with his dreadful memories? His nightmares had almost ceased, except when he was reminded of his old life, like when hobos sat on our front porch eating any stale bread I could scrounge up. Last week, Fremont dreamed a boy drifter fell between the boxcars and got crushed. He woke up sweating and shaking. I wish I could help him.

Some evenings, Fremont would sit outside with the men we fed. He'd reminisce with the scruffy young hobos, speaking a different language, using words like "banjo" for a small frying pan, or "glad rags" for fancy clothes, and many other words I didn't understand. Fremont explained them all to me when I asked.

"Things could be mighty worse."

I scolded myself for being so hard on him. Amazingly, Fremont seemed content with our life. Except for his occasional nightmares, he never seemed too concerned about the troubles we encountered. That was him, calm and steady.

He looked around absentmindedly, and then glanced at me again, this time with his sweet grin. He shook his head, and suddenly, I couldn't remember why I was upset. My anger slid away in a flash. His eyes, shining sky-blue in a sooty, black-smeared face, still made my heart beat faster than the Santa Fe locomotive. "Don't worry so much," he said. "The good Lord'll take care of us."

He could defuse my frustration unlike anyone else. His heart shone like silver. I scooted near him and put my head on his shoulder, not caring if I got dirty. He wrapped his arm around me, and I tried to picture Papa treating Mama with the same kindness and reassurance. I could not. In fact, I couldn't remember Papa ever holding Mama's hand or hugging her.

A Model T Roadster pulled into the filling station, and Fremont rushed over to pump gasoline and wash the windshield.

When I thought about how many times Fremont had calmed me down, reassured me of his love, and held my hand, dismay dogged me. Deep down, I knew he loved me, but I doubted he liked having a moody wife. Here was a hardworking man who deserved more, and I determined to try harder to be the kind of wife he deserved.

Chapter Twenty-Nine
February 1934

Then, just like that, another crisis.
    I was pregnant.
Again.

But the worst was my family's disappointment. Their reaction to our news was worse than a red wasp's sting.

"You're what?" said Mama. "You can barely manage one baby, what makes you think you can take care of two? What were you thinking?"

I agreed. Having babies was the toughest thing I had ever done.

"You should get rid of it," Papa said bluntly. "In this economy and married to Fremont, a man who can barely support himself, it would be the wisest thing to do." Papa only pushed the sting in deeper. Why did his words always hurt?

Even Mother Pope crossed her arms in a gesture of disapproval and did not congratulate me when we shared the news. I was frustrated and tearful. I needed them to be happy and supportive, but they were making the situation worse with their disapproval. That evening, as we left the Pope home, Mother relented and said to me, "Don't you go worrying so much. God promises to take care of you through the good and bad times alike."

How many times did I have to hear that? Where was God now when I needed Him? I really tried to accept His will. Mother Pope had shared a verse with me. Psalm 42:5. "Why are you so cast down, oh my soul? Hope in God."

Hope. Yes. I did believe in God, but I would need more than my belief to make it through the future.

Most of my friends had continued on with their lives, moving to the big city, leaving me stuck in a pauper's life on the south side of Shawnee. A useful life of helping the poor seemed farther and farther away. I was so busy caring for Margaret that I had not helped with the soup lines for months. Impoverished people were scattered throughout the streets of Shawnee, gaining numbers like a slow-moving epidemic, and it frightened me. It frightened us all. As I looked at all the needs, the hungry mothers and children, the out-of-work fathers and grandfathers, I prayed. As Mother Pope often told me, even if I couldn't do anything else, I could pray. Surely the Lord would help.

This pregnancy didn't treat me any better than my last. Most days I was so sick I could barely lift my head. Though it was a struggle the next day, I heated water on the stove and poured it into the washtub for baby Margaret's bath. She giggled, knowing I would let her splash for a bit. She smiled sweetly at me as I cried.

I needed to relieve stress. To rest and recover from the sickness. To think about a second child. To clear my mind. Fremont encouraged me to take Margaret to his parents' house for a few days. Mother would love it.

"Please watch her close," I said when I arrived the next morning. "She can pull herself up on chairs and get into cabinet drawers." I handed Margaret to her and placed a few diapers and clothes on the chair. Dad Pope had enough goats' milk to feed a dozen young ones, so I wasn't concerned about her going hungry.

"Don't you worry, child. I'll take good care of her," said Mother Pope. "I'll keep her as long as you need. You just get some rest, you hear?"

"Thank you very much." I'd never felt so grateful. My own mama said her child-rearing days were over and Margaret was my business.

I lay abed the rest of the day and agonized over a bleak future, my sick pail beside the bed.

And then, my asthma resurfaced. The familiar feeling of pressure in my chest settled on me, suffocating me, and I felt like I was trapped in a small closet unable to escape. I choked. Gasped. Nothing helped. I wished Grandma Bennett were here to comfort me like when I was young, although I could do without her nasty turpentine mixture.

Fremont left for work and I stayed in bed all day, my face buried in pillows. Fearful. I cried more than when Grandma died. I was so miserable I wouldn't have known the Shawnee Mill three blocks away burned down if it hadn't been for the smell of charred wood pervading the air, causing me to gag.

Finally, at about dusk I fell asleep. I didn't notice when Fremont came home from work. He worked so much these days, sometimes he didn't get home until way past nightfall.

From my bed, I heard rattling in the kitchen, dishes being stacked and water running. He was cooking. I felt guilty for not being able to make dinner, but I couldn't get out of bed.

Fremont walked into the room. "Honey, can you sit up? I brought you some supper."

I didn't answer.

"You need to eat something. You can't go on like this." His voice was soothing.

I opened my eyes and looked up at him. His powerful shoulders leaned over me, his sweet blue eyes watched me, tender and concerned. He arranged the pillow behind my back and set the tray in front of me.

"Now, you don't have to do anything. Mother sent over some chicken soup, and I heated it up for you. Here're a few crackers to go with it. See if you can eat."

I felt so weak, I could barely whisper. "Thank you. I never had anyone treat me like this before."

His eyes crinkled, and tenderness passed between us, a connection that was always there. Sometimes I pushed it away, too afraid to admit my deep feelings for him.

"I love you, my dear little wife," he said, "and I love this new little baby you're carrying. You mean a mighty lot to me, and I sure don't like to see you sad."

I could barely keep from crying again. I knew deep down I loved Fremont, cherished him, but it was so hard to say the words.

171

No one in my family ever said "I love you," and it was hard to get past that upbringing. I felt like I didn't even know how to say it.

"Don't let the troubles fool you, honey. We're going to be all right." He leaned over and kissed me on the cheek.

Chapter Thirty
March 1934

The quarrels in the Trimble home escalated. None of my family seemed to have any peace, and peace seemed more important to me now than ever. I felt obligated to visit Mama often and check on my brother and sisters.

Mama and Papa married twenty-five years ago in 1909 after a two-year courtship. Papa purchased a house, but had some trouble related to his job and transferred to a bank in Clinton then later to Wewoka. The past five years of their marriage, Papa spent most of his time away from home auditing banks across Oklahoma. He rented an apartment in the City.

With Papa gone most of the time, Mama flew around like a crow searching for carrion, as sour and bitter as gall. She ranted about Calvis, who, at sixteen, was learning to drive the Chrysler. Calvis had been picked up by the police for speeding and Mama had to go to the police station to bail him out.

"I should have left him in jail to learn a lesson." she grumbled to me afterward. "Or until his Papa got home. Where's your father when I need him?"

Every time I visited Mama, she had some new complaint.

When Papa did show up at home, he and Mama squabbled like geese fighting over their territory.

One of their recent arguments had to do with Mama's volunteer work. Papa, a Mason for years, attended meetings in the new brick Masonic Temple Hall on Bell Street. Seemed to me that Masons ran the town because most city officials belonged to one or another of the eight chapters in Shawnee.

Papa often expounded on the noble Masonic ideals and lofty principles. "The rightist groups must amend their thinking and practices, or they'll find themselves discarded by the leaders and instructors who have been found wanting."

His words made little sense to me, but Papa was a busy man, probably stressed out over the bank closings.

Despite his own volunteer work, Papa's temper blew when he found out that Mama voluntarily sang for the Eastern Stars. He raised so much Cain, Mama said she thought the house would explode.

That was the way of my parents' household; Papa didn't like *anything* Mama did. Mama didn't like what Papa did.

I tried to understand but usually left the family visits crying. I thought they should be more sympathetic to one another. Little did I know.

The next week, I pushed the baby carriage toward Mama's house, sauntering through the fresh-smelling town. Spring had arrived. I loved the fresh green grass of the park, the bright daffodils and clean smell of early spring as I walked through town to visit. But I steeled myself as soon as I stepped through their front door.

I had listened to Mama's complaints for weeks now and thought she had expounded on every misconduct Papa could possibly have. She stood at the front door with her latest details.

"Your papa came home edgy as all get out last Saturday afternoon," said Mama as she helped me unload the baby. "He handed me forty dollars for the month like usual, but started asking about everything I'd bought last week."

Mama never kept track of her spending the way I kept track of ours. She never had a reason to, so when Papa asked her to give an account of where the money had gone, she couldn't.

"Then your father said, 'You must be getting along all right. You saved enough to buy a new-fangled electric sewing machine.' He actually accused *me* of not feeding the kids enough. Can you believe that man? I flat out told him I needed a few extra dollars for piano lessons, if he could spare the money. After all, he does work for the state. It must pay *something*."

I nodded as I bounced Margaret on my knee, her dark curls springing up and down like bed springs.

My mother stomped back and forth across the room. She had auditioned for the new radio station in Shawnee, KGFF. They liked what they heard and she began singing weekly while Mrs. Marlow accompanied her on the piano for an hour-long show. Mama's operatic voice bellowed Johnny Goodman's tunes like they were never meant to be sung. Before Mama sang, Mrs. Collins from next door dramatized ghost stories and poems. The slot after Mama's singing belonged to Marjorie's husband Kelley, who played country music on the guitar.

"I'm not just an Eastern Star now, I'm a radio star." Mama boasted. "Even if the money's not enough to buy a used hanky."

I imagine Papa did not see any humor in Mama's job singing on the radio.

"'Rubbish,' he said. Then your Papa stepped out on the front porch and stared at my Chrysler."

Papa had purchased the car for a thousand dollars just two years ago. Recently, because of the distressed economy, many people had to sell their cars, even if they sold them at a loss. Surely my rich Papa couldn't possibly need the money, so what *was* he doing?

"When he came back into the house," Mama continued as she sat down beside me on the sofa, "he told me there's a man in the City who wants to buy the car. The fellow needs to take a look at it first."

I shook my head along with her and she seemed pleased, assuming I was on her side. I was most of the time. Except when her bitterness surfaced.

"Papa stuck out his hand and demanded the keys. He started backing the Chrysler out the driveway. But wouldn't you know it, the car slid toward his precious red Cannas. He barely missed them and almost hit the hedge. So I ran out and yelled at him. He was going to ruin the Chrysler *and* the flowers. He got out of the car and let me back it out for him. Before he drove away, I told him to get a good price for it."

Mama scrunched up her lips in a smirk.

"But what will you drive?" Besides daily trips around town, excursions to church and Eastern Star meetings, every few weeks Mama drove to Sulphur to visit Grandpa Bennett and her relatives.

"He said I could use his old Buick coupe. Can you imagine?" She snorted and shook her head. "Can you believe that beat-up old thing still runs?"

We continued to discuss the implications of Papa selling her car. She was suspicious and resentful, and although my allegiance wavered, I still held loyalty to Papa because I believed he had good intentions. But blazes, my childhood promise of devotion to him and his beliefs were fast becoming an irritating, nagging nuisance. If not downright difficult.

The cherished dark green Chrysler was gone and Mama said he came home by taxi the next morning.

I had always considered my folks a safety net. Now I wondered if there was any net at all. Hopefully, my marriage would not become like theirs.

Chapter Thirty-One

Papa's next time home was a disaster.

Calvis was always into mischief. Last summer he was showing off Mama's new wringer washing machine to his best friend. He turned on the Maytag machine and stuck three fingers in the running wringer to demonstrate how it worked. He screamed when the rollers scraped the skin from the back of his hand. Mama had to drop everything and rush him to the doctor.

This time, it happened in the garden. Papa had planted ten poplar trees at the back of the property when we moved into the house in twenty-seven. He also planted two cherry trees and an Alberta peach, and during the fall, the fruit trees produced enough for Mama to make pies and enough jam to last all year. Papa's iris beds began blooming early in the spring, but even more than the irises, Papa's fish pond was the focus of his backyard paradise, his pride and joy, where a dozen goldfish were meticulously fed and pampered.

Calvis, an hour late getting home, snuck into the house through the back door, hoping to not get caught. The rascal had been down the street visiting a girl.

Mama and I bustled about in the kitchen baking cookies for a church bake sale. The floor squeaked. Mama's ears perked up.

"Calvis Trimble!" she yelled. "You get over here right this minute! You've been out gallivanting all over town, haven't you? Sometimes you act just like your father."

"Sorry, Mama."

"Hurry and burn the trash before Papa gets home. He's due any second, and he'll be angry if you don't have your chores done."

Calvis grabbed the trashcan, ran outside, and dumped it into the burn barrel at the back of the yard. He ran to the shed behind the house to grab the gasoline can. When he sprayed gasoline on the trash, in his hurry, some fuel landed on his pants. When he lit a match, his pants caught on fire!

I heard a high-pitched banshee scream. When we ran out to the back yard, Calvis' pants were blazing. In his panic, he jumped into the fishpond to put out the fire.

And then, Papa stepped through the back door. All he saw was Calvis sitting in his previously immaculate fish pond. He grabbed his whip and ran to the pond, where he pulled Calvis out by his shirt sleeve. As Papa raised the whip to switch him, Calvis tried to run away, but Papa caught him and swung.

"No!" I yelled and ran to them. Papa got in several hard licks before I got there. I pushed myself in between them. "He's burned! Look at his legs!"

Papa stopped and looked down at Calvis' scorched pants. Dismay crossed his face. Mama and I dragged Calvis into the house. Papa followed us, shaking his head and muttering, "That boy doesn't have a lick of sense."

Calvis was severely burned from his knee to his ankle. Mama called Dr. Fortson, and while we waited for the doctor, I brought in some aloe vera from the plant in the yard.

When Dr. Fortson arrived, he soaked Calvis' leg in cold water and then applied Mecca Ointment and dressed it. "He'll have to stay in bed under a tent with a light in it," the doc said. "I'll come back tomorrow morning to check on him. We'll watch him close every day for a while, but it'll be months before he can get up."

"How long will he be in bed?" Mama asked.

"About three months. You'll need to contact his teacher and have his school work sent home."

No one told Papa what a cruel thing he had done.

And he acted like nothing had happened.

But I knew.

Papa had overreacted something fierce, jumping to beat Calvis without finding out the specifics.

He seemed out-of-control, not like himself lately, and I didn't know if he was worried about his job, the economy, Mama's spending, or his children. Whatever it was, I couldn't understand what was going on or what I should do to help.

Chapter Thirty-Two
April 1934

"Can you take care of Margaret while I run to the store?" I asked Mother Pope one warm afternoon. She was always willing to watch Margaret, so I left the baby in her care, took a big bag to carry my purchases, and headed downtown.

I had several errands to run and planned to be gone for a couple of hours. As always, I purchased a few books first. *Murder in the Calais Coach* by Agatha Christie had just come out. I had recently re-read *A Farewell to Arms* by Ernest Hemingway, and its story of love and pain had embedded in my mind.

I sauntered down Main Street, reveling in my afternoon of freedom, so glad the morning sickness had improved. I walked with the air of elegance that had been part of my life before marriage. The brown waves of my hair fell over my shoulders, and I enjoyed the way my locks moved as I tossed my head. I took pride in making my own dresses, which were simple and perhaps not the latest fashion, but I carried myself like I had when I'd belonged to the Shawnee Country Club, playing tennis in the cool mornings with eligible bachelors or sipping sweet iced tea on the patio.

As I meandered through downtown, several groups of shabby men lounged or squatted in front of stores, cigarettes in hand, hats pulled down over their eyes. Heads turned as I passed, and I pulled up my chin and went on. More men dawdled around town than they had when I'd worked for Mr. Weston, lots more. I ignored them and went about my way.

I hurried to the union offices. It had been over three months since I'd last volunteered, and I felt guilty. Today I was going to let them know I planned to help in the soup lines for a couple of months, at least until my baby was born.

There was no one behind the desk in the Women's Organization office. I decided to try the Salvation Army group down the street. They fed lines of transients daily. I awkwardly made my way back through the desks of union men.

"Ah, the banker's daughter."

I turned when I heard Mr. Weston. He sat near one of the desks and nodded for me to come over. "Pregnant again, I see. Can't seem to help it, can you?"

I felt no need to respond to such a rude question. Mr. Weston had always been a little too pushy.

He asked how I was, how my husband fared, and seemed especially interested in what Papa was doing these days. I answered his questions in a generic tone. I couldn't be unfriendly, even if he did irritate me. After all, he still owed me $27 back pay.

"Heard your papa's getting cozy with the big boys up in the City," he said. I assumed he was talking about Papa's bid for the Assistant Bank Commissioner job. Even if I'd wanted to, I was not going to discuss it with *him*. I didn't know much more than anyone else. The conversation, and this whole place, was uncomfortable. I rushed away.

I hurried back to Thurman's on Beard Street to grab some groceries. I was already frustrated by bumping into Mr. Weston, even more so when I realized I didn't have the ten cents to buy the pound of ground beef I wanted. I had just enough pennies to pay for soap. Pennies.

After picking up the few items I could afford, I rushed back toward the south side of town with just enough time to pick up Margaret before rushing home to begin dinner. I was always late for everything, one of my biggest annoyances with myself. Mama said I'd been late for my own birthing.

Irritated at myself, I would be late getting home to fix supper. I hoped Margaret was ready to go home.

I found Mother Pope bathing Margaret in the backyard and bubbles overflowing the washtub. My child's dark curls clung to her head and with her blue Fremont eyes. She looked like a kewpie doll covered in mountains of suds.

"Margaret. What are you doing in there?" I scolded, as if my toddler could be responsible. I pulled her from the dirty sudsy tub.

Typically I did a good job controlling my tongue, but it got harder the more frustrated I became. "Now I'll have to change her clothes before we go home."

Mother Pope quickly stood. "It isn't her fault. She got muddy, so I decided to bathe her. We were having fun, and time got away from me."

"I'm sorry," I said with a gentler voice, feeling immediately remorseful.

As I dressed Margaret and put her in the carriage, I heard Mrs. Pope muttering about how it took time to learn to be a good parent. I sighed. I would apologize again tomorrow. I agreed with her. It was taking a long time for me to learn parenting skills. Fremont had proved the better parent, much better than I. Parenting came naturally to him.

Would I ever be as good a mother as Mrs. Pope? I pushed Margaret in the baby carriage and shuffled home feeling lousy about my impatience. Every bump in life left me feeling that I could handle no more. My life seemed to count for so little. My dreams, developed by Papa's influence, had almost died the moment I got pregnant and married. God had washed me clean, but surely not to sit at home and do nothing. Did He give me a fresh spiritual start simply to become one of the suffering? Did He know I wanted to be a leader of world change? Why would God give me a sharp, inquisitive mind and not give me an opportunity to use it? Being stuck at home taking care of my child and pregnant with another made me feel restless, bored, and unhappy.

As we walked the few blocks home, I noticed Margaret's downcast face, and that brought tears to my eyes. I didn't want to hurt my little girl's feelings. I didn't want to be like my own mother, forever criticizing. I wanted to be a better mother whose children were happy because they knew they were loved.

I stopped, knelt down on the side of the road, and talked to Margaret like she could understand. "Mommy is so sorry she yelled," I said gently. "I'll try not to get upset with you again. Please forgive me." She wrapped her tiny arms around my neck and we hugged, my heart filling with love and sadness.

I could not live like this anymore, depressed and snappy. Would leaving Fremont be a solution? I wanted to open up and share my problems with him, but he was so preoccupied with work, we hardly ever talked. Even when we spent time together, he could not understand my discontentment.

Papa would know what to do. Despite everything that happened, I still talked to Papa. I vacillated in my belief, still trusting his motivation was proper and his life views true, at least most of the time. Maybe after I had my baby, he could help me find a well-paying job in the City. I could send money back to Fremont and the children, like many other mothers did. We needed money desperately. They would miss me, of course, and truthfully, I would miss them.

What was I thinking? I didn't want to leave my family. I loved them too much to abandon them, even to find a job and send money back home. We would have to be poor together. I would stand in soup lines if I had to. I would *beg* if I had to. So, why did doubt so often intrude?

Chapter Thirty-Three
May 1934

In the days that followed, questions rolled around in my head. I wanted to know why the sun rose on time but the rain failed to fall. Why the workers were so plentiful and the jobs so few. Why God had planted me in this town, at this time, within this family. I wanted to know why this marriage and why these dire circumstances?

There were so many things I wanted to know but mostly, I wanted to know what God had in mind for me. When I was younger, Papa implanted in me a purpose for my future. I believed that by following his plan to become a leader and change the world for the better, I could matter. Could I still hold onto that dream? Or was I just a wife and a mother now, tethered to these roles?

Fremont arrived home late the next Saturday evening after I had put Margaret to bed for the night. Earlier that day I bought a chicken leg for a quarter and made a delicious soup with rice, carrots and onions. I served the dinner to my husband and then put my questions to him.

"Do you think God expects more from us than simply going to church every Sunday?" That seemed to catch him off guard. I continued, "I mean, I've been thinking. We barely have enough flour in the house to make biscuits. How can that be God's purpose? Your mother told me God can use everything in our lives to help us grow. But what about poverty? Can He use that?"

"Only God knows," he replied gently. "We don't need to worry about it. Just do our best."

I continued to struggle with finding purpose in our humdrum existence. I wanted to find peace in my world and my circumstances. Fremont held a simpler view of religion than I did. My abstract questions baffled him. He embraced concrete concepts like hard work, honesty and determination. To him, telling a prospective client that he needed a battery when he did not was wrong, while helping a neighbor repair his roof was right. He saw black and white. I saw gray.

Fremont never got upset at me when I considered these things aloud, as I was doing tonight. He listened closely, but my questions baffled him. Questions like, how could I determine right from wrong? How did poverty contribute to anything good? Surely God didn't want children to starve to death, did He? Why didn't He help the thousands who came through town begging for a bite? I didn't understand.

"I don't know," he said. "I just don't know. Maybe you should talk to the pastor about it."

Pastor Burton was a good, honest preacher, but sometimes he droned on too long. I couldn't imagine him understanding me or my dilemma any better than Papa did.

After we married, it seemed natural for us to go to Fremont's parent's church, Calvary Baptist. It was smaller than First Baptist but bigger than I thought it would be, with attendance around fifty or so. Fremont grew up regularly attending church with his family and as an ingrained habit, he did not think twice about whether it was the right thing to do. It was just a part of life.

What did I believe? The pastor's sermons may have been boring, but I detected truth buried inside. I suspected God wanted more from me than mere words. He showed truth by his actions, didn't he?

Fremont admired his father and tried to emulate him. Mr. Pope was considered wise by everyone who knew him. He never spoke up in church, his religion such a deeply personal matter that he refused to pray in public. But how many times had I heard that Mr. Pope silently passed a dollar to a needy person or helped with fieldwork if a man was unable to get his crop in? When Mr. Pope bowed his head, everybody believed God listened to him. God would listen to a man like Fremont, so like his father, who put the commandments into action.

The lessons I learned in the Pope family were in stark contrast to Papa's lectures. Mr. and Mrs. Pope's Christianity centered on the individual's relationship to God. This was different than what Papa believed. He believed the intention of Christianity was to improve society. He told me, "As we force people to follow Christ's way of sharing the wealth, purge the obstinate souls, utopia can be reached, and everyone will have food. Simple concept. It will just take a few more generations to teach the masses the ways of Christ."

I contemplated Papa's idea that we should force people to share their fortunes. In the long run, what good would it do to make people give up part of the wealth they worked hard for? Would taking the working man's profits only make him resentful, or quit working altogether?

My mind went in circles trying to digest the differences in our family's beliefs and to determine the truth for myself and in my life.

Chapter Thirty-Four
June 1934

The spring had not lasted long, and the days quickly heated up. Little rain fell, ponds dried up, and hard-packed soil cracked into gaping gulleys. The previous year, God had granted a slight respite from the blowing dirt and tornadoes, but this year, the sun caused vegetation to wilt. I read in the paper that many elderly people and babies died from the heat, so I took extra care with Margaret and checked on our parents often.

Fremont felt obligated to help people on the road to California. Many of their cars needed a mountain of repair, so he spent most of his time at the station. Although I didn't want to admit it, he was my rock, and I missed him. He was the opposite of Papa. He expected little out of me and always gave me love and tenderness. Nevertheless, I wished he didn't have to work so hard or be gone quite so many hours even if he brought home a bit more money

He seldom had time for church, so this Sunday morning, I alone pushed Margaret in the baby carriage toward the church.

We lived only a few blocks from Calvary Baptist. The new church building on the south side of Shawnee was built in 1927 and replaced the old clapboard structure, which had had a hitching post for horses. This building was two stories high with classrooms around the balcony.

Margaret was almost a year old, and I was more than six months pregnant. My belly was huge, which made me miserable and awkward, especially in the sticky, unbearable heat.

When we arrived, I left Margaret's buggy outside the door and carried her through a tiny square vestibule into the cozy church, the dark pews adding to the intimate feeling. Mr. Pope, in his best overalls, stood at the back of the auditorium as a deacon welcoming members and visitors. As I passed, he patted Margaret on her disorderly dark hair.

I chatted with church members, asked after their health and inquired about their children. I met many nice people at Calvary, people who lived on the south side of town, farmers from the outskirts, gray-haired couples, and newlyweds like Fremont and me.

"Good morning, dear," said Mrs. Pringle, an older lady in the church nursery. "We're so glad you came today."

I hugged Margaret before handing her over to Mrs. Pringle, who would watch her in the nursery during the morning service. Margaret was a quiet child who liked people. She seldom cried. "Margaret toddles around quite well now," I said, "although she doesn't talk much. Please come get me if she cries."

"She'll be fine, dear, just fine."

I walked to the front of the small auditorium and sat on a wooden oak pew next to Mother Pope. She wore a peach print dress, starched and ironed, looking immaculate and stately as always. With my huge pregnant belly, I felt awkward and self-conscious beside her.

The whole congregation stood and joined in the singing. Mother Pope sang loudly and although her voice was not as trained as Mama's, I sensed the sweet sincerity in the words. "Blest be the Tie that Binds our Hearts in Christian Love."

People's hearts were knit in love, a connection not apparent to me when I attended First Baptist. Throughout the opening services, my heart weighed heavily. Did God still listen to me? I watched Mr. Pope pass an offering plate and wished Fremont was sitting beside me instead of working on someone's old rattletrap.

The Popes' faith renewed my desire for spiritual growth. How many times did Mother Pope quote scripture? How many times had I seen Dad Pope bow his head and pray? I yearned for that kind of peace and godliness.

That day, the pastor's sermon touched my heart. The words from Jeremiah chapter three about repenting had a harsh ring of truth, especially considering the economic predicament most people found themselves in these days. When the pastor spoke of backsliding, I felt as if the message were directed at me. I had sinned. I had done wrong. The guilt and responsibility for my actions before marriage engulfed me. Papa's teaching never mentioned personal repentance so this was a new idea to me.

When the sermon ended, I stood for the traditional altar song. Suddenly as the congregation sang the words to "Just as I Am," tears streamed down my face. Mother Pope glanced over at me and rested her hand on my shoulder. A sympathetic look graced her face.

After church, she walked with me to retrieve Margaret. My baby looked up with her bright blue eyes and smiled happily at Mother Pope, ignoring me.

"You seem troubled, dear," she said as she gently handed Margaret to me. "God knows the stone you carry in your heart. He loves you very much."

The guilt was strangling me. Words would not come. Deep inside, I knew something in my heart had to be dealt with before it destroyed me with bitterness and resentment. I yearned to be right with God, but I was just learning how to make that happen.

Chapter Thirty-Five
September 1934

A frantic Blanche stood on my front porch, looking as if she had run the entire way. "You'd better hurry over to the house," she huffed. "Things have blown up and Mama needs you." Abruptly, she turned and ran off towards my parents' home.

Fremont and I rushed over. I carried Judson while Fremont lifted Margaret onto his back. I could hear weeping coming from Mama's room. My youngest sisters were huddled close together on the couch, their faces drawn and pale, my father and brother nowhere in sight.

"What's going on? What's wrong? It isn't Grandpa, is it?"

Tears poured down Frances' face. "Papa's moved out," she sobbed. "They had a fight."

"Don't be a baby," Blanche said. "Mama kicked him out. He deserves it."

A wave of shock washed over me. Did Blanche, the one who adored Papa, the one who thought the sun rose and set on him, had she said Mama had forced Papa to leave home?

"Good riddance," Blanche said icily.

Mama appeared in the doorway. Her eyes red. "Blanche Harriet!" she scolded. "Your papa may be a dirty scoundrel, but you should never talk like that." She sank into the couch beside the two girls, her tangled hair falling on her face. She looked terrible. "Oh, I can't believe it, after all these years."

"Mama, get a hold of yourself," I said. Fremont and I slipped into the closest chairs. "What happened?"

Mama threw her arms into the air. I could hear the pain in her voice as she spoke. "That lying, no-good sleaze of a man has gone too far this time. He's keeping another woman in the City!"

My mouth fell open and my stomach lurched. "Surely not."

"Whose side are you on anyway?" Blanche glared at me, a frown pleating her forehead. "Papa treats Mama like dirt, and you act like it's nothing."

"I didn't say it was nothing. I just can't believe it's what you think."

"He hit me. Look! Your papa hit me!" Mama pointed to the crimson mark on her cheek.

No. Not *my* papa.

My mother stood and stomped around the room. "How could he do such a thing? I don't care what anyone says," she cried. "I'm never letting him back into this house!"

Fremont shook his head, stood and scooped Margaret into his arms before ducking into the kitchen. I wished he would speak, let me know how he felt about all this, but he never liked the constant drama in my family. I knew he would wait until things calmed down before he voiced his opinion.

"Calm down, Mama," I said. "Tell me what happened."

"Marjorie went up to Oklahoma City. She saw it all. Papa's other life. Last month I visited his apartment and he wouldn't let me in."

I nodded. She had mentioned it.

"Well, it seems he has a *lady friend* living there."

"Marjorie could be wrong," I said. "Where is she, anyway?"

Frances spoke up. "I knocked on her door, but she wasn't home."

"Just like her," said Blanche. "She came over, dropped her bombshell about Papa and left. She starts chaos and disappears."

Mama paced the floor and clenched her fists. "Marjorie visited his apartment and saw women's dresses and toiletries lying around. So he's rich enough to keep house for a little housekeeper."

"Her name is Gladys Means," Blanche spat out. "Marjorie told us. She was a waitress at the Masons' banquet at the YWCA. Can you *believe* it?"

"Blanche," I said. "What were you doing? Eavesdropping?"

"Of course, I heard." Blanche jumped up and placed her hands on her hips. "They were loud enough for the neighbors down the street to hear."

"And Marjorie found another mink stole in his apartment," Mama said, "Identical to the one he gave me. How could he? Give a mink stole to his girlfriend?"

"Papa called Mama a prude and a nag," Blanche added.

"So I pulled out the leather suitcase and began to stuff my clothes into it. I should have left that man years ago."

"But you can't just move out and leave the girls here by themselves," I said. "Papa couldn't take care of them."

"That's what I told her," said Blanche. "I ran to the suitcase, picked up Mama's clothes and hung them back in the closet. And—"

"I pointed to Papa and said, 'If you'd rather live with a slut than me, then just move out.'" Mama put her hands on her hips as she talked. Her oldest house dress hanging on her like rags.

Blanche imitated Papa's voice again, "He said, 'Why should I be the one to leave? I own this house. Besides, she's a far better woman than you'll ever be. Got more than half a brain, too.'"

"He said that?"

"Yeah and that's when I yelled at him to stop talking to Mama that way."

"And that's when he slapped Blanche." Mama stopped her pacing and stood in the middle of the floor.

"He hit Blanche, too?" I asked. "Why?"

"I called that lady of his a whore. And she is, too!"

"A fourteen-year-old shouldn't be using words like that, Blanche," I said.

"Papa flew across the room in two winks, and I thought my head was going to spin in a circle when he hit me." Animosity distorted Blanche's face.

Now I understood. Papa had never struck Blanche before, never struck any of us. Not that Blanche never had it coming. Arrogance oozed from her pores like sweat in August.

Mama and Blanche raged on. Blanche's anger at Papa's behavior rivaled Mama's. Frances merely sat on the floor taking it all in. Hate boiled up in Blanche's face for the man she'd once idolized. Papa's fall from our family's grace was complete.

In a screechy high-pitched tremor, Mama declared, "Your papa's not worth talking to ever again. Anyone who speaks to him betrays the rest of the family. Especially betrays me."

"Where's Calvis?" I asked. "Does he know what's going on?"

Blanche shook her head. "Calvis walked in at the wrong time, right in the middle of the fight, idiot that he is. He asked if he could go to his friend Nathan's until things calmed down. What a dope."

"I got mad at him." Mama seemed almost sorry. "I lost my temper. He's just so much like your father, and...oh, I feel terrible now. I told him he should go with Papa."

I looked from Mama to Blanche and back.

"He's better off with your papa."

It couldn't be true. "You mean he—?"

"You heard me," Mama said. "I told him to pack up his clothes and leave."

Heartbroken, I could imagine my seventeen-year-old brother's astonished face.

"What about his trombone and his drums? Where's he going to go to school? How is Papa going to take care of him?"

"I did what I thought was best." Mama's face flushed red. "You should feel sorry for me, not him." She fled to her room again and slammed the door.

"See what you've done now?" Blanche said. "You think you're so hotsy-totsy. Like always, you're no help. Right when the family needs you most, you can't decide whose side you're on."

"How can you say something like that?" I shot back. "You know I care."

"Well, it doesn't seem like it. Looks like I'm the only one left to take care of Mama."

I burst into tears. Blanche's criticism stung almost as badly as Mama's heartbreak and Papa's atrocious behavior. My head swam until I thought I might collapse.

There must be some reason for Papa's behavior. He would never abandon his family. Not the Papa I admired. The man who taught me to dream of a world without pain could not have inflicted this pain on his own family. Could he?

On the way home, I feared Fremont's reaction to the whole situation. I hiccupped from crying and walked a few feet away from him, not wanting to be close to him or anyone. He carried Margaret while I pushed the empty buggy. I had tried so hard to change for Fremont, to become an upstanding, righteous person, and now my family was tearing itself apart. I would never be good enough to be his wife, not with a family like mine.

Pain struck my heart as I realized that perhaps I was more comfortable with Fremont than I thought. I loved him more than I'd allowed myself to believe. My life seemed more and more confusing every day. What would I do if Fremont left me like Papa had left Mama?

I began to worry about the stability of marriage, of my marriage or any marriage. Would Fremont and I ever be as close as I wanted? Could we find common goals and dreams? Was it even possible to have both a happy family and fulfilled dreams? Achieving my purpose in life might require a lot out from me. I would have to dig down deep in my heart to find out what I really wanted to do and who I wanted to be.

Chapter Thirty-Six

As Fremont's nightmares subsided, mine began. Days after I learned of my parent's separation, I dreamed of a pillow pressed over my head, suffocating me. I flailed about in terror and woke gasping for air, my heart pounding in my ears as loud as a church bell. I felt strangled, like I did during asthma attacks. In my nightmares, I was sinking, drowning, unable to breathe. I struggled to inhale, my heart racing. My promise to Papa ate into my soul. Was I still obligated to please him? Would I always be a disappointment? Was I prone to be a failure?

My questions raged on and on. How did I get trapped here? How did this happen? My passion for life faded, drained away by worry. I felt useless, my life's dream buried under tons of broken expectations.

I could stand the turmoil in my heart no longer. One midnight a few days later, I got out of the four-poster bed quietly and put on a robe. I crept into the living room and knelt by the worn sofa, and sobbed.

"Why, Lord? Why did this happen to me? How did I get here?"

God did not answer.

I waited.

In my heart, I heard something like a whisper, *follow me.*

"How? I can never be pure enough to take Your path." Guilt washed over me as I realized my whole life had been centered around my plans and my needs. Why did I always do the wrong thing without thinking? I recalled a Bible verse from a recent sermon, Romans 3:10. "No one is righteous...they do not know the way of peace because there is no fear of God."

Certainly, I was not the only person to do wrong, not the only one to go my own way instead of God's way. My self-centeredness had created the chasm between me and God.

"Please, Lord, I've made so many mistakes...please forgive me," I whispered.

I broke down sobbing again, but this time with tears of peace as God's love rained over me. My heart flowered open as sweetly as one of Papa's irises, and I felt loving forgiveness. A weight lifted from my shoulders. Relief flowed through me like a breath of fresh mountain air, like new life.

I determined to follow God more closely; sure that He still had a plan for my life, a role for me in society. Hope as fresh as spring-water bubbled up in my heart. Perhaps my dreams and my reality could be reconciled. Perhaps a purpose could be found. I was so relieved and elated that I laughed out loud for the first time in weeks. Forgiveness was refreshing. Joy had found me!

Chapter Thirty-Seven
October 1934

Fremont paced less during the labor of our second baby. I occasionally heard the coins in his pocket jingle, nervous as I was, I assumed. I lay in the tiny room surrounded by Mama, Mother Pope, and the doctor. Their busyness grated on me. I wished this birthing could be done in private.

I smelled coffee perking in the kitchen and heard small talk from the living room where our family members waited.

Our baby boy was born October 20, 1934, exactly on his due date. Born in the same small house, in the same four-poster bed as his big sister Margaret. And he was delivered by the same rotund doctor, Dr. Fortson.

I heard the baby's first cry, and then the tiny bundle was laid in my arms. I smiled as Fremont entered the room. He kissed me on the cheek, and I think his face was as damp as mine. Then he gently took the baby into his arms. Such a loving father. I overheard the conversation as Fremont took the baby to the living room. I watched through the open door.

"A boy, Dad!" Fremont proudly handed the wrapped package over to Dad Pope as if presenting a Christmas present. "He's a mighty small thing. We named him Judson Lamont Pope."

"Son, you've done well." Dad Pope's face beamed with joy.

I nursed Judson, wondering how it could be so difficult. This time, I felt no depression and prayed it would stay away, even after I was left alone to care for him.

Papa dropped by our house a few days later. He'd spent most of his time at his apartment in the City, but occasionally he came to Shawnee on business and would sometimes visit with us. He didn't hold my baby but merely stared at him. "That's all this world needs— another destitute, undernourished child."

I didn't respond. Oh, how I wished I could turn back the clock to redo some of my life choices. I would take back my choice to get involved before marriage. However, being with Fremont was something I would never want to undo. Just one look at our tiny bundle, and I knew I would never regret having children either. I loved this little boy.

I would especially take back my promise all those years ago to blindly follow Papa. Would I ever be free of that childish promise?

A distasteful look crossed Papa's face before he caught himself. "This is my third grandchild in a year and a half, and I'm not sure I like being a grandfather any more than I like being a father. Being a grandparent is not all people say it is."

I had no words to say to him.

"My dad was one of fifteen children, as you know," he continued. "And at the rate you're going, you'll have a mountain of offspring. And twins—keep in mind that my father had a twin sister. Twins run in our family. Sibyl, think what will become of you if you don't stop this nonsense."

I understood Papa's concern, but I didn't plan to have fifteen children.

"If you need help, let me know. I can loan you money. For a good cause, that is."

Before I could answer, he turned and walked out the front door. This time, I was glad to see him go. His presence only brought gloom and I didn't need that now, not during such a happy time.

That evening, Fremont hummed softly to the newborn bundle in his arms. I saw tears well up in his eyes as he rocked back and forth, and my heart melted as I watched. My Fremont. My children. I was so blessed.

"A son! What every fellow wants," Fremont said. "I'm not worthy of such a wonderful wife and children. Not me. Not a poor boy like me."

Not even a month after Judson's birth, we had cause for another celebration. The Popes bought some land. My mother-in-law cooked a big pot of black-eyed peas with ham hocks and made sweet cornbread. I made a cream pie.

It wasn't often these days that anyone bought land, but Mr. Pope was able to purchase four lots a block west of their rented house, right at the west dead end of Farrell on Tennessee Street. He paid a hundred dollars cash and signed a two-hundred-dollar mortgage payment. The Popes hated debt, but they gave in to purchase the land and build or move a house on it so they wouldn't have to rent any longer. They still owned eighty acres of pastureland out in Waco, where they hoped to move back some day.

It was clear to me that my father-in-law, Mr. Ollie Pope, never gave up on his dreams. If he could hold onto his goals in this desperate economy, why couldn't I?

Chapter Thirty-Eight

January 1935

A new year dawned. After the turmoil of the previous one, I needed a new chance at a good beginning.

I sat at the kitchen table sewing a jacket for Margaret from Fremont's old navy blue corduroy coat. Lately, I'd spent more time tearing apart old garments to reuse than sewing new fabric. Mother Pope taught me this valuable skill. I wrote down all the clothes I remade, proud of my accomplishments and all the money we saved because of it. Fremont and I laughed when I showed him my list. We were proud of how we were making our life together work.

Over the past year, my mother-in-law had taught me many things, from housework, to health care, to how to live a victorious life and overcome any obstacle that fell into my lap. I took her advice seriously. I especially wanted to talk to her about my parents' separation. I wanted to understand how it happened because it affected me more than I liked.

I was lost in thought when a knock sounded on my front door. Before I could pull my foot off the treadle machine, Marjorie hollered through the screen. "It's me, sis. Don't get up."

As stylish as ever, she wore a bright emerald dress with a cape collar and a fashionable sconce hat perched at an angle atop her blonde locks. She smelled of talcum powder.

"Well, it's about time you came by to see me."

She smiled as she joined me at the table. I reached back to straighten the kerchief over my hair, which was loosely tied in a bun. I wore my old calico house dress and was embarrassed by how faded and plain it looked in comparison to my sister's outfit. "I think I'll make Margaret an Easter dress, one with ruffles and petticoats underneath. What do you think? Maybe a pink bow for her hair?"

"I know nothing about all that, lovey," Marjorie said. "I'm glad I don't have to worry about little girl dresses. I don't sew any more than I have to." She fidgeted with the white collar on her dress. The edges were frayed. She had taken an old petticoat and re-sewn it, able to make fashion out of next to nothing.

"I came by because I need to talk," she said.

"Looks like you could use a cup of coffee. Is something wrong?" I rose and opened the kitchen cabinet. "Would you like some cold biscuits? I have some peach jam."

"Coffee sounds good."

I saw Marjorie eyeing the platter of biscuits, so I placed one in front of her and poured us both a cup of coffee. I picked up Judson, my lightweight of a baby.

"Kelley's cheating on me again," she blurted. "I don't know what to do."

"Surely not. You're just imagining it." I wanted to believe the good in everyone, even someone with a questionable past like Kelley.

"Don't be so naïve, lovey. He's been stepping out on me since we first married. He wasn't even home on our wedding night. He went out drinking." She drew a deep breath and then grabbed a biscuit and stuffed it into her mouth. She sat up straight, determined to be brave.

I didn't know what to say. Kelley Walker had not made a good husband from the first, but I would *never* suggest she leave him. Disgrace always followed divorce. And I didn't think Marjorie could survive alone in the midst of this jobless depressing country. "Maybe he needs time to grow up," I said. "He's still young."

"That's not it. I'm starting to believe what Mama says. Men can't be trusted. It might be better to make it on our own. Have you ever thought about it, Sibyl? Leaving all your kids and financial problems and calling it quits? Papa can find us jobs in the City. I don't want to run back to him, but hey, we could move on up to the bright lights."

I couldn't imagine Marjorie's bright lights, but life *had* been full of ups and downs. I rubbed my forehead. No, I couldn't leave my children. Motherhood was too important. But would I consider finding a temporary job in the City?

"There'll be a turnaround in the economy," I said, "and our financial circumstances will improve. Soon I hope. Keep your spirits up. I'm trying to keep Fremont from getting down in the dumps."

"Perhaps Mama and Papa's troubles are affecting us," Marjorie said. "I want to do something different, but I don't know what." My sister leaned forward, looking into my eyes.

I stopped and reconsidered. Maybe Marjorie was right. Was I destined to have ordinary children, an ordinary husband, to live in an ordinary town? Impossible. My life was meant to be more than that.

"Kelley and I are still trying to make it," she said, massaging her forehead. "If you call living in a dumpy place by the railroad tracks on Main Street 'making it.' Larry has no one to play with. We don't even have an icebox. We eat lots of potatoes and cornbread, and Kelley didn't come home again last night. I think he's ashamed because he batted me around a few days ago."

"He what? Marjorie, I don't believe it."

"It was nothing. Didn't really hurt. I should have seen it coming and kept my mouth shut." She swished her hand in the air. "Oh, did I tell you? Kelley wrote some new cowboy songs to play on the radio."

"Wait a minute. Don't change the subject," I said. "You should call the police or something."

"No way. I'd never do that. If we're going to stay together, then I can't get the police involved. I can't imagine how Kelley would react to that."

"Maybe Fremont can speak with him," I offered.

She shook her head. She didn't want anyone involved, not even Fremont.

"Is Mama still singing?" I asked after the awkward pause. "I thought I heard her on the radio the other day."

"Um-hum, right after Kelley, but I don't think she cares much for Kelley's music. What she said is 'He isn't bad, but he isn't too good either.'" We laughed at the tone we knew Mama used.

"I heard Mama's trying to make things work with Papa," I said. "Maybe all this will blow over and they'll get back together. Sometimes people separate, then think better of it and patch things up."

"Hope so, but I don't know. Mama's still pretty mad."

"How's Larry?" I hadn't seen my nephew in several weeks.

"He's with Mama. She takes good care of him." Marjorie turned toward me with widened eyes and an innocent look. Her I-can-do-what-I-want look. "Now, sis, I don't need another lecture about how to look after my boy."

"God's been a big help to me, and He can help you, too."

"I don't need God. Maybe when I get older, but right now I can take care of myself."

I didn't say what I wanted to say. She was not doing an adequate job taking care of herself or her son, not in my opinion. "What are you going to do? You can't keep on like this." I searched my memory for spiritual words from Sunday sermons or verses from Bible class that could help, but nothing came.

"I'm okay, sis. If I could make it on my own, I might leave him. But then I'd have to go to Papa for help, and I don't want to do that, even if I say I do. Kelley's not so bad. He's talking about heading out west like hundreds of others. Trouble is, those fellows don't always come back."

My parents' marriage had almost disintegrated, and now Marjorie's was rocky. What could I say about a good marriage? Heavenly days, I didn't even know what God said about marriage. All I knew was that trouble was brewing all around.

"Marj, your future's a blank page, ready to be written on. Don't just sit there. If Kelley's treating you badly, then do something about it."

"I'm all right, really I am. Besides, I still love him."

I longed to talk to her more about God, but I still questioned if God could help. Then I remembered the time God had soothed my soul by offering forgiveness for my indiscretion, my untimely pregnancy. Church had become an important part of my life. I had joined a Sunday school class and began to sing in the choir. Perhaps Christ offered the strength I didn't have. Maybe He could do the same for Marjorie.

"You're in a bind," I said. Doubt squirmed through my mind like a snake in the petunia patch, but the words came from some deep knowledge inside. "I know God can help, so I'll pray for you. Come by here anytime. We can talk."

After Marjorie left, I sat at the sewing machine, but couldn't focus on my sewing. I paced the tiny room, a caged lion analyzing my options. My doubts scared me. One minute I wanted my marriage to work out so badly it hurt, the next I felt depressed and wanted to escape. Why did I go back and forth? I tried to ignore my rampant emotions because the desire to leave Fremont could not be from God. I felt as if a battle raged inside me, so I prayed for help. I needed God's wisdom, needed more understanding than I got from a Wednesday night sermon. I knelt and pleaded from an anguished place deep in my soul.

"Help me, God."

Chapter Thirty-Nine
April 1935

One hot Sunday afternoon, daytime turned into night. We were half-way home from church when we noticed a dark cloud on the horizon. Within minutes, dirt blocked the sun. I reached for my children. The air was so thick it was difficult to see them through the dust cloud. I grabbed them and ran toward home for cover. I rolled up towels and cloths and stuffed them in the window sills.

I prayed for Fremont to hurry home. He was probably stuck alone in the filing station, where he would wait for the storm to clear.

An hour later, I still didn't dare venture outdoors. A wet handkerchief over my mouth could not block the suffocating feeling of the dirt-filled air. Asthma threatened and I took several deep breaths.

I washed my children's faces with damp cloths and stripped them to their underwear so they could stay a bit cooler. It was warm, too warm, and sticky. Gritty sand stuck to our bodies and lingered in the air. Our lunch tasted like coarse, dry dust. This was the worst dust storm we'd ever experienced, and later the *Shawnee News* termed the day, "Black Sunday."

I hated the dust more than I hated being poor. Poverty could be endured and overcome, but the dust-soaked air left me choking. I coughed constantly. The darkness felt like the Angel of Death passing over our small town. And death passed over a lot in the thirties, the dust storms too frequent in our drought-stricken land. The fierce winds lasted all week, driving the dirt all the way to the east coast.

Could life get any dirtier? My spirit sunk lower each time we were confined to this tiny room. Despair rolled over me.

A week after the big storm, Fremont arrived home late from work. He had been out in the dryness trying to get a migrant's old tin jalopy running again after the airborne grit smothered the engine to a standstill. I pulled off his heavy work boots and put them by the door as he eased into a metal chair at the kitchen table. My carefully prepared dinner waited for him, as it did every evening.

He crumbled a piece of cornbread on his plate and I ladled steaming brown beans over it. He scooped a spoonful of his mother's homemade green tomato chow-chow and plopped it on top.

As he ate, I announced in my best soap-opera voice, "There's a sale downtown at C. R. Anthony's store tomorrow." He didn't reply. "Do you think we might go? Look around?" Being confined in our small house during a dust storm made me want to get outside, go somewhere.

"Is there something we need?" Practical as always. "We're mighty short on funds right now."

"Of course," I said. "I know it as well as you do." I turned my back to him to hide my frustration and stirred the pot of beans and ham hocks on the stove top.

We lived from paycheck to paycheck, never able to save money, except the few coins I had managed to hoard for a real emergency. We were unable to afford a car or a better place to live, barely managing rent and groceries. I tried to make ends meet the best I could, but poverty ate at me. If only Fremont had a better job, I wouldn't have to count pennies as much. I knew he'd graduated from high school, but had he ever tried to get a better education?

"I'm trying to work hard. You can't accuse me of not trying."

"Of course not."

The rest of the meal was eaten in silence and Fremont seemed to regain his depleted strength. I checked on Judson. The little thing couldn't seem to gain weight like most babies his age. I worried about him, thinking I might need to feed him again soon. He was sound asleep. Margaret, too, was sleeping, her curls flaring out around her head. I kissed them on the forehead. I wanted so much more for them. Piano lessons. Nice clothes. A good education.

Back in the kitchen, I sat across from Fremont and could not stop myself. Insensitive words popped out of my mouth. "You might have a better job now if you'd gone to college."

I didn't say *we wouldn't be in this mess if you'd gone to college*, but that's what I meant. I gritted my teeth to hold back more mean or unfair things, because so often, my words came out flat out uncaring.

His face seemed to fall a thousand feet, and tears came to his eyes. The last thing I wanted to do was hurt him, but I was worried about our situation. Our future.

I stood and took his empty plate, put it in the sink and began to clear the rest of the table.

He watched me thoughtfully. "I always wanted to go to college to study engineering. Maybe someday I can."

"Why didn't you?"

"Nobody could afford college," he said quietly. "Least, not anyone I knew." He leaned his chair back on two legs and linked his hands behind his head, balancing his words as carefully as he balanced his body. "Not that college is much easier now."

"Maybe you just didn't want it badly enough."

His chair hit hard against the floor. "Didn't want college? I never tried so hard for anything in my life. You think I wanted to live in poverty?"

"I'm sorry. I didn't mean that."

"During high school, I worked mostly in the hayfields. I saved as much money as I could for college, but I didn't have enough. Most of my paycheck went to help my family. Someone always needed bread or gasoline or shoes. I wrote letters to relatives to let them know my plans, people I thought might help me get to college. Uncle Charles Castleman lived in Illinois and owned a timber company. I asked him for money and he wrote back. I memorized his letter."

Fremont lowered his voice. "'By all means get all the education you can. A fellow faces a hard time these days if he doesn't have something more to offer. Hitch your dreams to a star and keep your eye on it.' A twenty-dollar bill fluttered from the envelope. You can imagine my surprise. My uncle's gift motivated me to fill out college applications. I saved up the ninety dollars for one semester's tuition, but I was ten dollars short. Sibyl, can you believe that? Ten dollars short."

How could I have questioned his sincerity? We looked deep into each other's eyes. My heart pounded loudly. My anger evaporated.

"I tried mighty hard to get admitted to college. I met with the dean on Bison Hill, promising to pay the ten dollars by the end of the semester. I even asked if I could take a class without credit. I tried four different colleges in Oklahoma with no luck."

Amazement must have shown on my face. Respect increased for this man I married.

"I finally went to a bank to get a $10 loan. Money was tight. Prices fell so much on cattle, you could practically buy a heifer for a buck. A mighty difficult time for a poor fellow to be looking for an education. 'Don't have a penny to loan,' the banker told me. 'Not a penny.' That's when I hopped on a freight train like thousands of other folks traipsing over the country."

I stood and kissed his curly dark hair. Here was a part of Fremont I hadn't known. Learning how hard my man tried to accomplish his goals increased my respect for him. There was so much more depth to him than appeared on the outside.

He would probably always surprise me. How lucky I was to be his wife. His misfortunes were not his fault. He, like so many others, had been caught in the noose of the world's financial collapse. Add to that the unforgiving weather Oklahoma had seen for years, and it was a wonder we were doing as well as we were.

Life lessons were so hard for me to learn, but this one I knew would stay with me forever. My husband did have ambition. He did want to try his best. The husband God gave me was a jewel. I should treat him like one.

Chapter Forty
May 1935

"Come with me to WMU," Mother Pope said. Lately she'd encouraged me to get more involved in activities such as the Women's Missionary Union at Calvary Baptist. "I think you'll be downright pleased."

The church ladies met every Tuesday afternoon at different women's houses. I would gladly attend the meeting, grateful for a diversion from family problems, financial worries and dull days. The best part was that Mother Pope would teach the class.

Having attended the Baptist Girl's Auxiliary and the Young Women's Association occasionally in my childhood and early teens, I knew the WMU offered missionary training. The warm memories I felt in those groups made joining the WMU natural. Maybe this would satisfy the urge to do something meaningful with my life as Papa always encouraged me to do. He had not meant church work, of course, but I didn't care.

"Do something useful, Sibyl," Papa would have said. "Use your head, not your heart. Church work is all useless namby-pamby heart work."

Somehow, even with Papa's nagging rhetoric in my head, this mission work felt right. I was excited to attend my first regular WMU meeting. I wore a starched but faded dress with the Peter Pan collar to look presentable, if not fashionable. Most of the other women in the group dressed similar to me.

"We're glad to have all of you today," Mrs. Pope said as we pulled up chairs. "We're studying mission work to prepare ourselves for whatever Christ calls us to do."

Mother stood in front of the circle of women, her sweet voice drawing our attention. "For example, Englishwoman Edith Cavell became a nurse during the Great War, helping wounded soldiers in a Belgium hospital. She made room for wounded enemies who were fleeing the Germans. And because she helped the enemies, she was arrested. Instead of lying, she admitted to helping over two hundred men escape."

"Two hundred!" I exclaimed out loud.

"Yes. She was caught, convicted and shot by the Germans in 1915. What might God ask us to do? Could you be as brave as Miss Cavell?"

She paused, letting the thought soak in. "Miss Cavell said, 'Patriotism is not enough. I must have no hatred or bitterness toward anyone.' She gave up her life for others. Could you do that? Remember, Jesus said whoever loves his life will lose it, and he who hates his life in this world, will find it."

Well, I was inspired. Mother Pope's thoughts on mission work, her Bible studies, and how I could apply her lessons to my life intrigued me. For the first time, I thought I could turn my dreams over to God. Studying missions and taking care of the unfortunates around the world was a worthy aspiration. It sounded loftier than Papa's speechifying. I would be *doing* something, not just talking about it.

"Let's give what we can to missionaries like Miss Cavell, who told others about God's love," she said as she passed a dish to the nearest woman.

I hesitated. The few pennies in my purse were for tomorrow's bread. The other women around me were giving, and I knew they had as little as we did. I pulled out two pennies and dropped them into the dish. My shoulders pulled back and I felt good, better than when I gave at Mama's church. This was a way to personally make a difference.

The more I learned about mission work, the more it caused me to want to help others. It was a way to change the world in a positive, meaningful way.

Mother Pope instructed us to invite a friend to next week's meeting. I brought two friends, Effie Douglas and Opal Davis, from my south-side neighborhood. All three of us were around the same age and newly married, and they had babies on the way. They joined the group that afternoon, as did many others.

I looked forward to the Tuesday WMU meetings. Everyone greeted each other warmly and helped with all the children. For instance, the wheels of our second black ornate baby buggy almost wore off. I put on miles from taking the children back and forth to church and visiting the ladies. One woman had a used buggy she didn't need any more, so I traded sewing for it.

The women surrounding me were young and had children. And they were restless, just like me. It surprised me, honestly. I wasn't the only one who felt trapped. These women were intelligent and understanding. They shared my feelings, and we uplifted one another. We sympathized without judgment. No one was critical. I had never experienced such companionship and acceptance. I didn't have to be a puppet on anyone's strings. Friendship, I learned, was an awesome gift from God.

Both Effie and Opal's baby buggies joined me as we walked to the meetings. Our missions group grew in numbers and knowledge. Within this safe place, my heart stretched out beyond the small world of Shawnee to others around the globe. With Mother Pope's guidance, I started to believe that I could, in some way, assist those less fortunate. Her steadfastness gave me strength and courage so I could share my desire to help others. My sense of poverty faded, temporarily forgotten, as I thought about the world outside of myself.

"You spend so much time with the Popes you've become a goody-two-shoes." Mama had dropped by and saw me baking cookies to raise support for workers overseas. "Shouldn't you spend more time with *your* family? You need that money yourself. How can you even think of helping others?"

I didn't try to explain it to her. She was too busy trying to hold herself together to understand.

Papa's child support failed to cover Mama's essentials and although she found odd jobs, nothing stable had materialized.

My desire to change the world grew. It changed course and direction as my participation in the WMU expanded. I tried to contribute information and insight at the weekly meetings. I began clipping newspaper and magazine articles to share. I read books from the Carnegie Library about Christian missionaries in China, Korea, and Mexico. There was so much to learn.

One afternoon, I sat on the sofa with newspapers and magazines spread around me. After I finished clipping what I wanted, I gave the children the remains. They seemed content with the cut up pictures.

Suddenly, the verse Mother Pope recently challenged me to memorize popped into my head—Second Timothy three-sixteen. *All Scripture is given by inspiration of God.*

Of course. I could find help in life by reading the Bible. I didn't have to struggle by myself. I could learn, not just from libraries and newspapers, but from God's own words.

Never before had I studied the Bible in the way I studied geometry, world history, or even shorthand when I was in college. I wanted to learn on my own, to read the Bible more, to find the answers to the questions that burned inside me. I'd finished high school in two years instead of three, so I knew I was capable. And, as an added incentive, more Scripture knowledge might give me the right words to help others. Even if it only helped me, Bible study would be worth a try. What did God have to say about families? Broken ones like mine? Did He have advice?

I remembered Grandma Bennett's love of reading the Bible and the stories of Jesus she shared. I didn't know where to begin studying, the Bible such a big, complex book. I sought God's guidance in this overwhelming task. *I will teach you*, I heard in my heart. That's what I wanted to hear. I wanted to learn wisdom, not facts. I found Romans twelve-two, which read, "Do not be conformed to this world, but be transformed by the renewing of your mind." That was it. I needed to renew the thoughts in my mind, focus on the good lessons God had given.

Elation rose in my heart and I felt like jumping up and down. My new purpose grew clearer.

Along with the weekly attendance at the WMU small group, I designed a systematic plan for my study at home. I could share information with others. My study was not only for my edification, but also to obtain knowledge needed to help others learn the Scriptures.

The next morning, after Fremont dashed out for work and before the children woke, I sat at the dining room table and opened my Bible.

Armed with fresh knowledge of God, I felt like I could take on anything. What problem could possibly stop me?

Chapter Forty-One
June 1935

Saturday evening, Fremont took off work early, and we strolled around the neighborhood. I loved walks. I liked the way we could get close while talking or amble comfortably without saying a word. The large baby buggy rattled as Fremont pushed it beside me. My husband, his handsome profile towering over me by a foot, walked tall and confident with his chin up.

I listened as he vented his frustration. Car parts were mighty hard to come by, and most old vehicles he serviced had seen better days. Then his worst news, "The Goodsons have gone bankrupt."

"No!" Not the Goodsons, not the owners of the service station. Were things that bad?

Fremont let out a long, frustrated breath. "Mr. Goodson told me he can't pay the wages owed for the past two weeks. He's broke. Mighty broke. His family's already packed up their belongings to head west." His pace quickened, and I grabbed his arm to slow him down. "Looks like I'm going to be out of a job."

We walked another block in silence, all the while my mind running in circles. We switched places. Fremont picked up Margaret while I pushed Judson in the buggy. We turned onto Beard Street and slowed down, the recently rebuilt outline of the Shawnee Milling Company towering over us.

"Maybe it's time for you and me to take off to California," he said. "We can hitchhike." He kicked a stone on the sidewalk, his confident stance gone.

"That's impossible," I said. "Hitchhike—with two children? How can you even suggest such a thing? Especially after what we hear about how bad it is out west." I dreamed of leaving Shawnee, but never with children to tend to along the way and certainly not without money for proper food and lodging.

"What if I set out, earn some money, and send back for you? You could ride a train out there."

"Fremont, you're being impractical."

He bumped my shoulder. "It would be mighty fun, now admit it," he teased.

"Oh, all right, it would be fun, in some ways. But there might be another way to survive here in Oklahoma. I saw Papa last week. He suggested we buy a filling station, what with all the growing sale of autos these days and your experience. He knows of a station for sale. Why don't we talk to him about it?"

"Own my own filling station? Honey, you're dreaming again." Fremont laughed as if I was joking.

"I know you can run it." I was silent for a moment. "The bank will loan you the money. Papa said he would put in a good word for us."

"A loan? I don't see any way."

I knew exactly how much money we had. For all of our marriage, I had kept proper accounts, listing our income and expenses. We were always short of money, no matter how much we scrimped. We had a better chance at getting ahead if Fremont worked for himself. If only I could convince him, Papa would approve and help us out.

"I'll keep the books, of course. I'll list auto parts on hand, cars serviced, and who owes money." I grew enthusiastic. Entrepreneurship seemed like the answer to our financial difficulties.

The stars glittered like gold by the time we arrived back home. We talked late into the night about the filling station, trying to convince ourselves that we could afford to buy it, considering ways we could make it profitable.

"Maybe it's an answer from God," I said.

The more Fremont thought about the suggestion, the more he liked it. He shared my enthusiasm and began to hope we could make a go of it. A reliable, steady man, Fremont wanted to succeed in life, to be proud of himself, and to be a vital part of the community. If it took hard work, well, then, he would be the best worker possible.

Fremont and I approached Papa for advice, but he carried on about social injustice, worldwide brotherhood, and how the evils of business and government shaped the economy. Then he got off on an even more unrelated tangent.

"The history of the past and the experience of our lives show us that if the intent is right, the result will also be good. And if the result becomes a cause, and if we have not permitted evil to creep into our actions by ignorance or deceit, then the resulting new effect can be useful, possibly to a much greater extent."

His statement was almost incomprehensible. What if our intent was right but something bad still happened to us? Did that make us evil? Anxious to change the subject, I asked, "Papa, did you get the Assistant State Bank Commissioner job you wanted?"

Papa stared at me before he spoke. "Not yet. My boss promised it to me when he left office, and I have wooed that position for two years now. I can't believe the officials are taking so long to make the appointment. With my experience and expertise, I'm their best choice."

I looked at Papa's expensive, fashionable clothes and his straight-back demeanor and could see him being a proud Commissioner.

"As to your request, Sibyl, how can you ask for such a thing when thousands of banks are closing? I submit foreclosure papers every single day, and you want to invest?"

What? What was he saying? "It was your idea, and it's a good idea, Papa. You said so yourself, and Fremont's a good mechanic. We can make it work. We'd be beholden if you could help us."

"I disapprove of Roosevelt's deficit spending because it will never revive the economy. But there's a slight chance it will make an effect. Property prices are extremely low right now and continuing to drop, so perhaps it might be an appropriate investment."

Papa stopped chattering and seemed deep in thought. I fretted, worried that yet again, all our dreams would come to nothing. And then what would we do? The thought of going to California, of leaving family and friends, terrified me. But if Papa didn't agree, what other choice did we have? There was so little work in Shawnee, and the rest of Oklahoma wasn't faring better. It seemed a million years before Papa spoke again.

"I'll speak to the bank for you. Fremont, you've got what it takes to make a good son-in-law. Just jump in there and take a chance. It's people like you who will change the world. Making a buck is what it's all about. You have a plan, and I believe you have the skills to make it work."

For all his faults, Papa hadn't let me down. I felt relieved. My breathing came easier.

Then Papa continued. "Of course, if this goes through, you'll owe me. I might need your support someday. Remember, my good name is on the line."

Papa intervened with the bank. A week passed before we finally walked to the State National Bank. Fremont and the bank manager hammered out details of the transaction and discussed rates.

"Guess I'll allow you a chance to make the station succeed," the banker said. "Most businesses fail. So few individuals are taking risks these days. I don't understand why, but Mr. Trimble is backing you on this. You wouldn't be getting this loan if it weren't for him."

I never realized having a bank auditor for a father could be so useful. Indeed, I did feel beholden to Papa, and I knew he would eventually expect something from me. But I didn't care. Surely having a successful business would earn his acceptance and fill that deep longing inside.

Fremont and I looked at each other and smiled. Business owners. It felt good. Joy leapt inside me. At the same time, a nagging fear pressed me as we signed the papers for a loan. Had we rushed in too quickly without seeking advice? Had we sought God's will, or were we too excited about the possibility of owning our own business? I shoved the disturbing thoughts aside.

I helped Fremont clean out the old station. We scrubbed the floor. We shined the windows with vinegar and old newspapers. We repainted the trim on the outside of the garage. We were elated, driven by the possibilities. A few days later, the place looked almost new.

Fremont talked to Mama's former gardener, Lester, about helping when there was too much work for him to do alone, and I purchased an account book to keep track of the finances, especially the mortgage payment. Then we had our first customer, old Mr. Willis.

Word quickly got around about the new owner of the filling station. More people dropped by, and our business grew. I could tell the difference in Fremont. He loved his job. He felt respected as a business owner and was quickly becoming an integral part of the community. With his newfound pride and vigor, Fremont climbed a bit higher on the pedestal in my mind.

We waited to see if our plan would work out. Much depended on the economy, and in 1935, Oklahoma had difficult days. Even with the topsoil blowing across the dining room table and hungry families coming to our door, we hoped our chance had finally come.

Chapter Forty-Two
July 1935

As the Depression continued, more hungry men roamed the streets than ever before. No longer could the law keep them hidden behind rear church doors and under alley stairs. A few hungry men came knocking on Mama's back door, but more came to Mother Pope's, since she'd helped out for so many years. She fed the transients egg sandwiches or cold biscuits and sausage, never letting a man leave hungry. I marveled at how she found the extra food.

I admired Fremont's mother. Instead of spouting pompous expressions of concern, as my family might do, she took action to fill empty stomachs. She didn't just talk about the needs, she actually put on her worn, flowered apron and went to work. I decided to do the same.

One day when I took Mother Pope some potatoes I had found at the market, she volunteered to watch the children for a few hours. The children loved spending time with her, except when she gave them a spoonful of castor oil, the nasty stuff that could clean out the insides of an old rooster.

Grateful for the free time, I planned to check in with the union offices again to see if I could be of help. I hadn't assisted much in a long time and not at all since Judson was born. I would sign up for two hours volunteer once a week. No one would know.

First, I walked down Main Street to see my old boss, Mr. Weston, to ask for my back pay. We needed it. Fremont's filling station had not picked up much business yet.

A young lady sat in my old desk in the reception area. She was dressed very perky with a white scalloped collar over a gray tailored blouse. I felt dowdy, old, and drab. Of course, I was a wife and the mother of two now, and I couldn't afford the latest fashions, even though I altered old clothes on the treadle machine as best I could.

The receptionist shuffled papers on her desk. My old desk was in disarray. With piles of papers scattered, it looked like Whirlwind Avenue. I had always been organized, my notes and folders neatly stacked. I raised my chin. It felt good to know I had been a competent secretary.

Mr. Weston sat behind his desk, papers spread over it too. He hadn't changed, his dark-rimmed glasses sliding down his nose, his bald head shining. He was wearing the same suit he wore the day he let me go.

"Well. Well. Sibyl Trimble. What brings you here today? Not needing an attorney, I hope." Mr. Weston's condescending voice still grated against my nerves.

"That's Sibyl Pope now, sir, and no, we don't need an attorney. I came to see if I could collect the $27 you owe me."

He tilted his head back and looked me up and down. "Can't say I have that much money to spare. You know how the economy is these days. No one's able to pay the full amount on anything. I'm barely squeaking by."

"Mr. Weston, we really need that money. Any part of it would help. I have two children now and my husband's new business is barely making the bills..."

"Everyone's hit pretty hard. I don't have anything to spare."

"I'm sorry to have interrupted your work." I said quietly. "I'll check back with you in a few months." I turned to leave. I would keep reminding him that he owed me. I wouldn't forget. We needed that money.

"Sibyl, I'm sorry to hear about your mother and father."

"My mother and father?" I spun around. Surely he hadn't heard about their marital difficulties.

"Mr. Trimble asked me to handle the *marriage situation* for him. I refused. Not that I couldn't have done it, but with the issues with the state banks and all, I felt it best not to get involved."

I wanted to crawl under the desk. Had the news of Mama and Papa's troubles spread across Shawnee? "What bank issues?"

"I'm sure you know all about it," he said. "Since your father is a bank examiner, he can see the books of almost every bank in the state. Bank records are no secret to him. The state Bank Commissioner Barnett has been in hot water lately."

"I read that in the paper, but what does that have to do with my father?"

"Remember the bankers who encouraged people to invest in their banks? Just before many of them folded? Seems that someone vouched for them. Signed off that they were solvent when they were most decidedly not. At least that's most people's opinion."

I gasped. "Are you saying my papa did something wrong?"

"Not saying anything, mind you. Been some talk. The way your father goes on and on about unreasonable governmental agencies unjustly treading all over the little man. Then there's this scandal with the Commissioner. Mr. Trimble can't seem to avoid trouble."

"What does my father have to do with the Commissioner and his problems? Papa's name wasn't mentioned in the newspaper articles."

"Can't tell you any more than I know, girl. Go on now. I've got work to do."

I stomped out, unsure how to respond to this devastating news. My confidence in Papa's integrity had taken a plunge when he abandoned Mama and my sisters. Now this new information dropped it even lower. Did I even know him anymore?

This particular charge Mr. Weston was referring to, the one against the Commissioner, had been in the news for almost two years. The case was scheduled to go to trial within a few months. The defendant, Voigtlander, admitted he purchased shares of Hillsdale bank stock, but claimed he was encouraged to do so through fraudulent representations. He said the bank had been presented as being entirely solvent even though the bank officers were fully aware it was not. His accusations claimed the bank commissioner audited the bank's books and knew the severity of the overextension prior to allowing the bank to offer its stock to the public.

I doubted Mr. Weston's reliability. He loved to gossip. On the other hand, there was a possibility that the particular bank in question was part of Papa's duties. After all, his job was to audit banks for the

Commissioner. Admittedly, Papa did offend people easily. He was pretentious and made it clear he believed he was smarter than Solomon.

This was news I would not share with Mama. It would only fuel her anger and bitterness.

I walked toward the union offices. Main Street was crowded during mid-morning. Housewives in stylish hats pushed baby carriages, and men in double breasted suits rushed in and out of stores. I stopped on Bell Street and looked at the window display in the four-story brick Mammoth Department Store. Just the price of one of those fancy hats in the window would feed my family for a week.

At the union offices, men still lounged around, waiting for jobs to become available. The atmosphere was much tenser than the last time I'd walked through. No coarse joking bantered across the room. No raucous laughter flew out the windows. I slowed down as I maneuvered the maze of desks and chairs to pick up what I could from their conversations. The voices were harsh and loud.

"This here New Deal was supposed to help, but what's it done for Oklahoma?"

"Yeah, the government's not doing a blamed thing to fight this depression."

"I'm scraping by just to get the mortgage paid."

"Did you hear about the strikes? One up in Toledo. Maybe we should strike, too?"

"The banks are in league with the government to take us down."

"If the Socialists had won the election, economy might be different now."

"I'm getting out o' here—leaving Oklahoma. No good can come out of this state."

"I ain't a going to be treated this way anymore."

"Sons, we gotta tighten up our belts."

I made it to the back of the room where the Women's Organization desk sat. My friend, Eula May, was absent.

I didn't recognize the woman who sat at the desk. I stopped in front of her and she looked up and asked, "May I help you?"

"I'm here to help feed the poor."

Chapter Forty-Three

It had been almost a year since Mama and Papa separated, and no one in the family had seen Papa in over a month.

Saturday morning while I was visiting Mama, Blanche picked up the current *Shawnee News Star* and said, "Listen to what I read this week: 'Mr. Powell, applying for a divorce, told the court he had seen his wife only three times. 'How long have you been married?' His answer: thirty-one years.'"

We all laughed.

"See Mama, your situation could be worse."

Mama spoke up, "Sometimes I think that might have been better."

A horn honked outside, and Frances looked out the window. "It's Papa!"

Mama skedaddled to the back room while Blanche and I went to look out the window.

Papa sat in the car that was formerly Mama's. He was waving from the passenger's side while a woman sat in the driver's seat. The green Chrysler was all shined up. Blanche and I looked at each other, not believing what we were seeing. He'd supposedly sold that car. I shook my head in disbelief.

When Papa saw us peeking out the window, he motioned for us to come outside. Frances ran out the door and Blanche and I followed.

"How's my princess?" he asked as he stepped out of the car. "Here's a package for you." He handed Frances a brown covered box and smiled at me.

My youngest sister tore open the package and pulled out a winter-green cardigan sweater. "My favorite color. How'd you know?"

"Lucky guess," said Papa. "Now Blanche, come get your package."

Blanche stood away from the car. "I thought you were going to sell Mama's car. You said you needed money."

"I thought about it, but decided to let Gladys drive it. She didn't have a car. You understand, of course." I stared at the woman in the driver's seat. Gladys was blond, buxom, and well-coiffed.

"If you really cared about us, you'd come see us more often," Blanche said. "But, if you really cared, you never would have left."

I couldn't agree more At a minimum, Papa should provide his daughters with proper food and clothing, which he didn't do, according to Mama. She also said she needed gasoline money to go to Sulphur and money to get Frances dance lessons.

He ignored Blanche just like he'd ignored her outspoken remarks since she was old enough to talk. He didn't seem to care that her antagonism was now directed at him.

"Come on over. I have a gift for you," Papa coaxed.

Blanche strolled to Papa's car, her arms folded. Her tall, lanky appearance accentuated her awkwardness.

"I brought you some chocolates." He held out the box. "I wanted to give you something you'd like."

"If you think all I want from you is a box of chocolates, then I don't want them." She threw the chocolates back to Papa, turned, and ran back to the house. Frances followed.

From the steps, she yelled, "And you don't need to come back. Ever!"

I watched Blanche disappear. I knew how she felt and considered following her, but when I turned, Papa beckoned me over. I seldom saw him anymore and wanted to discuss several things, mostly Mama's predicament. Her lack of funds. Her need for money. I would have to listen to his banter first, of course. I nodded to the woman in the car and leaned against the hood. He started talking about politics and business like usual. Despite everything, I'd always felt honored that he would trust me with this insider information—the banking practices back east that caused business difficulties all over the country, the stock market crash, and how banking problems grew more desperate every day. I felt like I understood Papa more than most people did.

"I'm sure you read about Huey Long's Share the Wealth Program, didn't you?" he started. "Well, I agree with most of his platform, but, in my opinion, it will never pass."

"Why do you think that?"

"He proposes to limit individual fortunes to a few million dollars. Now isn't that what Socialists have been saying all along? Take from the rich and give to the poor? This proposal will allow the American people to share in the wealth."

He kept talking for the next ten minutes without stopping. I tried to no avail to interrupt his discourse to ask about the Bank Commissioner lawsuits. Several more lawsuits had surfaced since my talk with Mr. Weston, and my questions were mounting, but Papa rambled on.

"I agree with Mr. Long, but I don't think it will pass," he continued. "The feckless heads of the established powers will never allow it. They are beholden to the wealthy who support their policies. What we need is someone who can stand up and make a difference."

"You should encourage women to run for office, Papa. Women can do good things. Look at Amelia Earhart."

He leaned against the Chrysler. "I read about her, the first woman to fly solo from Hawaii to California." He turned and looked at me. "Not like you—you've chosen to stay mired in this mess of poverty affecting our country. Child, you should pull yourself up and do something useful."

"Like what? I can't change my situation."

"Make some choices. Take advantage of this depressed economy. There are lots of opportunities, like that filling station you just bought. Use that head of yours to see how you can benefit from others' failures."

I examined the grass, dying right in front of me.

"Marjorie and Larry have moved in with me temporarily. She made a poor choice getting involved with Kelley. She needs to quit acting like an irresponsible teen."

Marjorie moved in with Papa and Gladys? Kelley must have disappeared again. She probably thought she had no other choice, but she had not even spoken to me about it. Poor Larry was shifted from house to house like an old useless lantern.

How could I help Marjorie? By first helping Mama. I opened my mouth to begin my plea for but was interrupted by shouts coming from the house.

Flapping her arms and raving from the porch, Mama yelled, "That's my car. And that...that little minx is driving it!"

"I bought the car, so I can do what I want with it." Papa turned away from me and hurriedly got in the car and drove off.

We went back into the house.

"I never want to see that man again in my life," Blanche said.

"I agree," Mama said. "The man who fathered my children is a down-right, no-good sham. We don't need him." She paused. "However, girls, we do need his money—and that box of chocolates would have been nice."

My sisters and mother laughed. I felt tears coming to my eyes. My parents might never reconcile.

Chapter Forty-Four
August 1935

Mama showed up mid-morning and my house was in chaos, toys and clothes scattered everywhere. I stood at the sink washing plates and glasses from the night before while Margaret and Judson sat on the floor playing, their laughter rolling out the open windows.

"I did it," Mama said.

"Did what?" I turned and looked at her.

"I filed for divorce."

I dried my hands on a towel and followed her to the sofa. "Why? Why did you do that?"

"Ah, Sibyl. I knew you wouldn't understand. That's why I didn't tell you I was filing. But I had to come and explain in person. We're bone-poor at our house, you know as well as I do. He hasn't given me money in three months, and before that he only paid $7 a week. How does that man expect us to live? I *had* to file to get him to support us."

Mama brought out several pieces of paper from her pocketbook and handed them to me. "Here, read this."

The top page was a court summons. I scanned the document, catching phrases here and there.

I noticed Mama's attorney, Abernathy, Howell, and Abernathy. Then I looked through the Petition. My hands shook as I read it. It claimed from June, 1934, to the current month, August, 1935, Papa neglected and refused to support his wife and children. Last year, in 1934, he abandoned and deserted Mama, and the children without cause. He had not been in communication with his wife but had expressed love and affection for another woman.

The defendant, Papa, employed by the State Banking Department of Oklahoma, had a salary of $250 a month. Plenty to support his family. Several properties were listed. First, the house on Beard Street where Mama lived. However, I didn't know the $2,000 mortgage was delinquent. It appeared no payments had been made on it since June of '33.

Next listed was our Wewoka home, the one we lived in before we rented it out and moved to Shawnee. That mortgage payment was delinquent. Mama claimed Papa collected the rent but did not pay the mortgage. That was also a big surprise to me.

Papa owned other acreages and tracts of land in Seminole County. The document mentioned the Jack Cudio land, Joe David land, James Johnson Tract, William Noble land, and Tyson property, which included royalties.

Mama, the petition claimed, was without fault, without funds, and wholly destitute. She asked for $125 a month.

Mama stood and, wringing her hands, said, "I didn't want to file for divorce, of course, but I had to. The next step is for the sheriff to find him and subpoena him. Maybe he'll take me seriously now."

But by the end of August, the deputy had still not served the summons. Papa could not be found.

Chapter Forty-Five

September 1935

I was sympathetic to Mama's plight and wished her troubles would disappear, that she'd find gold dust under her pillow or Papa would get on his knees and apologize, but none of that seemed likely. If Papa would only come clean, confess he had been seduced, or at least admit he was tempted and beg to come home, Mama might forgive him.

While sympathetic, I was also irritated. Mama only saw the bad side of Papa. I had admired him since childhood. His gifts, his exuberance, his love of gardening.

Mama clamored on about the disgraceful way he treated her, preoccupied with her *betrayal*, as she called it, raving on about no-good men in general. She thought her children should share the same attitude. Consequently, even though I wanted to listen and be there for Mama, I dreaded the time and energy a visit with her required. She could not see her own bad behavior.

"Papa's up for the State Commissioner job," I said, thinking she might be interested.

"How can you be interested in him?" she chided bitterly. "He left me for another woman and doesn't want to keep up his own children. What a low life. Our problems are his fault."

"I didn't mean..."

"I need money—desperately. Your Papa's given me almost nothing since he left. I drove his old Buick Coupe down to the used car lot on Philadelphia Street and bargained with the salesman for as

229

much as I could. I sold it for fifty-five dollars and paid off the grocery bill."

"I'm sorry, Mama, I'm sorry."

"I don't want to ever see that man's face again or hear his name spoken in this house." Her hatred was so entrenched in her heart that she pushed him completely out of her life—and wanted him out of ours.

I struggled with believing Papa could be disgraceful. He had been my hero since I was a child. His beliefs and lofty views had been mine, and I still yearned for his approval, defending him, hoping the stories about his atrocious behavior weren't true. When I listened to Mama's tales, I kept my doubts to myself. As the evidence against Papa mounted, he didn't even try to hide his behavior.

He had seen other women for years.

He refused to help Mama with finances.

He ignored his children.

He bought both his wife and his girlfriend the same silk Japanese pajamas, Marjorie confided. How could he?

The information went on and on. Divorce seemed inevitable. This kind of notoriety could ruin Papa's career and jeopardize his standing in the community. Of course, he didn't want a divorce. He was satisfied with things as they were.

I empathized with Mama's animosity. How could Papa disregard his family so easily? Any woman spurned this way would be angry.

My rosy view of Papa dimmed. Although I didn't understand his actions I couldn't bring myself to completely turn away from him. However, my indulgent image of him had tarnished.

During the next week, with all the stress brought on by my parents' situation, my temper began to flare at the least thing. The more I tried to control my feelings, the worse they became.

I fussed at Margaret for tracking dirt into the house. I let Judson stay in his dirty diaper longer than I should. I dropped an egg on the floor and cried. Sharp words flew from my mouth, and tears followed apologies. I didn't understand the tension building inside me or know how to release it. I knew no one, absolutely *no one,* who was divorced. Bad marriages, yes. Separations, yes. But divorce? It was unthinkable.

I found relief in scrubbing the house five times in three days, from the ceiling to the drab kitchen floor. I cleaned every corner of our small home, each broken tile and cracked window pane, working like a whirlwind. In the past, I would have danced away my frustration, but with children, that was impossible.

I read in the *Shawnee Morning News* that two more people had died from the dust in the Panhandle. "Clouds of silt continue to sweep stricken areas...a constant threat to the respiratory organs." This horrible weather wreaked havoc on Oklahomans' lives. My heart sank. What else could go wrong? I shut my eyes, and discouragement nagged my mind. Hopelessness threatened to close in. If God was testing me, I was failing.

Later, when Fremont didn't notice the extra-clean house or my desperate feelings, it seemed my life slowed to a snail's pace. I didn't fully understand that his struggles to keep the business and feed our family were preoccupying him. Instead, I thought he didn't love me anymore. The housework frenzy over, I flopped to the opposite extreme. Exhaustion overtook me. I slept late, barely able to rise from bed to fix meals or take care of the children.

One evening, Fremont came home from work and found dishes piled in the kitchen sink and clothes strewn throughout the house. Our children, still in pajamas, played on the floor right outside our bedroom door. He must have known something was wrong. Last week, I had been prickly as a cactus. Now, I was listless as a sloth. My moodiness had grown worse since my parents' breakup. I wasn't sure how long my marriage could survive the stress. Or I, for that matter. Did life have to be this difficult? And the weather? I felt like Moses in the desert.

I heard my husband washing the dishes and cleaning up as best as he could. He fed the children and tucked them into bed, kissing them goodnight and promising to read *Alice in Wonderland* the next evening.

When he ventured into our bedroom, I was curled up under the quilt. I lay motionless. He tiptoed to my side of the bed and sat next to me. I smelled the dust and grease from his long day at work.

"Honey, what's wrong?" he whispered.

"Nothing," I mumbled. "I'm not feeling well."

Fremont drew on the patience he'd cultivated, the patience of Job. "You can talk to me."

"I'm sorry. I just can't believe my parents." I spoke weakly. "How could they want a divorce after being married for so long? Is anyone ever happy?" I longed to share my confusion about wanting to leave our marriage one moment and then the next, needing it so badly it hurt. I wanted to talk about how I wanted to be loyal to Papa but was losing faith in him. My emotions went up and down like a bouncing ball. I couldn't talk about any of these things. I just didn't know how.

"I don't understand either," said Fremont, "but we can't let their problems control our lives. Sometimes mighty bad things happen, but we can't give up because of difficulties."

I turned my head toward him. He cradled my chin in his strong hand, leaned over, and kissed my forehead. Tears ran down my face. He wiped them off and wrapped his arms around me, holding me as I cried. I had held the tears in for too long. I sobbed like a cry baby.

"Why does life have to be so hard?" I looked into his blue eyes, eyes that looked about as sad as I felt.

"I don't know, honey." He held my gaze. "But it helps to remember what the Bible says. God promises to be with us always, no matter what."

"Right now, that's hard to believe."

Fremont drew me to him again.

"Please, don't leave me." I cried and tightened my arms around his neck. "Don't ever leave me like Papa left Mama. Don't run off with another woman. Promise?"

"I love you, Sibyl. More than you know." He stroked my hair. "I would never do that."

I had never actually told Fremont I loved him. My family didn't use those words. But a warm feeling spread through me like sunshine. "I love you, too," I said. "I should have told you a long time ago, but it's true. I love you, Mr. Fremont Pope." I wanted to bury my head on his shoulder and cry, it felt so wonderful to share my heart.

He pushed the hair back from my face and smiled his tender smile. Our eyes met. "I knew all along you loved me, but it's mighty good to hear you say it. I won't ever leave you. I don't want to be with anyone but you. I'm right here." A familiar grin flickered across his face. "After all, you're my Cinderella."

"In this old dress? Oh, Fremont, what are you thinking?"

"You're my Cinderella in cleaning clothes?" His eyebrows lifted. "And I'm not going anywhere, even if you try to run me off with a pogo stick. I'm staying."

I did not deserve him. I truly did not deserve a man as good as Fremont.

Chapter Forty-Six

Fremont and I sat in rockers on my in-laws front porch watching Dad Pope push our children in a swing hanging from the Catalpa tree. When the children tired of that, he rolled them up and down the hill in the wheelbarrow pretending it was a racing motorcar. The wheelbarrow tumbled over and the children rolled onto the grass in a heap.

"Must have hit a rock," mumbled Dad Pope as he picked them up off the ground. "Come on now, let's sing, 'You are my Sunshine, my only Sunshine'!"

Even though he was thin and scrawny, Judson had more energy than the rest of the family could muster. It challenged everyone to keep the little guy out of mischief. His temperament was nothing like any child's I had ever seen. Not a year old yet, he threw tantrums normally reserved for two-year-olds. He screamed. He grabbed hair. I couldn't let him out of my sight because either a table would be knocked over or dishes broken or some such disaster.

The children tired out their grandfather. Fremont's dad wore beat-up overalls and a worn brown hat covered his bald spot, tufts of white hair sticking out. He plopped down on the porch swing while Fremont and I pulled our chairs around him. I smiled at his overalls, wondering if he had a half a dozen identical ones in his closet.

Earlier that afternoon, Mother Pope had prepared us a delicious meal. She set everything just so on the table, using real napkins even when no company came. We devoured the tasty chicken and dumplings, served with green beans from their garden that she had canned the previous year and flavored with bacon, along with fresh hot buttered rolls. Fremont's family might not have much money, but his mother knew how to prepare a luscious meal.

Mother Pope pushed open the screen door and stepped out carrying bowls heaped with blackberries from the vines by the creek. They were topped with fresh sweet cream.

"Son, Betsy's got enough milk for all of us," said Dad Pope. "Between that and the eggs from the chickens, we'll make it through this here depression." For a man with no more than a third-grade education, he seemed confident. "If the wind stops blowing away all the topsoil out on the farm, I can plant again. Those seeds I planted last week have already flown to Alabama."

"We're doing mighty fine, considering the times," agreed Fremont. "And if you buy another one of Butler's hogs to butcher, we'll make it through even better, long as you don't eat it all up yourself."

Dad Pope chuckled and pulled at his mustache. A long chain tucked into a bib pocket of his overalls linked a brass watch on the side. He unclipped the chain, wound the watch and handed it to Margaret. She held the sparkling, mechanical trophy in her chubby hands and listened to it with great fascination.

"Remember that time in Wynnewood, Fremont?" Dad Pope asked. "About twenty-six or so. Wiley Post used to fly in to visit his parents. He landed in a meadow strip beside the house. He needed gas from Uncle Hugh's filling station before he headed back."

As I listened, I realized where Fremont got his flamboyant story-telling traits.

"I remember, Cousin Olin and I would take gas out to him," Fremont continued. "We kept a fifty-five-gallon drum on the back of our truck to hand-pump gas. Wiley'd put about ten gallons in his plane. One time, we stood around talking and he said, 'Would you boys like to go for a spin?' Was I ever excited! Olin and I piled in together on the passenger side of that little plane so fast the engine sputtered. We circled the town, and this old world looked mighty tiny from up there." He laughed. "I never saw such a sight."

"Too bad about what happened to Wiley," Dad said. "Least he died doing what he liked to do. Hey, Mother, this here's about the best blackberries and cream I've ever ate," Dad Pope said licking his lips and looked at me. "Don't you agree?"

"Fiddlesticks." Mother Pope stood and dusted off her apron. "You're just asking for more." She marched into the house to refill the bowls with blackberries.

"Those were the days." Dad Pope said. "We looked out over fresh cut hay in Waco, knowing the winter wouldn't bite us, 'cause we was nestled down in a cozy little cabin." He stopped talking as he looked down at Judson, who was playing on the ground with something shiny. Dad's watch. The child had somehow gotten ahold of the treasure and was covering it with dirt.

"Good gosh almighty! I declare, that child needs to be tied up." Dad scuttled down the steps. He picked up his watch and dusted it off. "Don't know as you'll ever be able to control him." He belly-laughed as he set Judson on Fremont's lap.

I watched, chagrined by Judson's behavior, thinking I should have watched him closer, but a stronger thought emerged. Dad Pope did not yank the boy up in anger and yell about what a rotten kid he was like Papa would have done. Our two fathers were as different as cushions and concrete.

The whole Pope family seemed secure and content in their love. Happy, even. I had never known people so confident, and I supposed it came from their faith. Mother Pope always spoke of Jesus as if he were swinging on the front porch beside us.

Mother's words broke into my reverie. "Remember when Fremont was the size of a jack rabbit? I rode that old quarter horse around the countryside raising money? Weren't we a sight?"

Everyone laughed except me. My thoughts kept me tied to my family's trials.

Mother Pope recalled the story about raising money for the Oklahoma Baptist College's first women's dormitory. "Our school needed a place for women to live and I was bound and determined to help raise money. We did it, too. Women would take a nickel or two of their sewing money and give it to the cause." She seemed to sit a little taller as she recalled those days. "Do you remember riding with me that summer?"

Fremont tilted his head back and laughed loudly. "How could I forget? I held on for dear life. We galloped from farm to farm like the fields were on fire!"

The Popes' faith had helped them through many challenges. Meanwhile my family, which seemed to have little to no faith, was falling apart, crumbling like a dried-up piece of cornbread. My mama's pain oozed onto everyone while Papa seemed indifferent and cold. My father's noble philosophy, along with his idea of a perfect world, now seemed like a fairy tale. My siblings each dealt with the hurt in their own ways. I tried to ignore how my parents' difficulties were affecting Fremont and me, but there were still days when it disarmed me and I couldn't get out of bed.

I felt torn between these two ways of life, between the positive and negative, trust and doubt. I could no longer hide my pain as we sat there with Fremont's family. I couldn't compliment Mother Pope on her berries and cream like nothing else mattered. I couldn't understand their contentment in the face of all the bad things happening in the world. I couldn't see how they could be so confident when their land and seeds were blowing away like chaff. And here they were, still so happy.

I wanted to be like that, content in the face of difficulty. An ache overwhelmed me. The pain boiled inside me until I could no longer stand it. I jumped up out of the chair and ran into the house.

Mother Pope followed me. "Are you all right, child? I know your parents' problems must have you all upset."

I could only nod. If she only knew.

"This is not your battle, Sibyl. It's theirs. Trust in the Lord, 'cause He's still there for you."

Deep down I felt like my parents' battle was also my battle. After all that had happened—my untimely pregnancy, my marriage, the crop-destroying weather, the people living like refugees, the world falling apart. And now my parents' divorcing? I didn't think I could endure much more.

Mother Pope wrapped me in her ample arms. "Don't give in to despair, child. Keep your head up. God has not abandoned you."

Chapter Forty-Seven
October 1935

Papa couldn't hide from the sheriff forever. Malcolm Calvis Trimble, as an employee of the State Banking Department, had to have an address on file somewhere. As we already knew, he was living on Ninth Street in Oklahoma City. The deputy finally found him and served him in person.

Two weeks later Papa showed up on my doorstep, livid. I'd been waiting for him to get served, but not to come see me.

"Your mother's insane," he said. "Why would she want a divorce? Can't she be content with the way things are? A divorce will damage my career, and she'll get even less than she does now. She's being unreasonable." He shook his head and stopped pacing. He grimaced at me and shook his finger. "In times like these, she should be grateful for whatever I give her."

Should Mama suck in her pride and cooperate more with Papa? Would that bring in the much-needed funds? Between Marjorie's contribution, the church's benevolence, and our supply of garden goods, she had survived. Would it be better to subpoena Papa for money instead of a divorce?

"That reminds me, Sibyl. I need your help. I've been asked to testify in Commissioner Bartlett's latest court case. It's going to take some time. But that's not your problem. I need your help at the divorce proceedings. Your mother seems to want this. I do not. I was perfectly willing to support her as a wife and live separately. This divorce situation will jeopardize my job. It already has caused no little embarrassment."

I froze. Looked down at the worn linoleum. "What are you asking me to do?"

"I need you to testify on my behalf."

I wanted to walk away. Ignore the request. "But Mama needs financial assistance, and Blanche and Frances still need to be taken care of."

"You have no obligation to help your mother or your sisters. This is not your argument, nor your problem. After all, you and your husband would never have gotten a bank loan without me."

And there it was. The favor I'd always known he'd ask for, as if helping his own daughter was a bartering chip. But I'd known, hadn't I, that taking Papa's help would eventually cost me. But this? Could I go against my mother, my sisters, in order to satisfy my father's demands? I was twenty-six-years old, married with two children, and still my whole life revolved around my parents' marital problems.

"Papa, I don't know. I'll think about what to do. And I'll talk to Fremont."

Would I have to choose which side to support? How could I do that?

I should have been able to detach from the emotional effects of their hatred, but I could not. My heart felt torn, pulled apart by parents who couldn't see any needs beyond their own. I fought off depression for the sake of my children and tried to make our home life happy, crying in Fremont's arms at night.

Predictably, Papa didn't like the turn of events. On October fourteenth, he filed a Motion to Squash Summons. I read the whole petition at Mama's house. While it didn't give a good reason to stop the divorce, it did state that the summons had not been issued, served, and returned according to the law. Whatever that meant.

Anger spewed from Mama's mouth like spittle. Unfortunately, my young sister Blanche mimicked Mama down to the intonation and syllable.

"That dirty no-good scum," Mama spat out. "How could I have ever married such a man?"

"Yeah. That dirty no-good scum," came Blanche's reply.

"He deserves that woman. She's just a gold-digger, and he's stupid enough to fall for it."

"You're right." Blanche said. "She's just a gold-digger."

I could have slid under the table. How could bitterness have been imbedded so deeply? Would Mama or Blanche or Frances ever get over the rejection?

Five days later, Mama's lawyers filed an Order for Alimony, which ordered Papa to pay $100 per month to support Mama and his two youngest children. He was also ordered to pay the court clerk fees of $25, reimburse Mama another $10 for court costs and pay $100 of Mama's attorney fees. Even I had to squint at that bit of bravery. Clearly her lawyer didn't know Papa's temper like we did.

Mama was elated when she read the order. Almost as if she'd waited all this time to get back at Papa. I hoped this was the beginning of the end. Tension felt like drawstrings on the whole family, strangling the good times we'd once had. I couldn't see how life would ever get back to normal after this.

Papa was given ten days to make an itemized and notarized list of stocks, bonds, deposits, autos, real estate, and mineral or other interests owned with the value.

Marjorie, who lived with Papa now, should have warned us that Papa was furious. I could tell, of course, when Mama handed me the Motion to Modify. The one his lawyer filed in response to her Order.

Papa stated he was not financially able to comply with the order.

He *had* been giving sufficient provision to Mama.

He *had* been taking care of and providing for the children.

He *had* provided a home.

He *had* been contributing approximately $50 per month to the family.

He *had* been unemployed in the past year and incurred certain expenses and debts.

His new job as an examiner for the Oklahoma Banking Department paid only $175 per month, seventy-five dollars less than he'd made before.

He *had* no other property to earn money and could not borrow, therefore, he was unable to do what the motion asked.

Then his attorney asked for thirty days to comply.

I looked up at Mama. She pulled at strands of hair and raised her eyebrows. The words I read tasted bitter, so unsure I was that it included the whole truth.

I shook my head slowly. Papa never liked anyone else being in control. He thought he would have the last say, but he underestimated his angry, desperate, rejected wife.

Chapter Forty-Eight

During all the back and forth motions, Marjorie fell ill. Mama called me worried about her, her voice ragged. I went over and telephoned Papa, asking for details while Mama fidgeted by my side. He was nebulous but wouldn't give particulars, except to say she had been taken to the hospital.

Mama burst into tears and I handed her my handkerchief. "I'll pay for a taxi to the city," I said, knowing Fremont would agree if he was here. This was an emergency. I wrote the hospital name and address down on a slip of paper and handed it to Mama. The taxi arrived within the hour and I watched her leave.

Mama came to my house the next morning, Larry trailing behind her.

I looked at her, my brow scrunched with unspoken questions.

She immediately explained. "Marjorie had an appendix operation but she'll recover. She doesn't seem herself yet. Larry was sitting in the hospital lounge alone. I don't know how long he'd been there. Probably all day and night. Kelley's disappeared again. That's why I brought Larry home."

I took a deep breath. My sister. What could I do for her? For her little son?

Mama let me know I should visit Marjorie. "She's crying a lot. Maybe you can get more information out of her. Help her in some way."

"I'll ask Fremont to take me."

The next day, Fremont drove me to Deaconess Hospital in Oklahoma City so we could visit her. As we drove, I noticed the many oak trees on the rolling hills along the way had already lost their leaves. Limbs were laid bare. Life was laid bare.

Fremont sat in the waiting room with our children while I went into the hospital room. Mama had visited the day before and brought Larry back. He had been sitting in the hospital lounge. Kelley had disappeared again. She told me Marjorie had had an appendix operation but would recover easily enough.

Marjorie's story was a little different than that. I hugged her and sat in a chair by the side of her bed. The hospital smell of paraldehyde and carbolic cleaning soap overwhelmed me.

"I ran to Papa when I discovered I was pregnant again." She whispered to the sickly air.

"Wait. Pregnant? I thought you had appendicitis?" I tilted my head in doubt. "So you're going to have a baby?"

"That's not what I'm trying to tell you." She sat up on the side of the bed, her thin blue hospital gown flowing past her knees. Her face was pale as white cotton.

"Maybe you should start from the first."

"I figured Papa's money could fix anything, so I told him about having another baby."

"What did Kelley say when you told him? You told him, didn't you?"

"That's when he took off for Phoenix. Ran off as quick as a jack rabbit. Said he doesn't need another kid. I should have known he'd leave me. So I *had* to go to Papa. I figured he'd understand my predicament better than Mama. That's why Larry and I moved into the spare bedroom at Papa and Gladys' apartment."

"Oh," I said. "Your move to the City makes more sense now."

"One day, when we were sitting on the front porch, Papa said, 'I'm not sure you can handle another baby, Marjorie. You're having a hard time taking care of Larry.'" I agreed, of course. So then he told me that I should do something about it."

"What did he mean by *do something*?" I asked uncertain I wanted to hear. My stomach lurched.

Marjorie spoke quietly. "You know exactly what he meant. I told Papa I'd think about it. And you know him. 'A girl in your

243

predicament has no time to think about anything.'" Marjorie mimicked his stern, convincing baritone.

I didn't respond. My sister continued to talk like she needed to get the whole story off her chest.

"I didn't want to be on the streets. I don't have a job and Kelley has skedaddled. Papa said he'd kick me out if I didn't listen to him. You can understand that, right? Without a man, alone and pregnant." She swallowed hard and turned her face away from me. She looked utterly helpless in the sterile white hospital bed. "Not that I wanted this child so much."

"Marj," I whispered.

She bawled, "I—I don't know if I can tell you."

"It's okay."

"Now don't go getting religious on me. You'd never do anything like this, would you? Of course not, you already have two children. But what's so wrong with me waiting a few years for another one?" Marjorie crawled back into the bed and covered her face with a pillow. I could hear her sobbing. I scooted over and sat on the bed beside her and placed my hand on her shoulder.

"There's nothing wrong with wanting that," I said slowly, though my heart beat like a criminal on the run like it couldn't survive more bad news and wanted out of there. I understood how my heart felt.

"I've overheard enough talk from girls who've taken care of this...problem. Slippery elm will do the trick," Marjorie said when she calmed down and glanced up at me.

I'd known it was coming, known from the moment she'd confessed the pregnancy. Still, to have her confirm it. The image of sweet little Larry filled my mind's eye. A little brother or sister who may have looked just like him, or like my own beautiful children. That baby would never be now. Never have a chance at life. Never have a chance at love.

I looked down at my little sister. A thousand terrible decisions had led to this, but who was I to judge? I'd made my share of bad decisions. I understood her fear. What was done was done, and right now, my little sister needed me. I wrapped my arms around her and pulled her to my chest.

"It was so painful," she said. "I lay in bed most of the day fighting the worst cramps. It was like knives stabbing me. And the bleeding...I thought it would never stop." Marjorie leaned away from me and wrapped her arms around her middle like she was experiencing it all over again.

I stood, moved around the bed and went to the window. I'd considered it, hadn't I? Considered how easy it would be to just end the pregnancy. My life would be so different now. But what if I'd never had Margaret? Or Judson? Think of all the joy I would have missed.

I turned back to my sister. "So then what happened?"

"Guess Papa came home from work and saw how bad I was. Said I was white as a sheet. I wanted Mama, but I was afraid to ask for her, knowing how they're supposed to go to court soon. He and Gladys drove me to the hospital, but I don't remember the trip."

Marjorie flung back on the pillow, her face and neck pale, her hand hanging motionless over the side of the bed. "Gladys called her own doctor, a German woman friend. She was trying to help. The doc operated and repaired the damage, something about having to tie my tubes. I don't know what that means, but Papa said I'd never be in this mess again."

I cringed at my sister's pain. It bonded me to her, pain deeper than I had ever endured.

"I lost the baby, sis. I lost him."

Marjorie stayed in the hospital several days. When she got out, she moved back in with Papa.

She visited Mama the next week and helped me line a matchbox with silk and place a slip of paper containing the baby's name and birthdate inside. I wrote out the twenty-third Psalm on another sheet of paper.

We put on our heavy wool coats and slipped out to the back yard.

Marjorie held the box while I dug a hole with a shovel. After a moment of silence, we buried the box among the irises in what had once been Papa's pampered backyard.

Afterward, Marjorie pretended nothing happened, but when I looked in her eyes, I could see a sadness that had not been there before.

Chapter Forty-Nine

My parents' divorce turned even nastier, which I hadn't thought possible. Details of the pending divorce came out in the social page of the *Shawnee Morning News*: "State Bank Aid Sued for Divorce." In a town like Shawnee, even a small classified ad prompted hours of speculation. Few people divorced in our area of the country, so this was shocking, not just to my family, but to the whole town.

Everyone knew my family. In our hometown, we were almost as well-known as one of my favorite radio singers, Rudy Vallée, whose wife, Fay, claimed their short marriage was doomed from the start. I hoped my parents' divorce did not end up as such a public hullabaloo.

People picked sides. Tempers flared. Most of the men understood Papa's complaints about a nagging wife and believed a socialite woman could not focus on making a happy home. However, most also agreed that leaving Mama destitute with children under her wing hardly constituted the proper thing to do, especially for a well-known, wealthy man. Town women sympathized with Mama while speculating about why she lost her man.

I was at the house visiting my family when I read in the paper that, along with everything else Mama had demanded, she'd accused him of "extreme cruelty" and asked for custody of the children.

"Extreme cruelty!" I exclaimed as I threw the paper down on the coffee table. "Mama, did you really charge Papa with extreme cruelty?"

"The attorney drafted the petition," Mama said, sitting on the edge of her chair. "Kenneth Abernathy is a state legislator and a good

247

lawyer. I'll do whatever it takes to set food on this table and get some decent clothes for the girls. That man brought them into the world, and it's his responsibility to support them. It's been months, and he still hasn't come to his senses."

"You're right, Mama." I got up and paced the floor. "But custody of Calvis? You know he won't come back here. And Papa should be supporting you. I don't understand why he's doing this."

"I've lived with that man for years," she said. "I should know him. In the end, if I don't completely destroy his reputation, he'll at least take care of his kids. I hope."

"Mama wanted to name Gladys the tramp as a correspondent in the divorce," said Blanche, "but Papa raised Cain about it. Personally, I think Mama should subpoena her. And, get this, Papa offered money to our neighbor Mrs. Collins to tell some dirt on Mama."

"There wasn't any dirt to get, I'm sure." I turned to face Blanche. "But why are you so involved with this, young lady? It's not your concern."

"Someone has to watch out for Mama." Blanche jutted out her chin. "And I'm going to testify, too. African lions couldn't keep me off the stand."

"I don't want to make your papa angry," Mama said.

It was too late for that.

"He'll do what is right," I said. "He'll come to his senses."

She sat at the dining room table, her head in her hands. "Sibyl, I have a request. You probably already know this, but the girls and I need money. More than your papa is willing to give. He's a skinflint and claims he never wanted his two youngest daughters. He said he never asked for these children and, therefore, should not have to support them. I should have expected this of him, but I didn't."

"You know I don't have any money to give you. But maybe I can help with sewing, or…"

"I need you to testify that your papa mistreated you and the children."

"Mama, I can't do that! It's a flat-out lie!"

"Not exactly. Remember when he spanked you so hard you couldn't sit down?"

I had to be careful. Mama's bitterness could easily overflow into my life. Her hostility toward Papa tainted every word she said.

I didn't know if she'd ever recover.

"The time I stole your earrings and gave them away? I deserved being disciplined over stealing. He didn't *mistreat* me."

"You don't have to say he mistreated you," Mama said, "Just fudge a bit. Make it sound like we're desperate. We will be if he doesn't help us out. I want to see him poor as a beggar on the street. He doesn't deserve to keep a penny. If he can support a floozy woman up in the City, then by golly, he can take care of me for the rest of my life."

"But Mama...."

"And since your papa knows the judges and attorneys in this town so well, and since he's a member of the Masons, we may not have a fat chance at getting cow feed. I need your help."

Chapter Fifty
November 1935

The court appearance was scheduled for the next day. November sixteenth. Town people expected a long, drawn-out affair. All five of us Trimble children had been asked to testify for either Mama or Papa. None of us wanted to.

Mama's living room felt like a funeral parlor, quiet and pensive. Everyone in the family preoccupied with the coming divorce.

"Frances and Blanche will testify for me about Papa's atrocities," said Mama. "They can describe the lack of food and clothing in the house since he left. They also might be asked if Papa hit them. I can certainly say he hit me."

Frances, only eight-years-old and too young to understand, echoed Mama. "I can say that, Mama. There's no food or heat in the house."

My heart ached. A child should never have to say they had no food. They should never be forced to choose between her parents. I would never ask that of my children, no matter what happened.

Blanche's anger over Papa's rejection instilled such a profound hatred in her that she would gladly take Mama's side. She was disgusted with him. "You bet I will say whatever it takes to get money from that old man. He doesn't deserve to keep a thing."

Even with her lawyer's help, the verdict looked bleak. The way Mama saw it, she was destitute. No longer was she able to gallivant about like before he'd moved out. The way Mama saw it, she'd done no wrong in their almost twenty-five years of marriage. She deserved to take everything Papa had.

I struggled with what to do. Our family seemed shattered and I went into mourning just like the saints weeping over Billy Sunday's death last week. We could use a spiritual leader about now.

I wavered over whether to testify or not, and whether to testify for Mama or Papa. I loved them both. Obviously Mama needed money. And Papa had done her wrong. Treated his children wrong. Could the judge be trusted to be fair? I felt guilty for not wanting to do as Mama asked, but what she asked me to do wasn't honest. I couldn't exaggerate. As the court date drew nearer I prayed for courage and confidence to make these decisions. Decisions that might tear my heart and our family to shreds.

I hardly slept the night before the court appearance. We had already dropped the children off to spend a few days with the Popes. About two in the morning, I sat up in bed. Since my tossing and turning had kept Fremont awake and he sat up, too. My dilemma felt like the looming shadow of a noose outside the cell of a condemned man.

"How about a cup of coffee?" he offered.

"It's the middle of the night."

"And you can't sleep, so we might as well get up and talk."

I grabbed a housecoat and pulled it on. We went into the kitchen, and I plopped down in a dining room chair while Fremont started water boiling for coffee. He always made it too strong, but tonight I didn't care what it tasted like. He also made us each a piece of toast, mine perfect and his burnt to his liking.

"What am I to do? What should I say? I worry so about her, about my sisters."

"The decision's yours. I can't tell you what to do, but I'll be praying for you."

Fremont's stability could calm my frazzled nerves. This night my emotions ebbed and flowed like the runaway wind.

"Papa will be furious if I let him down. I've sided with him all my life. I can't face his anger. Yes, he was wrong to cheat on Mama. He failed to be the husband and father he should have been. On the other hand, he helped us get the bank loan. And, he's my Papa." I didn't say

251

that I felt a deep loyalty to him because of the promise I made many years ago.

"He'll be your Papa no matter what happens."

"Papa said we owe him, that we should stand up on his behalf. He thinks highly of you, Fremont, or he wouldn't have helped us buy the filling station. I don't know. Maybe he has reasons for what he's done. Maybe it was all a misunderstanding."

My husband's eyebrows rose. "A misunderstanding?"

I nodded. My toast still in front of me. The thought of food turned my stomach.

Fremont stood and brushed bread crumbs from his fingers. He finished making the coffee and placed a cup in front of me. "Have you talked to Calvis and Marjorie?"

"They're going to testify for Papa." I was not surprised at their responses, but I had to hear from them directly myself.

Calvis had been adamant. "I have no choice," he had said. "Living off Papa is awkward, especially since Gladys doesn't care to have me around, but what else can I do? Papa promised to send me to college. Even Mama understands why I have to stand up and testify for him."

Marjorie had recently left the hospital, still weak from her *operation*. Medical bills had been mounting, too much for her to pay. "Without Papa's help, we'd be out on the streets, practically starving to death. Mama can't help me. Papa has more money than anyone I know, and he promised to pay my bills. Said if I testify for him, he'd help me financially in other ways too, like rent money. I don't have a choice but to help Papa, no matter what he's done."

I turned to Fremont. "What about Frances and Blanche? He should be helping them. And how do we know he'll really help Marjorie financially? So many questions."

Fremont shook his head as if he had no answers. I continued. "With two siblings supporting each parent, and considering I'm the oldest, my testimony might make a difference in the court's decision. I'm torn. Neither one is in the right and neither one is completely wrong. I never asked to be in the middle of their war."

Fremont reached across the table and took my hand. "Think about it, Sibyl. You don't have to be a part of their war. You just have to answer for yourself and do what is right." But what was right?

Chapter Fifty-One

The Pottawatomie County Courthouse, newly built earlier in the year, was an imposing three-story stone building designed by Davis & Sons on North Broadway. It sat on the edge of Woodland Park next to the Carnegie Library. The front steps led up to three double doors separated by fluted stone panels. Above the doors were elaborate windows framed in metal with medallions depicting the head of an Indian, the scales of justice, and the head of a pioneer. The day was cool but dry.

Inside the building, Fremont and I walked up the concrete steps to the second floor to find Court Room Two. Our footsteps echoed. The ceiling tall and the concrete walls cold.

Although we'd agreed to arrive thirty minutes before the session began, we did not make it that early, thanks to my usual tardiness. Papa was nowhere in sight, so we walked to where my mother and youngest sisters stood in front of the double doors of the court room. The stern look on Mama's face forbade any discussion.

As we prepared to go inside the court room, I motioned for Fremont to wait as I went downstairs for a drink of water. I needed to be by myself for a few minutes. I needed to breathe and tell myself to remain calm.

I had walked down the stairs and rounded the corner when I saw her. Well-endowed and overdressed. Smoking a cigarette beside the water fountain.

She was leaning against the wall, her coiffured hair in curls on top of her head. Her pocketbook dangled delicately from her shoulder.

She looked as immaculate as if she'd just stepped out of *Time Magazine*.

I didn't want a confrontation, so I turned to go back upstairs.

"Well, if it isn't the eldest daughter."

With a sigh, I walked toward her. We'd never had a conversation, so I had no idea what to expect.

"Gladys? I'm surprised to see you here today." It seemed bizarre that Papa would bring his girlfriend to his divorce proceedings.

"Wouldn't miss it for the world. I'll be glad when your Papa's free of your mother. She's out to strip him of everything, you know. A bitter woman's never satisfied."

"Maybe my mother has reason to be bitter."

"Don't worry, girl. She's never going to win. Your father and I talked it over. He won't let her ruin his career and his reputation. I'll see to that." She blew smoke in my face. A vile taste rose in my mouth, almost as if I had chewed on a rotten leg of lamb. The audacity.

"Your Papa said you were on our side in this, so I don't mind telling you. He'll give her nothing." Gladys's smile was wide, and I was sure if I looked closely enough, I'd see dollar signs in her eyes. "She doesn't deserve it. Actually, he said he never loved her anyway. Couldn't. How could he love a nagging, cold, hard-nosed woman who only cares about herself?"

My temper rose. "How can you say that about my mother? You're the one who took him away from our family."

"Oh no, girlie, your mommy pushed him away. I'm simply here to make him happy."

I rushed down the hall to the ladies' restroom, vomit rushing up through my throat. In the restroom, I almost fell against the wall, shaking uncontrollably, and threw up. How could this have happened to my family? To my parents? Regardless of what that woman had said, she was at least partly to blame.

No. I clenched my teeth. *No.* I would not let Papa or his *lady friend* get the better of me.

I stood up straight and walked back up the stairs. Fremont, I thought. I need to be with Fremont.

Chapter Fifty-Two

Fremont was waiting by the courtroom door. I was still shaking and my stomach ached. The large hall was empty, Mama must have gone inside. Thankful she could not see my distress, I walked up to Fremont, waiting in the corner.

Fremont looked at me curiously, put his arm around me, steadying me, before pushing open the heavy wooden door. People were streaming in, looking for a place to sit. We slid onto benches at the back of public gallery. Friends? Neighbors? People who knew about my family's disgrace? My stomach turned nauseous again. I hoped not to be caught up in the dramatic performance at the front.

Mama, Blanche, and Frances sat in the front on the left side of the courtroom. They all wore dark dresses with matching hats. Papa sat on the right side dressed in a suit with a double-breasted waistcoat and a pocket handkerchief and matching tie, Daddy Warbucks without Little Orphan Annie to change his attitude. Calvis and Marjorie sat immediately behind him. They wore church-going clothes. Larry, his rowdy hair slicked down, sat on Marjorie's lap.

I scanned the room. People crowded in close on the packed benches. The overflow stood along the back. News of the prominent, wealthy man and his estranged wife had been broadcast statewide. Few people had experienced such a publicized divorce hearing. Around the perimeters of the courtroom, cameras were set up and popping flashes. Although there had been a drive to ban cameras in the courtroom, it had not reached Shawnee. Newspaper reporters lounged together with pipes in their mouths and pens and sketchbooks in hand. The audience waited and grumbled.

Papa's paramour sauntered into the room and walked up to sit beside Papa. He put his arm around her and pulled her close. Mama's eyes flared with indignation. How could he degrade her by allowing Gladys to be present?

Things got worse when Mama's attorney failed to show up. A young associate, probably her lawyer's son, who I was told had just joined the firm, rushed down the aisle. He slid into place and leaned over to whisper to Mama.

A gloomy silence descended over the room as the black-clad judge entered. People stood, wordlessly, shuffling bodies the only sound while the judge walked in and settled in his place. Then, the bailiff directed us to sit.

Papa's lawyer made his opening statement. His bald head shone from where we sat. His voice grew louder and louder as he berated Mama, going on about what a bad wife and mother she had been. From his tone, you'd have thought that Mama was on trial for murder! She hung her head as if avoiding a physical blow. It was hard to see her like that. More accusations followed. My heart sank at the display, and as the hearing went on, I wanted to scream, "Don't do this. Don't do this to each other. Don't do this to our family!"

Blanche was the first of my siblings called to the stand. My fourteen-year-old sister stepped up and swore an oath to tell the truth. After a few preliminary questions, Mama's substitute lawyer asked, "Did your father ever hit you?"

"You bet he did. He slapped me so hard I thought my head would spin. Of course, a head can't spin around in circles, nor can it come off, but if heads could, mine would have been rolling on the ground!"

The audience roared, voices resounding off the wall.

Blanche's youthful, vivid words brought laughter from the spectators. It seemed like the hatred emanating from such a young girl tickled the crowd. I wanted them all to stop laughing. It wasn't funny. I listened to her caustic remarks as the questions continued. I squeezed Fremont's hand until he nudged me and I realized what I was doing. I let up but still I clung to him, grateful for his presence. I looked at poor Marjorie sitting behind Papa.

Then I saw Mama chasing Larry. The three-year-old, unruly as always, ran through the courtroom, clambering through spectators' feet and under the benches. Mama dashed around and caught him. She carried him back to Marjorie and said loudly enough to be heard at the back, "Keep him here!" Poor Marjorie. Kelley had disappeared from her life when she needed him most.

After Blanche stepped down from the witness stand, Frances's name was called. She balked and turned her face to hide on Mama's shoulder. I stiffened. She was just a little girl. How could Mama put her through this? She shook her curly head of hair and in a fragile baby voice said, "I don't want to."

The attorney asked her again.

"No. No!" she screeched. "I can't."

The room became quiet as people watched my youngest sister cling to Mama. Her anguish broke my heart. I wiped tears from my cheeks as Mama relented and asked the attorney to release Frances from testifying.

Mama looked back at me, her eyes wide and questioning. But how could I testify on her behalf? She would gloat for the rest of my life if I took her side. I could see bitterness in her rigid face and anger at anyone who disagreed with her. And what about Papa? Was I ready to spurn the only father I knew? Lose the close relationship we'd had since I was a child? I didn't agree with his principles any more, but was I still loyal to him?

Mama turned away, and the procedures continued.

Papa's defense began, and Marjorie was called to the witness stand. Her pale, beautiful face was as still as a faded orchid. It was clear she hadn't fully recovered from surgery. I bit my lip as I listened to the questions posed to her. Marjorie's voice was weak and she never looked in Mama's direction. Marjorie stated that her two younger sisters were doing fine without financial help from Papa. In a monotone voice, she testified, "Papa has always been a good father to me and the other children." Her comment left a nasty taste in my mouth.

Next, Calvis was called to the stand. By that point, the court hearing had become a shouting match as the attorneys argued at each other and people voiced their opinions out loud. The judge pounded his gavel and threatened to throw the nosiest interlopers out of the courtroom.

As Calvis walked to the front, he was thinner than the last time I saw him. He nodded no, declining to answer any questions, saying he could not choose between his parents. He said nothing more. His head drooped, his eyes unable to meet anyone's. Then he stepped down from the witness box.

Papa's young lawyer stood and faced my way. He called my name as a witness to come to the front. I let go of Fremont's hand and started walking down the aisle between the wooden benches. I stopped at the front railing by the entrance to the stand.

I was speechless. Mama needed money and the girls needed to be taken care of, but my childish promise and devotion to Papa held me captive.

I felt resentment over being expected to choose one parent over the other. If I chose Papa, Mama's upturned face would refuse to look at me, rancor swelling in her eyes. She would shun me for years. I could imagine Papa's proud, arrogant eyes, gleeful at having inflicted injury, like the winner of a dog fight.

If I chose Mama, she would give her smirky little look and regale her supporters with comments about her children repudiating their father and the disgracefulness of all men. Papa would feel betrayed. He would never trust me again, never sit and have long political chats with me, never discuss the state of the country. He would withdraw any semblance of respect and love, and I would lose him. What was right?

When I looked up, Papa was glaring at me. I knew what he wanted. He had always controlled me with those disapproving glares.

I couldn't let Papa control me now. But I couldn't let Mama control me, either.

I could hear Fremont's encouragement from the night before. I only had to do what was right. And what was that? Neither parent had behaved well. Neither deserved my betrayal of the other. One was unfaithful, the other, petty and hateful. I loved them both, and if they loved me, if they loved my sisters and brother, they would never have asked us to choose. Suddenly, I knew what I had to do.

I would do what was right, not what was expected of me. Even if that meant breaking my mother's heart. Even if it meant breaking a long-ago promise to my father.

I looked at the black-clad judge, then at the attorney who'd summoned me. "I won't testify."

I watched the judge as he processed my words. The decision was left to the judge's discretion. One child had testified for each side. Three children had declined. I prayed he would be wise and fair as I turned and walked back to my seat beside Fremont. I was sliding in when I heard the judge say, "Noted, Sibyl Pope refuses to testify."

Papa was called to the stand, where he offered a final plea. "Judge, I have no responsibility to help them financially. My son, Calvis, will be an adult within months, so he needs no financial support. I never wanted the younger children, and they do not want me. Therefore I do not feel obligated to the youngest two children."

I winced as his words. Somehow, I had held out hope that in the end Papa would live up to the man I'd always believed he was. That in the end, he'd be a man of honor. A man of goodwill.

In the end, my father lost my respect.

It stabbed through everything I had ever believed about his honor and goodwill. Not only did he not want what was best for his children, he didn't care. We were useless to him and his goals; therefore we had no value to him. I felt the bleeding inside, a pain that might never heal.

We waited. The judge wrote hurriedly on paper before walking out the side door. Camera flashed. Reporters scribbled notes. The voyeurs chattered.

Would the judge buy Papa's foolish argument?

The judge walked back into the room, and people quieted instantly. The judge began to speak. He agreed about Calvis, but he decided Papa was indeed responsible to support Frances and Blanche. "I order you, Mr. Trimble, to pay twenty-five dollars per child each month. You must also recompense Mrs. Trimble the nearly twenty-three dollars she has already expended toward attorney fees as well as up to one hundred dollars to cover additional costs. Is that clear?"

Mama received physical custody of my little sisters, a small child-support payment each month, and little else. She would be stricken.

Papa didn't ask for the right to visit Blanche and Frances, but the court granted unsupervised visitation with the girls twice a month.

For their twenty-five years of marriage, Mama received the two houses. One in Wewoka. Papa had not kept up the mortgage payments nor paid the taxes on it, and Mama had no financial resources, so that house would immediately revert back to the bank. She would have to make the mortgage payments on the house on North Beard, where we had lived since 1927. I wasn't sure how she would do this.

Papa kept all the rest of the property, including oil and gas leases and all bank accounts, some of which were not listed in the court documents, or so Mama claimed. The rest of Papa's assets—acreages and many tracts of land and their royalties—were not mentioned in the final divorce.

Despite all her hopes, Mama didn't get what she'd hoped, nor did she get, in my opinion, what she needed. She wouldn't even be able to pay the mortgage on her home with what Papa would pay her.

Meanwhile, Papa and Gladys would be fine. Just fine.

Chapter Fifty-Three

Court adjourned and Papa turned to face the crowd. Anger crimsoned his face. He reared his head back and roared, "My rights have been disregarded! I demand a re-trial!"

Newspapermen swarmed around him, and camera bulbs flashed. I hoped he could keep the proceedings out of the news.

He turned my way, and our eyes linked. His were filled with disgust that bordered on hatred. Mine were filled with tears. I forced myself not to cringe before his hardened face as I had done in the past.

I turned to my husband. "I have to talk to Papa." I rushed over to the side door to catch Papa as he tried to escape the press.

"Papa," I reached him and touched his shoulder. "I know you won't understand, but I had to follow my conscience. Do what I thought was right."

Reporters continued to flash bulbs and scribble notes. Shout questions. Surround him. Time stood still, and I saw an instant of weakness on his face, a feeling of loss or rejection, but it quickly turned into anger. Our relationship would never be the same.

"I don't have time for you." Papa turned and put his arm around Gladys. They rushed down the stairs and out toward the back door of the courthouse, Papa practically pushing her in haste.

I took a deep breath and turned. I saw Calvis and dashed forward to catch him in the hallway. I hadn't seen him for several months, and he was taller than the last time I'd seen him, thinner, with whiskers budding. Gaunt, stiff, and uneasy, he stood with his hands shoved deep in his pockets.

"How are you?" I asked. "Are you all right?"

Calvis shrugged. "Papa said he'd pay for my college. He also said he'd find me a job at the bank. One that pays well," he muttered. "Of course, today may change that."

"Are you going to stay with him?"

"I don't know."

"You can move back home with Mama."

He sighed, shrugged. "I have to go. Papa'll be waiting."

As Calvis disappeared, I watched Marjorie go down the stairway to meet Mama in the lobby. Her eyes were glazed and empty as she held her sleeping son in her arms. She stopped about two feet in front of Mama. She was unsteady on her feet. I stood beside her, wondering if I could catch her if she fell.

Ignoring me, Mama spoke to Marjorie. "Well, what do you have to say?" Her face looked like a stone wall. "Are you proud of yourself?"

"I'm sorry, Mama. I had to do it. Please understand," Marjorie whimpered with a tiny voice. Her eyes filled with tears. I had never seen her meek before. Surely, she hadn't wanted to speak out against Mama.

"Can I come home with you?" Marjorie pleaded.

"Of course not," Mama snapped. "I never want to see you again." She turned and stomped away without another word. Blanche and Frances followed dutifully behind her.

Marjorie shrugged. Head down, she turned toward the rear doors behind the courthouse where Papa would be waiting.

I clenched my teeth and stood in shock as Marjorie left. Anger threatened to engulf me. How could my parents do this? Neither were acting like responsible adults. A flash of heat rose up through me. I wanted to hit something, tear something down, or shake the two of them until they understood their crassness.

My parents had always insisted on a proper public appearance. But now. Now they had publicly shown their true natures. Malicious to each other and their children. I had misunderstood Mama and Papa my entire life.

How could Papa, a man who loudly paraded his principles, have created this situation?

He never applied his beliefs to his personal life. In fact, he didn't apply any of his utopian rhetoric. He theorized but had no strength of character to put his words into practice. Apparently, he didn't care about anyone's welfare but his own.

But I was not my father. And I was also not my mother.

Fremont took my hand and led me out of the courthouse. I felt drained.

A weight lifted from my shoulders—the weight of trying to please Papa. My belief that he wanted the best for others fell away. I wanted no part of his way of life. Just because my parents' marriage was over, my life was not over.

As we walked down Beard Street, I reviewed every word said in court.

I decided to examine Papa, my childhood idol, through more perceptive adult eyes.

Papa's philosophy was flawed. He favored a collective philosophy primarily because it generated a new ruling class, a upper echelon he could take part in. Even a socialist government needed leaders. Papa and his cronies personified what was wrong with the socialistic belief. There was no room for individual freedom and no attempt to permanently improve the lives of everyone, especially those who disagreed with him.

Papa's philosophy of life was different than Dad Pope's.

Papa didn't care about the working class. Dad did. Papa' political ideals offered personal opportunity. Dad helped individuals.

Dad Pope may not have been active in politics, but he generously gave to others. I had never seen a more humble man.

Papa was wrong and Dad was right. I was ashamed I'd ever agreed with Papa's principles and regretted I'd been so desperate to win his approval that I couldn't see his self-centered manipulation. The need for his approval had blinded me.

That night, I knelt beside my bed to pray. Dazed and exhausted I wept bitter tears as I pleaded with the Lord to help my parents and siblings. To help Fremont and I. God was still in control.

I sought guidance so I could follow my heavenly Father, a good father who truly desired the best for His children.

Chapter Fifty-Four
December 1935

"Honey, can you carry this for me?" I turned to Fremont, who stood in our kitchen with his hands behind his back. "I can come back and get it if you don't have time."

"I don't mind at all." Fremont grinned at me. "Gives me a chance to follow you around." He seemed at ease carrying a pan of hot rolls in one hand and a gallon of tea in the other. Margaret and Judson trailed behind us.

I walked beside Fremont with the chicken casserole I'd made, the delicious smell wafting in the air around me, the children following us. We were headed to the house of a church woman who had just had a baby. Mrs. Ellis's husband left to find work in California two months ago, and she had two other children at home to feed. With most people low on supplies, I knew that the Ellis family could use whatever we could spare.

Papa might not be my hero any longer, and Mama might be mad at me for years, but I had Fremont, who stood with me through the mayhem of life. With him by my side, I would never be alone or hungry. This man knew how to cherish his wife and children. He knew how to build a family. And he knew that the love between people was a reflection of the love of God. I didn't have to earn Fremont's love, I just needed to love him as wholeheartedly as he loved me.

We delivered the food, expressed our congratulations, and admired the newborn before we started home. My mind still reeled from what I referred to as the "Trimble Turmoils," but even after all that, I could sense a turning point in our marriage. Now that my eyes were finally open about Papa, I could see my husband and our life together more clearly. I didn't expect a perfect marriage. I had a more realistic view. My future was safe with this man who had literally fallen at my feet. He would never hurt me nor leave me, nor disregard the needs of our children. I appreciated him more every day and felt enveloped by his loving acceptance of me.

By the time we arrived home, the children's nap time had come. I put them in their beds and went to talk with Fremont. I felt the need to unload some secrets. I wanted my relationship with Fremont to be open and honest, not secretive as my parents had been. "Fremont, did you know I work in the soup kitchen some times?"

"Yes, ma'am. I knew you were sneaking out during the day to serve beans," he replied with a serious look on his face, a smirk hiding in his eyes.

"You knew all along?" I had tried to keep my volunteer work secret so I would not have to explain to him. "Why didn't you say something?"

"I figured when you were ready, you'd tell me." He grinned his sweet grin. "I have to say, I'm mighty proud of you for your determination to help people."

"Do you think it would be okay if I continued volunteering? I know I'm busy with the kids and the business and the housework, but—."

"Of course it's okay." Fremont reached out and pushed back the unruly curl around my face. "Christ expects us to serve others."

"Maybe we could start a soup kitchen at Calvary Baptist." I scooted over closer to him on the sofa. "So people wouldn't have to go all the way across town to get a meal."

"Sounds like a great idea. I can help you evenings after work. We can collect food from church members. Some of those ladies can make a feast out of a turnip stump. I've tasted their goodies at the church potluck. I bet they'd be willing to help. Then me and the guys can set up tables in the parking lot."

"Whoa. You're getting ahead of me." I laughed. "I haven't even thought it all the way through." My heart warmed knowing Fremont wanted to jump in to help. I loved that we shared this desire to help others. I loved that we could work together. I'd been so busy being the "poor little rich girl" trying to please her father that I had not always realized the true value of this man who was my husband. My love for him multiplied, growing deeper every time I learned something new about him.

I no longer had to try to help my father's faceless masses. My dreams of helping others could become a reality as side by side, Fremont and I reached out to help real people in immediate ways. We could become the difference that Papa's speechifying could never bring into being.

That night, I walked into the children's bedroom and silently watched Margaret and Judson. Sleeping angels, God-given angels. God knew I needed children in my life instead of political pamphlets and fliers. I had so much to do. Mother Pope's WMU class needed nickels and dimes. Research and funds were needed for the flood in Florida and soup had to be made for a neighbor whose husband had lost his job. Soup line volunteers needed to be lined up. Women needed to be called.

I was overwhelmed and wanted to find paper and pencil to start a list. Instead, I sat in the rocking chair and watched my babies sleep. God was in control. I was His servant, and He'd help me accomplish everything He called me to do.

I went into the living room and looked at the calico curtains I'd made, the four walls we'd stripped and painted together, the meager biscuits left over from lunch. This was our world, and it was more than enough.

Fremont was seated on the sofa, his normal place to relax. I stood in front of him and smoothed down my dress. He looked at me, and we smiled at each other, a long, warm, embracing smile. The song "It Had to be You" played softly on the radio.

"Remember this song, Fremont? We danced to it right after we met, on the first evening we went to the Blue Bird." I reached out and slipped my long fingers into Fremont's calloused hand and urged him to stand. I might never dance in a speakeasy again, but I could enjoy a private moment with my husband.

"Come on, I'll teach you the steps."

Fremont's gorgeous blue eyes danced. I was the luckiest girl in the world.

He rose and put his arm around my waist. We danced, slowly at first, methodically, my graceful movements staying in harmony with his doggedly clumsy steps.

We waltzed. Our steps glided together as in an orchestra, the strings of the sensitive violin complimenting the deep, steady beat of a drum. So different, but, oh, what a wonderful melody we could make together.

The end.

Author's Notes

I began research for this book in 2001, a book based on my grandparent's story. I interviewed many of Sibyl and Fremont Pope's friends and family members, reviewed documents, and organized data. Most of the anecdotes are true, extrapolated from books written by the individuals involved. I also spent time researching the colorful and sometimes dismal 1930's. I collected mountains of enlightening information. My husband claims I enjoyed the research more than the writing. That may be true. Errors in this manuscript are not intentional, but likely. I found much more information that I could ever use and I tried to stick to as many known facts and dates as possible.

Sibyl Trimble loved to write notes. When we ran errands together later in her life, she would list the places she needed to go. I thought it silly until I began doing the same thing as I aged. She left many detailed notes about her life scribbled on bits of paper. Her ongoing asthma problems were also true.

She was known to be brilliant, a bit moody, and loved God with her whole heart. She graduated from Shawnee High School in 1927 when she was sixteen years old, almost seventeen, and from there went to Shawnee Community College before starting work. The drastic change in her circumstances could have made her a bitter person, but instead drew out her strengths, a dream to change the world, and a love of sharing information.

Fremont Pope left Shawnee, Oklahoma, after his high school graduation and rode railroad trains across the country to California and back. He was gone about one year before he came back and met Sibyl. *Calvary Baptist Church, 60ᵗʰ Anniversary Celebration, 1920-1980,* gives a list of the church's pastors, and there's a picture of a youthful Fremont Pope on the same page. When describing Fremont's attempts to go to college, I quoted a letter I found written to Fremont as "Nephew" hand-written on letterhead of Castleman Bros Timber Co, Springfield, Illinois. Signed Charles. No date. The tales about Wiley Post and Babe Ruth come from the many times I heard the stories reenacted as a child, confirmed by family members who also heard.

Their marriage license states Fredrick Freemont (sp) Pope and Sibyl Agatha Trimble, were married in Lincoln County, Oklahoma, on February 7, 1933, and was witnessed by Mr. and Mrs. Taze Teeples.

Malcom Calvis Trimble, Sr. proclaimed himself a dedicated Socialist in his book, *Our Awakening Social Conscience-The Emerging Kingdom of God.* Most of the Mr. Trimble's rhetoric in *A Promise to Break* is taken directly as quotes from this book. However I did have to simplify much of it. Malcolm's biography on the flap of his book states that he was with the Reconstruction Finance Corporation having previously served as Special Assistant to the Bank Commissioner of the State of Oklahoma.

Trimble probably would have attended the political meeting in Shawnee that took place in the Convention Hall. (The Convention Hall burned down in the twenties.) Agrarian Socialism, a strong force in Oklahoma during this time, supported Jack Walton for Oklahoma Governor. Walton was inaugurated as the fifth Governor of Oklahoma on January 9, 1923, afterward throwing a gigantic feast. He was impeached in November of that same year.

Mable Bennett Trimble with her daughter Blanche Trimble wrote *Nothing but the Truth, Autobiography of Mable Trimble,* and self-published it in 1982. The first part of the book is about Mable's history, but it latter gets into a lot of boring family gossip, boring even for me, and it's my family. Much of the information in this book, such as Papa's Iris garden, Sibyl's engagement to James, and her work for an attorney (and the debt owed) came from Mable and Blanche Trimble's book.

The marriage of Malcolm Trimble and Mable Bennett was announced in the Sayre Oklahoma Local News Section. They were married on Sunday, September 19, 1909. The announcement states that the groom was a young man of splendid business ability working as a bookkeeper for the First State Bank. It states that the bride worked in the post office and was a favorite among the young society people. The new couple went to Doxey, where they boarded a train for their honeymoon. In Little Rock, Arkansas, they visited with the bride's family. I thought it interesting that rice and old shoes turned up at the toes were thrown as they left.

Fremont's parents, Willie Ollie Pope and Eva (Castleman), lived on South Pottenger and worked at the Shawnee Mill according to the 1932 Shawnee City Directory. Ollie's father, John Pope, registered a one-hundred-sixty-acre homestead with the Territory of Oklahoma, Pottawatomie County, on November 26, 1906, recorded in Volume 175, Page 135 of the directory. Waco, a ghost town now, is listed on a *Map of Pottawatomie County, Ghost Towns in Chronological order from Origin to 1907*. It took a while to verify it actually existed. Through John and Amanda Pope, our family traces its heritage through the Oklahoma Genealogic Society to the First Families of the Twin Territories.

The Application for Marriage License of W.O. Pope and Eva Castleman, in Pottawatomie County, Oklahoma, dated April 24, 1910, states that he was from Texas and she from Missouri. Information about her activity in the WMU and assisting the first Women's Dorm are correct. According to a Warranty Deed, Ollie Pope purchased property in Shawnee from a Mr. Gowin on November 8, 1934.

Marjorie Trimble's story has been debated. An article in the Shawnee News Star, October, 1935, states that Mrs. Trimble visited an ill Marjorie Trimble in a hospital in Oklahoma City. Statements from Blanche Trimble say that the accurate diagnosis was an abortion. Marjorie's only child, Larry, denied the claim but stated that his mother did in fact lose a child after he was born and could not have any more children. Frances Trimble remembers being told that Marjorie had an appendicitis operation, but later in life when Marjorie had surgery for cancer, her appendix was removed. So for this story, I am assuming that the abortion actually did happen.

Blanche Trimble, the most colorful and opinionated of the daughters, had an excellent memory and so was a wealth of information. Her salvation lay in the fact that she had never lied, as she told me, so I believed every word she said. I spent hours and hours interviewing her, copiously taking notes. The chapter about Papa helping Fremont get the filling station was from her, as were such details like Sibyl's wedding dress, the time Papa gave her chocolates, and her knowledge about the movies. She loved details.

Margaret's birth certificate from Pottawatomie County lists her as Margaret Katherine Pope, born on August 18, 1933. Fremont Pope was listed as an auto mechanic and Sibyl as a housekeeper. She was born in the home. The birth certificate was amended in 1998, to reflect the name she had always used, Margaret Kathryn Pope. I was named after my mother.

Information on Grandma Bennett, Cordelia Harriet (Clay) Bennett, was gathered from the Sulphur, Oklahoma, obituary, listing her death on March 29, 1933. The obituary, also listed in the Shawnee News, stated, "She died in the home of her son, Lewis Bennett of Sulphur, until recently made her home here with Mrs. Trimble." According to the 1910 U.S. Census, George Bennet was born in 1856 in Michigan and Cordelia in 1858 in Ohio. According to the 1930 U.S. Census, Cordelia's father was born in New York, and her mother in Connecticut. Yankees, all of them.

The stories of Sibyl's brother, Calvis, are basically true. The fish pond story occurred earlier, when Calvis was about ten years old, but I moved it up to include it in this book.

I found the divorce documents in the basement of the First American Title Insurance Company in Shawnee. Lots of them. Mrs. Trimble filed a summons to Mr. Trimble on August 13, 1935. The total cost of the summons, including tax, was a ridiculous $2.95. However, the first summons was returned and signed by Sheriff Stanly Rogers, who'd stated that the defendant could not be found in Pottawatomie County. Another summons was filed and Trimble was served papers in Oklahoma City. I won't go into all the back and forth motions, special motions, order for alimony, etc. It was a difficult time for the family. I have a copy of the article in the Shawnee News Star, *State Bank Aid Sued for Divorce: Wife says M.C Trimble Neglects Her and Children,* dated 1935. Even though the divorce court was held in November 1935, the divorce decree was signed on January 6, 1936.

I have had so much amazing encouragement over the past years, I can never claim to remember each person, but without that continual push, I would not have completed this work. Thank you. Thank you all.

Many writing buddies along the way have helped me grow, develop, and advance my skills. Without them, this book would still be sitting in my closet. The list is long, and I fear leaving someone out, for there have been dozens who helped, from sharing one basic idea to getting me to revamp the whole project. All were important, vitally important. Thank you.

And then to my editorial team, your work helped drag this manuscript out into the open. Thank you Amber Beaman, Gina Dabney, Bonnie Lanthripe, and Mary Ruth Hatley Sadler. Without your help, this information would still be in an unreadable, convoluted form. You are the best. Thank you!

Interviews with others of Sibyl and Fremont's family have helped immensely. Since my interviews, some have since passed one, a reminder that we must hear and record the stories now and not wait until some convenient time in the future. I interviewed Sibyl and Fremont's friends still living, Opal and Carl Alexander and Anna Clark. I appreciate the openness, honesty, and lack of criticism. The tidbits of information or mountains of documents helped bring this story to fruition. Thank you so much.

To my extended family, the hundred or more who claim heritage from Sibyl and Fremont, I would like to remind you that this is also your story. Their faith can be your faith. No matter what difficulties they faced, they committed their lives to sharing the message of Christ, so don't let their dedication be wasted. Thank you for the joy you bring to my life.

My immediate family, bless them, have endured my slow-paced walk toward publication. My husband, Bill, especially deserves thanks for his support, along with our awesome children and grandchildren, those souls who shower me with love. Thank you for your love.

So to tell it all, most of this book is not from my imagination. Most of the anecdotes and stories told are true, including the story about Papa canning cantaloupe and Fremont's dancing ultimatum.

I simply organized the information and filled in the blanks with dialogue and historical description. This story has fascinated me for years. I hope you enjoy reading it as much as I enjoyed researching and writing it.

Kathryn Akin Spurgeon

About the Author

Award winning author, Kathryn Spurgeon has published over a hundred stories and articles, plus poetry books and devotionals. She is on the Writing Team of Henderson Hills Baptist Church, which has published eight compilations books. She holds a bachelor's degree from the University of Oklahoma and has pursued Creative Writing at the University of Central Oklahoma. She is a retired CPA from Oklahoma and loves to research Oklahoma history for her novels. Kathryn and her husband, Bill, have six children and twelve grandchildren.

Kathryn blogs at www.kathrynspurgeon.com and can be found on Facebook and Twitter.

Reviews on Amazon or Goodreads would be greatly appreciated.

Sources of Information

Public Documents

Calvary Baptist Church Minutes, Shawnee, Oklahoma
Oklahoma History Center
Pottawatomie County Historical Society, Shawnee, Oklahoma
Shawnee City Directory, 1930, R. L. Polk & Co. Publishers, Kansas City, MO
Shawnee City Directory, 1932, R. L. Polk & Co. Publishers, Kansas City, MO
Shawnee City Directory, 1935, R. L. Polk & Co. Publishers, Kansas City, MO
Shawnee News Star, Microfiche Newspapers from 1932-1935
Shawnee Public Library archives
US Bureau of Census 1930, Pottawatomie County, Oklahoma

Books and Articles

The American Writer and the Great Depression, edited by Harvey Swados, The Bobbs-Merrill Company, Inc., 1966

Calvary Baptist Church, 60th Anniversary Celebration, 1920-1980, Published by Calvary Baptist Church, S. Market and Farrall, Shawnee, Oklahoma, 1980

Chronicles of Oklahoma. "Fifty Years Ago in Shawnee and Pottawatomie County" By Ernestine Gravley, page 381.

Egan, Timothy, *The Worst Hard Time,* First Mariner Books 2006

Gaskin, J.M., *Baptist Women in Oklahoma*, Messenger Press 1985

Green, James R. *Grass-Roots Socialism- Radical Movements in the Southwest 1895-1943.* Chapter 10. Louisiana State University Press,1978

Perry, Bob, *Brothers of the Cross Timbers*, Bob Perry 2011

Shawnee, 1895-1930, Forgotten Hub of Central Oklahoma, reprinted by permission for the Historical Society of Pottawatomie County.

Soden, Dale E, <u>The New Deal Comes to Shawnee</u>, Chapter 10 in *"An Oklahoma I had Never Seen Before": Alternative Views of Oklahoma History,* edited by Davis D. Joyce, University of Oklahoma Press, 1994

Trimble, Mabel and Blanche, *Nothing But the Truth, Autobiography of Mabel Bennett Trimble,* Self-published 1982.

Trimble, Malcome C. Sr., *Our Awakening Social Conscience-The Emerging Kingdom of God,* Vantage Press, 1958.

Trimble, Sibyl, *History of Sibyl Agatha Trimble Pope*, handwritten about 1960.

Yarbrough, Slayden, *The Lengthening Shadow: A centennial history, heritage and hope of the First Baptist Church, Shawnee, Oklahoma 1892 – 1992*, published by First Baptist Church, Shawnee, Oklahoma, 1992

The Promise Child
Faith, Loss and Hope in the 1930s
Book 2 in Promise Series

Kathryn Spurgeon

Sibyl Trimble, a young woman from a wealthy banking family, married a former hobo. She suffers the burdens of the changing world and troubled economy

The Depression rips through her hometown of Shawnee, Oklahoma, leaving in its wake dying stores, repossessed farms, and countless men and women out of work.

Based on a true story, Sibyl wants to make the world a better place. She worries about her divorced, destitute mother and siblings. With two children of her own, she struggles to keep food on her table, and love alive in her heart —for her family, her husband, and for God. She does her best to listen to God, even in the bleakest times.

Changes come—a new baby, a new job with the PWA, and a promise of a bright future. Will that be enough?

Many people have already headed west to save their families. Will Sibyl and Fremont abandon Oklahoma and their hopes and dreams, for the promises in California? Or will they find a way to make it work in Shawnee?

www.MemoryHousePublishing.net
http://amzn.to/2szydtf

A Promised Hope
Faith, Prospects, and Dreams
in the early 1940s

Book 3 in Promise Series

Kathryn Spurgeon

Sibyl Trimble, a wealthy banker's daughter, gives up her status and wealth to marry a penniless hobo. Fremont Pope, her handsome, blue-eyed, husband stands by her side through the Depression, the dust storms and other difficulties in life. Just when life starts to get better, they experience one more disaster.

Why does God allow bad things to happen to her and her family? Can she continue to trust God through adversity?

Based on a true story, this novel follows Sibyl and Fremont through some difficult trials. She must find the strength to grow through the hard times and learn to trust on the Lord's overall goodness.

www.memoryhouepubishing.net

Made in the USA
San Bernardino, CA
07 August 2017